THE
SECRETS
WE
BURIED

THE
SECRETS
WE
BURIED

BECCA DAY

First published in Great Britain in 2023 by

Bonnier Books UK Limited
4th Floor, Victoria House, Bloomsbury Square, London, WC1B 4DA
Owned by Bonnier Books
Sveavägen 56, Stockholm, Sweden

A CIP catalogue record for this book is available from the British Library.

ISBN: 9781471415692

This book is typeset using Atomik ePublisher

Embla Books is an imprint of Bonnier Books UK
www.bonnierbooks.co.uk

For my husband Sam, who will dutifully buy this book but won't read it, so someone's going to have to tell him about this dedication.

TRANSCRIPT

Video published 17/06/2022

Subscriber count: 128

Hello everybody, welcome back to my channel. Thank you for joining me for more true crime craziness. Now, I know I've been a little AWOL recently but you're going to be glad you've stuck around as a subscriber. I've covered seven true crime cases so far since I started this channel, but do not make the mistake of assuming that this is going to be just like those, where I'm just reeling facts off the internet. There are many, many true crime YouTubers out there. I imagine you're subbed to quite a few of them. But no one has done what I am going to do here on this channel before. This is going to be a true crime deep-dive like nothing you've ever seen.

We're going to be investigating the murder of *Copperdale Street* soap opera star Geneva O'Connor, and when I say 'we', I really do mean that. You're coming along on this journey with me. I want you in the Comments. I want to hear your theories and your suspicions. And when I say 'investigating', I really do mean that too, because Geneva O'Connor was murdered slap bang in the middle of Millionaire's Row in Sandbanks, which just happens to be a fifteen-minute drive from the flat I am bringing this video to you from. That's right. This murder happened practically on my doorstep exactly five years ago today. And while many a true crime YouTuber has covered this case, we're not just going to be talking about the information that's readily out there in the newspapers and online. No, no.

I'm taking you to the scene of the crime. We're going to talk to her neighbours, her friends, her family. We're going to walk her footsteps from that fateful night. We're going to figure out what happened to Geneva. Because if you've heard of this case before, you've probably also heard that the husband did it, right? He was never convicted, but that's what everyone says. Elliot O'Connor killed his wife. It's always the husband. But what if it wasn't? What if, in doing this, we clear an innocent man's name? What really happened on the night of Saturday, 17th June, 2017?

Of course, we don't have access to forensics or any of the information that the police likely have buried away somewhere, so we're limited as to what we can actually find out. However, I believe someone knows something. Something they've kept secret all these years. And if we talk to the right people, we only have to discover enough to create a shadow of doubt. Maybe everyone jumped to the wrong conclusion. Maybe Elliot didn't murder his wife. Maybe Geneva's real murderer is still walking the streets just fifteen minutes away from where I live.

Are you as excited as I am? Be sure to smash that 'like' button to let me know, and subscribe to make sure you don't miss a single moment. I cannot wait to get started.

Chapter One

Friday, 17th June

Frankie

Millionaire's Row is on the farthest end of Sandbanks, as far as you can go without driving into the ocean. It's not really called that. The road Frankie once lived on is actually called Panorama Road, but it gained the nickname Millionaire's Row for obvious reasons. Everyone who lives there is minted. You have to be in order to afford one of the thirteen properties on the waterside street. It's the most expensive stretch of coastal real estate in the world, mocking the likes of Miami and Monte Carlo, with breathtaking views of Poole Harbour, luxurious multi-million-pound mansions perched along the peninsula and the ability to boast that your home once belonged to a celebrity legend like John Lennon.

And Frankie can't think of anywhere she'd less rather be.

She knocks her car into sport mode, the Mercedes letting out a gentle electric moan as it cruises down the tidy-looking dual carriageway. She's driven this road hundreds of times, and it brings a foreboding sense of déjà vu, coming back here. The familiar salt in the air might prove comforting in any other situation. Had she left for another reason. Had her departure been simply due to life moving on. In that instance her return would feel nostalgic, as if she were coming home. But that's not the situation, and she does not feel like this is home. Not anymore. Instead of the glamorous seafront welcoming her back with open arms, she's overcome with the knowledge that she should not be here. She's taking a huge risk in coming. The fact she's got away with what she did for these past five years with barely a whiff of suspicion floating her way should have been enough to ensure she never, ever returned. If it hadn't been for Eleanor passing away, she probably never would have.

As she drives past the road leading to the ferry port, the houses become grander, the driveways longer, the landscaping cleaner. Though no amount of money can change the fact that this road is still in rainy old England. If you google Sandbanks, you'll be presented with glossy, sun-soaked images that look like they belong in an exotic paradise holiday brochure, but this is the reality. Grey and miserable, to match the day perfectly.

Each house in Millionaire's Row is slightly different; unique pieces of architectural art. The plots of land here are long and surprisingly narrow, the houses crammed in against each other, though the lack of space either side of the buildings is more than made up for by the views each provides. Unlike the homes on the beach, where tourism saps any ounce of privacy, here on the harbour side the only thing you can see is the water, with clusters of boats and yachts sailing idly by.

Frankie slows her car and pulls up outside Zara's house, gazing at the terracotta-tiled building. A shiver travels down her spine. The windows that once gleamed with the warm glow of wealth and luxury now seem ominous, telling her to turn the car around and speed off before it's too late.

Zara's driveway, like the others on this road, is long enough to fit a good ten cars, but already they are starting to spill out onto the street.

'God help me,' she mutters, as she tries to estimate just how many people might be inside. There were so many people at the church, half the mourners had to stand outside in the rain, peering in through the doors and craning to hear the vicar, but Frankie had hoped the wake at Zara's house might be a little more private. She understands, of course. Zara's mum, Eleanor, was so well liked around these parts. Though born into money, she was never afraid of getting her hands dirty, often volunteering at the homeless shelter in Westbourne and organising litter-picks on the beach. When she got really sick and Zara had to hire a live-in carer, she received endless gifts and care packages to keep her comfortable while she faded away, and when she eventually passed away last month, Frankie's Facebook feed was full of nothing but heartbroken posts and photos of the good old days. Still, as much as she understands why so many are here, the thought of being in such a crowd sends her stomach turning.

As she clambers out of her car, Frankie checks her phone, half hoping there might be a text from Mike telling her the kids need her at home. But there's nothing, just the beaming photo of her brood of six serving as her wallpaper. Typical. If she had decided to take a day for herself at a spa, she'd be bombarded by questions of what to feed them and how to get the baby down for a nap and where Louis' EpiPen is, but when she really needs Mike to be a useless arsehole and beg her to come back, he becomes super-dad.

Mike was the one who wanted to leave Sandbanks. Frankie had a hard time letting go, even after everything that happened. For so many, Millionaire's Row is the ultimate pipe dream, and it felt wrong, ungrateful, wasteful to abandon it all. They traded their harbour mansion for a townhouse in London, closer to the robotics development centre Mike owns but less family friendly in every way. Once there, however, Frankie realised how much she needed it. She couldn't walk this street anymore, couldn't pass that godforsaken beach without feeling physically sick. Even now, five years later, it's like Geneva is still haunting this place, her memory imprinted in the very paving stones. Unwittingly, Frankie's eyes flick from Zara's mansion to the one two doors down, more modern in style with huge expanses of glass offering unobstructed views of the glistening Poole waters. For a split second, she thinks she can see her. Geneva. Standing in the window, gin and tonic in hand, smirking down at her. But, of course, there's no one there. The house is empty, has been since Elliot left, or rather, was forced out. As far as she knows, he never sold the place. It's just sat there like a morbid museum. A shrine to his dead wife.

Tugging at the hem of her black dress, the one she reserves for funerals, she gives herself a little shake and makes her way to the front door. It's propped open by a potted bay tree, which Frankie is grateful for. She didn't want to have to ring the bell and draw attention to herself. She is painfully aware that she is no longer 'one of them'. The elite. The top of the social ladder. In these parts, you turn your back on lunchtime mimosas at the golf club and you've turned your back on acceptance. She doesn't even have to meet anyone's eye to feel the silent judgement and repressed sideways glances. As she shuffles deeper into the belly of the house, it's like the walls are closing in, trapping her in a world of affluence and power she no longer has any desire to be a part of.

Luckily, it doesn't take her long to spot one of her old friends. Nadine is instantly recognisable, with her sleek dark hair, tailored outline and black leather bag that she's never seen without – a picture of impeccable elegance. Frankie's heart starts to pound. She'd purposefully avoided both Nadine and Zara at the funeral, preferring to pay her respects to Eleanor at the back of the church in privacy, but here she's going to have to speak to them.

'Hi, stranger,' she says, placing her hands behind her back so Nadine can't see her wringing them.

There is a moment when Nadine doesn't seem to recognise her, but it's gone almost instantly and a sad smile crosses her lips.

'Frankie.' She pulls Frankie into an embrace, squeezing her tightly, and while Frankie initially stiffens, she's quick to hug her back. There was a time she thought she'd never see Nadine again, not in person anyway. Of course they've sent the obligatory 'Happy Birthday' messages to each other when Facebook reminds them, but beyond that they've become practically strangers. It isn't until she actually sees her, smells the familiar Jo Malone Pomegranate Noir perfume and feels the warmth of her embrace that she realises how much she misses her.

'How's Zara doing?' Frankie says as they separate.

'I'm not sure. I haven't had a chance to speak to her yet.'

Frankie tilts her head to one side inquisitively. Nadine lets out a small sigh.

'We've sort of grown apart since you left. It was just . . . too hard to not think about Geneva, you know?'

Frankie does know. It's strange. You hear about murders happening all the time on the news, but until you're actually part of one, until it's your friend who is dead, it's impossible to imagine just how all-consuming it becomes. There is no such thing as normal anymore, regardless of how hard she tries to make it so. The life she had before Geneva died is water cupped in her hands, trickling through the cracks in her fingers, and no matter how much she attempts to scoop it back up, there's always a little less of her old self each time. That's what guilt does to you, she supposes. Even having moved away from where it all happened, she's never not thinking about it. With a different group of friends, they might have found comfort in each other, knowing they were the only other people who truly understood what it was like. But not for them. There were too many secrets sitting heavy like solid masses between them.

She offers a reassuring smile to Nadine that says *I know just how you feel*, and glances around the entryway. It looks exactly the same. Clean and minimal, with a sweeping staircase curving up to an interior balcony, from which Zara is peering down at them. Despite the tear-stained face and red-rimmed eyes, she still looks stunning as ever in a tight-fitting, undoubtedly designer, dress. Neither she nor Nadine have kids. Zara is all about the glam life. She didn't really need to pay her way through her BA in biology, Doctor of Medicine degree and postgrad in plastic surgery by modelling for glossy magazines in her underwear – her mum would have happily forked out the cash – but even she admitted she enjoyed the attention. Now she owns a cosmetic surgery clinic promising her celeb clients plumped-in-all-the-right-places bodies, just like hers, and she's starved slim and would never be seen dead out of stilettos. Nadine is all about her career; she's a hotshot family solicitor specialising in high-profile divorce settlements. Frankie's the one who opted for the mum route, and though she knows she picked the correct path and would rather have her four daughters and two sons over Zara's weekly nail and hair appointments, she can't help but feel intimidated by her appearance.

Zara makes her way down the staircase, her heels clicking on the marble floor, and steps towards them.

'I'm so sorry,' Frankie says once she's close enough, which prompts Zara's eyes to water. She swipes at them with the back of her hand. They hug, strange yet familiar, just like when she hugged Nadine, and Zara gives her a squeeze before they release.

'Thank you for coming,' she says.

Frankie nods. 'Of course. The service was beautiful. Very Eleanor.'

'Yes. Mum would have loved to see everyone together like this. I suppose it's worth all the effort that goes into it.'

A knowing smile creeps onto Frankie's lips and her eyes flick across to Ana, Zara's housekeeper, who is flitting from person to person with a tray of canapés. She is fully aware that Zara will have played little to no part in her mother's funeral or the wake, nor will she be the one to clean up once everyone has gone home.

'Is your dad here?' Frankie asks, scanning the crowd for any sign of Zara's normally absent father, who'd dipped in and out of Zara and her sister's lives after his divorce from Eleanor. Zara's snort of derision is all the answer she needs.

With this, the three of them fall into awkward silence. Frankie's heart aches for Zara. Her flawless exterior masks a multitude of scars. She's been through so much; first losing her sister in such a tragic way all those years ago, and now this. Frankie swallows and fiddles with her wedding ring, searching for something to say. Before Geneva died they were never short of topics to chat about. Frankie had found it easier to talk to the girls than to Mike. But it's as if Geneva was the glue holding them together, and they're not really sure who they are without her.

Before Frankie can think of something sensitive to say to her grieving friend, Nadine flicks her hair over her shoulder.

'You're still planning on keeping quiet, right?' she says.

'Nadine!' Frankie stares at her, mouth gaping open.

Nadine shrugs. 'What?'

There is another loaded silence, before Zara shakes her head. They're both used to Nadine's way.

'Nothing has changed,' she says coldly, then turns and disappears into a swarm of sympathetic hugs.

Frankie returns her gaze to Nadine. 'You do know how to be tactless, don't you?'

'Oh, like you didn't want to ask the exact same thing!'

Frankie doesn't respond to this, because she knows Nadine is right. Aside from offering her condolences, she has to admit part of her motivation for coming here today is to ensure they're all still on the same page. Eleanor was a big part of why Zara agreed to keep their secret. The last thing they need is for her to have a sudden attack of conscience now Eleanor is gone.

'You could have at least talked about the weather first,' Frankie says eventually.

Nadine just rolls her eyes. She's always been a to-the-point straight talker and she'll never change. At least they always know where they stand with her.

Zara doesn't return to them for the remainder of the wake, and Frankie doesn't blame her. A few people come over and ask how she's been, what her life is like in London, if they could see photos of her kids. She smiles her way through the conversations, busying herself with dainty finger sandwiches and wondering how long she needs to stay, out of politeness. Nadine doesn't seem fazed by the crowd, but then again she still lives here. She still sees these people every day, has been living their lie day in and day out for the past five years, has got used to the crippling fear of being discovered and the hell that would break loose should that happen. It must come naturally to her by now. She always was the most confident of the group anyway, after Geneva of course.

Eventually, Frankie notices a few clusters of people leaving, and takes that as her sign that now is an appropriate time to say her goodbyes. She gives Nadine another hug, though this time as she goes to pull away she's met with an odd tugging sensation in her stomach. Part of her is desperate to get out of this house and part of her doesn't want to leave. She can tell Nadine feels the same way because when they do separate, her eyes are glossed over. All those years of friendship reduced down to this. Empty social media messages and occasionally seeing each other at funerals.

She squeezes through the circle of people surrounding Zara and offers her a regretful smile.

'I'm going to have to head off,' she says. 'I need to be back for the kids.'

Even though that's not strictly true – Mike is more than capable of coping for one day on his own – she does ache to be back with them. Callie, her eldest, is visiting from uni this week, and Frankie's sure she hasn't been eating properly. Of course, the typical uni diet doesn't tend to be the healthiest, but she's gotten so thin Frankie wonders if she's remembering to eat at all. She does tend to get like that when she's got a lot of coursework or exams on. Frankie has tried suggesting that it doesn't matter if she doesn't get perfect marks, that there is more to life than academic success, but that's just what Callie's like. Always desperate to be an overachiever. She was the same when she was sitting her exams in secondary school, and it's even worse now she's nineteen and thinking about life after education, barely speaking to her mother. She must get it from Mike. It's certainly not a trait she's inherited from Frankie.

Zara places her wine glass down on the nearby console table. 'Of course. Say hi to Mike for me.' She leans in and gives her a gentle kiss on the cheek, which takes Frankie by surprise. Zara is more of a hugger than Nadine, and yet this goodbye feels stilted and forced.

'Listen,' Frankie says, lowering her voice. 'I'm sorry for what Nadine said.' She shouldn't be the one apologising, but she knows Nadine won't.

Zara waves her hand as if she were swatting a fly. 'Pay no mind to it.' But even though she's trying to sound casual, Frankie can tell it's bothered her.

Gulping back the lump in her throat, Frankie shuffles to the front door and steps out into the cool air. It was stuffy in there from the sheer number of bodies, and now she's outside she feels she can finally breathe. She fumbles about in her clutch for her car key, and is just about to press the button when a hand rests on her shoulder, making her jump. She spins around to see a woman she doesn't recognise, with platinum-blonde hair and heavy makeup with thick eyeliner wings. She's not dressed in black, and Frankie's sure she wasn't in Zara's house.

The Secrets We Buried

'Sorry!' the woman says, lifting her hand off Frankie's shoulder. 'I didn't mean to make you jump. Are you Francine Crawford?'

Frankie nods dumbly.

'I'm sorry for your loss. You knew Eleanor quite well, didn't you?'

'Thank you. Yes, she was my best friend's mum.'

She feels her eyebrows push together. What does this woman want? Why is she approaching Frankie to offer her condolences instead of Zara? Her eyes follow the woman's hand as she reaches into her tote bag and pulls out a camera.

'My name is Juniper Rose. I wondered if I could have a quick chat with you for my YouTube channel?' she says, pressing a button and holding it up between them.

'YouTube channel?' Frankie instinctively takes a step back.

'Yes. It's called *True Crime Over Wine*. I discuss true crime cases while drinking wine. Thought that was quite a good name, don't you? Anyway, I'm doing a kind of documentary-style deep-dive into the Geneva O'Connor case. I wondered if you could give me any insight. You were one of her best friends, correct?'

'No comment,' Frankie says quickly, pushing the woman's camera away and making a beeline for her car. Nausea bubbles in her gut. The imposing mansions loom over her. *We tried to warn you*, they seem to whisper. *You should have stayed away.* As soon as she's in the driver's seat, she revs the engine and slams her foot down on the accelerator, her car beeping furiously at her for not wearing her seat belt as the speedometer climbs. Her hands stick to the steering wheel from sweat. Once she's sure she's out of anyone's sight, she finally allows her foot to ease from the pedal. She presses the brake, the car rolling to a stop. She leans over and yanks open the glove box, retrieving her emergency stash of cigarettes and lighter. Trembling, she lights up and presses it to her lips. The only sound is the squeaking of the windscreen wipers scraping against the glass, and the hammering of her heart in her ears.

There have been countless YouTube videos posted about Geneva's death, though Frankie could only stomach watching a few of them in the early weeks, before deciding it was better for her mental health to steer clear of all of them. The internet calls these people 'amateur detectives', and for the most part they've just slagged off the police for not making sure Elliot O'Connor rotted in prison for his wife's murder. But this has never happened before. No one has actually approached either her, Zara or Nadine in person.

Sucking in deep drags of her cigarette, she attempts to quieten her racing thoughts. It's probably nothing to worry about. By the time Frankie gets home, everything will be back to normal and that Juniper Whatsherface will move on to another, more recent, murder case to exploit for views and likes and subs.

But even as she tries to convince herself, a terrified voice at the back of her mind tells her she needs to run and hide now, before it's too late.

Chapter Two

Saturday, 18th June, 2022

Nadine

'OK, how about every other weekend with you?'

'Absolutely not! I raised him just as much as you. Fifty-fifty custody or nothing!'

Nadine rolls her eyes as discreetly as possible. She's used to these kinds of discussions. As a family solicitor specialising in messy divorces, custody is one of the most common points of contention. If it were a child this particular husband and wife were arguing over, she would handle this situation with all the understanding and compassion that she normally does, but it's not. Mr and Mrs Evans have spent the last fifty-five minutes of Nadine's valuable time arguing over Doodles – their pedigree poodle. She's starting to lose patience.

Mr Evans' solicitor seems to be experiencing the same wavering professionalism, because he looks just about ready to fall asleep. Unable to bear it a second longer, Nadine scoops up her paperwork and bangs the edges against the table a few times, bringing the heated argument to a pause.

'Let's revisit this tomorrow,' she says, her voice making Mr Evans' solicitor start. 'We've made some good progress today.'

She has, despite the poodle row. She has expertly managed to secure Mrs Evans their entire marital home, even though she was the one who cheated on him. She doesn't have to like her clients or even agree with their actions in order to get them what they want. That's why they go to her.

As she leads the unhappy couple through the glass doors of the conference room and ushers them towards the lobby, she catches sight of her colleague, Andrew, smirking. He knows exactly the kind of day she's had. He's probably been listening to the ridiculousness and thanking God that Mrs Evans is not his client.

Once the Evanses are safely out of the building, Nadine slumps down in the chair opposite Andrew's desk.

'Remind me why I deal with these people?'

The corner of his mouth twitches up. 'Because they pay you the big bucks.'

'Because they pay me the big bucks,' she repeats, nodding. She glances over to the Rolex clock on the wall. It's home time, near enough, but she's not sure she wants to go home just yet. The reunion of her and her friends at the funeral yesterday left her feeling hollow. Nadine has always quietly enjoyed having her own space, but on the rare occasion, arriving home to an empty house causes the loneliness to set in. She doesn't want to ever get married – couples like the Evanses remind her of that on a daily basis – but she does sometimes yearn for a little company.

Her eyes flick over to Andrew. He's fairly good looking, she's always thought so. The suits he wears to work do a fantastic job at highlighting his arm muscles. He's also easy to get on with. They have a jokey, informal relationship, which is a pleasant contrast to the rest of her colleagues who all take themselves far too seriously. Nadine knows she finds Andrew attractive, but it's never occurred to her to make anything of it. Not until today, that is.

'Andrew,' she says, plucking a pen from his pen pot and twirling it around her fingers. 'Would you like to go to dinner tonight?'

It's possibly not the best technique for asking someone out – blunt and to the point – but Nadine doesn't know how else to be. She can't stand pussyfooting around, subtly flirting in the hopes that he may potentially one day ask her out. Better to just come out and say it.

Andrew raises his eyebrows. 'With you?'

Oh. Perhaps it's not better to just come out and say it.

Nadine feels the heat rushing up her cheeks and prays that the mortification isn't showing on her face. She presses her lips together, forcing her expression to remain neutral.

'Never mind.' She stands, dropping the pen back into the pot, and makes a start towards her own desk.

'Wait, that came out wrong.' Andrew follows her as she collects her coat and bag. 'I just meant, you never struck me as the kind of person who would *want* to go to dinner. You don't seem like the . . . dinner sort of person.'

'You're right, I never eat dinner.' She hauls her handbag onto her shoulder and heads towards the lobby.

Andrew lets out a frustrated growl. 'Can we start over? Yes, I would very much like to go to dinner with you. Though I can't tonight. I'm babysitting my friend's kid. How about tomorrow? Six o'clock? I'll pick you up from yours and you can choose the restaurant?'

Nadine pauses inches away from the exit, her fingers hovering over the door handle. Andrew has embarrassed her, which is not a good indicator, but he does seem to be willing to do a suitable amount of grovelling. She glances back at him over her shoulder.

'I'll have to check my calendar,' she says, the tiniest hint of a smile playing on her lips.

Without the company of a man to distract her, Nadine taps her long nails against the steering wheel as she drives, contemplating her options. She briefly considers heading to the golf club. She's not sure why she still goes there. The club used to be their domain before everything happened. The place they went to drown their sorrows in Chardonnay, Swedish massages and hot gossip, and, on occasion, a place to catch the eye of a wealthy businessman or two. After Geneva died and Frankie left, Zara stopped going. Nadine continues though, not because she particularly likes any of the women there, who, despite her wealth, still seem to look down on her because she's young and attractive and happily single, but because it's routine. Comfortable. Reassuring.

She knocks the windscreen wipers onto the next fastest setting as the drizzle outside picks up, beating down on the glass. The rain hasn't let up since Eleanor's funeral yesterday. It's as if the sky is crying right along with them, tears streaking down the windows. She won't go to the club today, not in this weather. Sighing, she resigns herself to an evening alone and heads for Millionaire's Row.

A flash of red hair, partially hidden by an umbrella, walking the pavement outside her house, makes Nadine blink. It kind of looks like Frankie, but she'll be long gone back to her family in London. Nadine often wonders if Frankie had the right idea in escaping this place and if she should have tried to get out too. She likes to picture Frankie's life, busy and chaotic with all of those kids running around, the perfect distraction from haunting memories. Maybe that's what she should have done; got herself a sperm donor and pumped out a few kids to take her mind off things, rather than sitting at the bar in the golf club every week and trying to pretend everything is still exactly the same.

As Nadine pulls onto her driveway, the redhead follows her, closing down her umbrella and giving it a shake. Nadine wasn't imagining things.

'Frankie.' Nadine steps out of her car, and Frankie gives her a half-smile before making her way over.

'I'm sorry to just show up like this,' she says, her words coming out in a flurry. 'I stopped by earlier but remembered you must be at work and wasn't sure if you'd be coming straight home after. If it's a bad time, I can go.'

'No, of course not. It's fine. Come in, come in.'

Nadine ushers her over to the front door, silently glad she didn't make plans with Andrew after all, and guides her through to the kitchen. Without even asking if Frankie wants a drink, she places two large glasses on the island and uncorks her favourite red. Frankie looks as though she could use one, and Nadine never needs much of an excuse.

Frankie perches herself on one of the stools, accepting the glass gratefully and taking a long, slow sip. Seeing Frankie sitting there, across the island from her, it's as if she's stepped back in time. The decor in her home hasn't been altered in years, and save for a few extra lines around the eyes Frankie hasn't changed much either. If Nadine didn't know better, she'd say Zara and Geneva would be flocking in any second too, ready for their weekly wine-tasting night.

'I thought you were heading back to the kids?'

'Er, yeah. I was.' Frankie starts picking at the skin around her nail. 'I ended up staying at the B&B last night. Something happened and I . . . I don't know. I just felt like I should stay for a bit. Mike's fine. I called him and asked if he'd mind me hanging around for a few days. He had this week booked off work anyway.'

Nadine frowns, studying Frankie. She's not met her eye once since she walked in. Whatever is bothering her, she's reluctant to tell her.

'What happened?' Nadine presses.

'This woman approached me,' she says, 'as I left the wake. Said she was some YouTuber.'

Nadine shakes her head, unsure where this is heading.

'Apparently,' Frankie continues, 'she has one of those true crime channels and . . .' She trails off, but she doesn't need to say anything else. Nadine understands.

After a brief silence she says, 'I wouldn't worry about it. It's not like she's the first.'

'No, I know.' Frankie takes another sip of wine, and as she does, Nadine notices her fingers are trembling. This woman, whoever she was, has spooked her. 'Something just didn't feel right. It seemed . . . different this time.'

Nadine moves to sit next to her, crossing her legs and leaning forward, her arms resting on the marble countertop. This whole situation is her responsibility. It's up to her to make sure the girls don't fall apart, that they can continue with their lives even after Geneva so tragically lost hers. She made it her responsibility that night, and if something has Frankie worried enough to stick around instead of running back to London, she has to take it seriously.

'Did she say what the channel was called?'

They spend a few minutes finding it on her phone. It's not a big channel. The woman, apparently named Juniper Rose, only has 128 subscribers and the views on each of her videos are pitiful. If there had been a thread of uncertainty tugging at Nadine's insides, it is now well and truly severed.

'There, see?' she says, giving Frankie a reassuring smile. 'Nothing to worry about.'

But Frankie doesn't look so convinced. Her brow is creased in concern.

'Listen to what she says though.' She taps into the latest video, the one entitled *Deep-dive Into the Murder of Geneva O'Connor*, and Juniper's bright voice spills out of the phone speaker. Nadine jumps to turn the volume down, as if there was a chance someone outside could hear them through the walls. They both lean in to listen to Juniper as she talks to the camera. Nadine has to admit, this is definitely different to anything they've experienced so far. It's one thing having these wannabe detectives talk about you in videos and podcasts. It's quite another for them to actually talk *to* them. That's a level of commitment to the case they haven't dealt with before.

'I really wouldn't worry,' Nadine says once the video ends, keeping her voice calm and measured despite the alarm bells ringing in her head. 'Go home to the kids. They'll take your mind off it until this all blows over.'

Frankie shakes her head. 'I don't think I can. I can't leave here until I know she's gone and isn't poking around anymore. You don't think . . .' Her eyes flick from side to side, on high alert. 'You don't think she'd have any way of finding out what we did, do you?'

Nadine places a hand on Frankie's. 'Trust me,' she says. 'There's no way. I took care of everything. You don't need to worry about this.'

Frankie nods but still doesn't look convinced. Nadine has to take control.

'If you really want to stay, why don't you stay here with me? There's no point in you sitting alone in a B & B, worrying. I've got plenty of room.' She doesn't say that at least if Frankie is staying with her, she can keep an eye on her and make sure she doesn't do anything stupid. 'Besides . . .' She eyes Frankie's dress – the black one she wore yesterday to the funeral. 'You could do with a change of clothes.'

Frankie *umms* and *urrs* for a while, but eventually agrees. Nadine has a way of making sure everyone does as they're told. Better yet, she can make it so that they believe it was their smart idea to begin with. And this Juniper woman is going to be no different. If she doesn't want to back off, then Nadine will make her.

They do their best to talk about other subjects while they finish their wine and Nadine refills their glasses in the hope that the alcohol might calm their racing thoughts, but the undercurrent of tension is thick. There's a sense of foreboding in the air which makes Nadine feel uneasy, and if there's one thing she doesn't like, it's uncertainty. Eventually, they do loosen up a little and migrate to the sitting room, where they proceed to scroll through the lighthearted films that Netflix has to offer. A girls' sleepover – how quaint. Maybe she should invite Zara and make a real night of it.

Nadine knows something is wrong before she's even fully woken up in the morning. Behind closed lids she can hear the beeping of trucks reversing, the screech of metal doors sliding open. Draping her silk robe around her shoulders and padding to the window, she peers out on the street below. Moving trucks. Four of them. She frowns. If someone had sold their house on Millionaire's Row, she'd know about it. It's a small cluster of houses and word spreads fast. So why would there be moving trucks parked up along the pavement?

She'd almost forgotten that Frankie had stayed the night. She's already up when Nadine makes her way downstairs, sitting in the kitchen nursing a cup of coffee, wearing a pair of Nadine's pyjamas that are way too big for her tiny frame.

'Morning.' Frankie smiles, but it quickly drops from her face as she clocks Nadine's expression. 'What's the matter?'

'Did you see the moving trucks outside?'

Frankie's eyes follow her as she heads to the hallway. 'No.'

It sinks in just as she walks out onto her front step, and Frankie, behind her, does the same. They glance at each other, and it's as if they can read each other's mind.

Frankie's face goes suddenly very pale. 'Is that . . .' She trails off, but Nadine doesn't need her to finish her sentence. She nods gravely as she follows Frankie's gaze to a tanned, black-haired man walking up the drive of one of the neighbouring houses, his hands buried deep in his pockets and his head bowed. He looks much thinner than the last time they saw him.

'Elliot,' Nadine murmurs. 'Looks like he's moving back in.'

Neither of them is sure of what to say. The shock has made Nadine's mind go blank, a numbness spreading through her like thick fog. Pressing her lips together, she flicks her eyes across to Zara's house, and sure enough Zara is standing at her bedroom window, arms crossed, staring down at Elliot as he disappears into the house he shared with Geneva before he murdered her.

Chapter Three

Sunday, 19th June

Zara

Zara forces her eyes to stay trained ahead of her, not daring to glance in the direction of Elliot's house, as she trudges down her brick-paved driveway, pulling her big green bin behind her. She's barely stepped outside since her mother died. There was the funeral a couple of days ago, and she visited the grave yesterday, but other than that she's cocooned herself inside as if the light of day might burn her skin. It was hard enough trying to face anyone in the thick of her grief. Now there's the prospect of facing him too. She had even considered just leaving the bins entirely, but Ana wouldn't start her shift in time to take them out before the bin men arrived, and the last thing she needs is maggots.

Her phone buzzes in her pocket. She pauses, standing the bin up, and peers down at the text message. It's from Mia at the clinic.

Hey, how are you? Any idea when you'll be back?

She purses her lips. When she had got word from their live-in carer that she'd found her mother dead in her bed two weeks ago, Zara had dashed out of the clinic so fast she barely had a chance to explain to Mia what had happened. She feels bad leaving Mia in charge, especially for this length of time. She's a more than capable surgeon – Zara wouldn't hire anything less – but their VIP clients, the ones who pay them the big bucks and keep the company in the likes of *Vogue* and *Marie Claire*, demand to be treated only by Zara. When you're a minor celebrity shedding out the small fortune it costs to go to Zara Garcia Cosmetic Surgery & Well-being, you want the woman herself, not some assistant.

She sighs and taps out a reply to Mia.

I need a few more days. Hold the fort just a little bit longer? I'll pay you double-overtime.

A voice cutting through the silence of the morning air makes her jump, nearly dropping the phone. She recognises the voice in an instant. Was he waiting for her to venture out? She should have waited until she was safely back inside her house to message Mia back.

'Zara!' he calls.

Pretend you didn't hear him. Just run back to the front door.

She knows that's what she should do but she's rooted to the spot. Stomach clenching, she steals a peek at him through the strands of her hair. He's wearing a black jumper with the hood up, plunging his face into darkness and shadows. She saw him early this morning, watched him through the window as he lugged furniture to and from the trucks, but seeing him walking towards her now sends a spark of panic shooting through her. Her knees feel like they might buckle at any second.

'Hey,' he says when he reaches her.

Zara's heart pounds. She swallows hard. 'Hey. You're back. How have you been?'

She winces at the ridiculousness of her question. He winces too, though she can't tell if he's bothered by her question or by the way she's edging away from him.

'Yeah, I . . . I felt like it was time. It's been long enough now.'

She nods forcefully, hoping that if she keeps things pleasant, this conversation will end quickly. For the first time in years, she wishes

Nadine and Frankie were with her. They'd know what to say to Elliot
to get him to go away.

'Where have you been staying?'

He shoves his hands into his pockets. 'I rented a place on the Isle
of Wight. Just somewhere I could be left alone, you know?'

She nods again, understanding completely. It was strange how
everyone's opinion of Elliot had changed so suddenly. One day he
was the 'it' man; the guy with the money and the looks and the suave
personality that made all the other women on the street a little bit
jealous of Geneva, whether or not they liked to admit it. And the
next he was the scum of the earth. The bogeyman. The one you had
to cross the road to avoid and who'd send shivers down your spine
every time he looked your way.

His whole being shifted after Geneva died too. Some said the
hollowing out of his cheeks and the greying of his skin was due to
grief. Most said it was due to guilt. It didn't take long for it to become
widely accepted that he was the one who killed Geneva. There wasn't
a whole lot of evidence – certainly not enough to convict him – but
rumours of their unhappy marriage and divorce being on the cards
had been enough to brand him the Murderer of Millionaire's Row.
For the first couple of months after Geneva's death, not a day went
by when Elliot's drive wasn't blocked by news vans, but even after
they moved on to other stories, he had no peace. The social media
frenzy that erupted was a circus. Something about rich people getting
murdered seems to pique the curiosity of wannabe detectives, and
every true crime podcast, YouTube channel and Facebook discussion
group was flooded with theories about why Elliot killed his wife.
Everyone was obsessed with the case.

The obsession wasn't just restricted to social media, though. Their
once private street became a kind of hot spot. Where tourists had
always flooded the beaches, now they ventured to the docks to see
the so-called 'murder house'. It started with kids spray-painting the
word 'killer' on his front gate. Then came the bricks through the
windows, the scratchings in the paintwork of his car, and once, most
disturbingly of all, a dead bird being left on his windshield. Maybe
that was the turning point. The moment when he decided he could

no longer live on this street and just upped and disappeared, quite unceremoniously, leaving the house a chilling, empty reminder of everything that had happened. For a long time, there was chatter about it being torn down, to erase any remaining traces of the tragic O'Connor family, but Elliot never sold the house and eventually the interest in their street died down.

And now he's back.

Zara desperately wants to ask him what made him decide to return to Millionaire's Row. If she were him, she'd never set foot in Sandbanks again. But if she continues to ask questions, he might want to come in for a chat, and she's not sure she can face that. Instead, she presses her lips firmly together and they stand in uncomfortable silence for a few moments.

'Listen, I . . .' he says eventually, staring at his shoes and rocking slightly on the balls of his feet. 'I know what everyone thinks about me. But I didn't kill Geneva.'

Every inch of Zara's body tenses. Why is he bringing Geneva up? Surely he wants everyone to forget about it, as impossible as that is?

Elliot's eyes flick up from the ground and he watches her intently. 'Do you believe me?' he asks.

The eye contact is too much and Zara tilts her head away, her heart hammering in her chest. Her mouth fills with saliva and acid, everything except a coherent response to his question.

She coughs and clears her throat. 'Of course.'

In all honesty, she's not sure what she believes. She certainly didn't jump on the 'Elliot's a murderer' bandwagon like the rest of the world seemed to. Part of her always doubted it. She just couldn't quite match up the man she knew with the man who would willingly take a life. But Nadine and Frankie were so sure of his guilt, so desperate for her not to cast doubt on the situation and draw attention to themselves and their own terrible part they had to play in it all, that she forced herself to keep quiet. As time passed, she managed to at least shut her disbelief away. With him gone, she didn't need to constantly turn over whether he was guilty or not in her mind. Things aren't so simple now.

She forces a smile onto her lips.

'I have to get back,' she says, before turning sharply and hurrying back towards her house.

'Maybe I'll see you around?' The hope in his voice is almost too much to bear.

'Yeah, see you around,' she calls. She can sense him watching her, his eyes burning into her back, but she doesn't turn round. Picking up the pace, she practically falls through her front door. Once it's closed, she leans against it for a few seconds, chest heaving.

Her hand brushes against the shape of her mobile in her cardigan pocket. Nadine and Frankie have sent her a few messages since they saw Elliot moving back in, asking her to call, and she's ignored each one. But now she's not so sure she can deal with this on her own.

TRANSCRIPT

Video published 19/06/2022

Subscriber count: 869

Welcome back to *True Crime Over Wine*. Since I posted the introduction video a few days ago, I've made contact with a few key players in this case, but before I go into detail about that, I thought it would be a good idea to recap, for any of you who don't know about this case, on what we know so far about the night of Geneva O'Connor's murder.

The body of Geneva Sarah O'Connor, thirty-two, was discovered on the beach in Sandbanks by a dog walker on the morning of Sunday, 18th June at around six o'clock, with a piece of metal wire wrapped around her neck. The post-mortem found that by this point she had already been dead for at least four hours, and she had a significant amount of alcohol in her system. The last time we know for sure that Geneva was alive was at just after eleven on the Saturday evening. Geneva, along with her best friends, Nadine Howe, Zara Garcia and Francine Crawford – Frankie to her friends – met regularly for 'wine' evenings at each other's houses. It was Nadine's turn to host that night. We know this because all three friends confirmed where they were that night, which was corroborated by these comments on one of Geneva's Instagram posts.

Instagram post displays on screen, showing Geneva taking a selfie with a glass of red wine and her friends Zara, Frankie and Nadine in the background.

Caption – It's the freaking weekend baby, I'm about to have me some fun. Nowhere I'd rather be. See you later for wine club sluts @nadinehowee @frankiecrawford @thezaragarcia

@thezaragarcia Omg, was that from last week? Talk about double chins!! Are we meeting at the club tonight?
Like   Reply   17 June, 2017 at 11:36 am

@genevaoconnor Nah. It's so busy at the moment. It's Nadine's turn to host, anyway.
Like   Reply   17 June, 2017 at 11:42am

@nadinehowee Sounds good. I have a bottle of Pio Cesare we can crack open.
Liko   Reply   17 June, 2017 at 11:49am

@frankiecrawford I'm easy. We're getting a babysitter in tonight. Usual time?
Like   Reply   17 June, 2017 at 11:56am

As you can see, the wine club was a regular occurrence among these ladies. Now, the police obviously interviewed all three friends after Geneva's body was found, and they said that they were all there at Nadine's house until just gone eleven that night. But that was the last anyone saw of her, which means Geneva was killed somewhere between 11.15 p.m. and 2 a.m. As the last people to have seen Geneva alive, I'm obviously very keen to speak to each of them, though this could be easier said than done. Frankie doesn't live in Sandbanks anymore, though she was there recently for a funeral, and when I tried to speak to her she was understandably very hesitant. The other two I have yet to make contact with, but I'm going to continue working on it.

One person I have managed to speak to is quite possibly the most important person in this case, and that is Elliot O'Connor, Geneva's husband. As you'll know if you've heard anything at all about the murder of Geneva O'Connor, it is widely accepted that Elliot is the one who killed her, though there was never enough evidence to convict him. Whoever killed her did a thorough job of not leaving a trace. No fingerprints on the wire. Nothing. Police did question him on Sunday, 18th June as to his whereabouts for the previous night, particularly those hours between eleven and two where it is believed Geneva was murdered. He claimed that he had been out with his best friend Mike Crawford – Francine's husband – that evening at the Cliff Poole Gastropub in Dorset until just after midnight, which has been corroborated with CCTV footage from the pub, but that after leaving the pub he decided to leave his car there and walk home. He eventually got home at 12.46 a.m. to find Geneva still wasn't home, though he later said this wasn't unusual and therefore he didn't feel the need to alert anyone to the fact she was missing, and it is that gap of time where he has no alibi that has made him the clear murderer in so many people's eyes.

– Cut to B-roll footage on Sandbanks beach –

Juniper: Have you heard of the Geneva O'Connor murder?
Person A: Of course. Everyone round here has heard of it.
Juniper: Who do you think killed her?
Person A: The husband. Without a doubt.

– Cut to B-roll footage of next person –

Juniper: Who do you think killed Geneva O'Connor?
Person B: Well, I didn't live round here when it happened so I don't know the couple, but everyone says it was her husband.

– Cut back to studio –

I asked a few more people who they think killed her and every single time I got the same answer. It was the husband. It's always the husband. You might wonder why I'm so disinclined to take this view myself. The truth is, I'm not really sure. I just have this nagging feeling that the reason the police couldn't find sufficient evidence to get a conviction is because they were focusing in on the wrong person. I've been chatting to him for a few months now in preparation for this deep-dive, and he's agreed to do a proper sit-down interview with me tomorrow. This will be the first interview he's agreed to do with me. In fact, this is the first interview he's agreed to do with anyone since he left Millionaire's Row five years ago. Before I speak to him, though, I thought it would be a good idea, for the sake of this deep-dive remaining impartial, to chat to someone who is absolutely sure of Elliot's guilt. Elliot's best friend Mike Crawford.

– Cut to Zoom interview footage with Mike Crawford –

INTERVIEW FILMED AT 20.38 ON 19/06/2022

Juniper: Thank you so much for agreeing to do this interview.
Mike: That's OK. Look, I haven't got much time. I've only just got the kids to bed.
Juniper: I promise I'll be very quick.
Mike: OK, well, what do you want to know?
Juniper: You were best friends with Elliot O'Connor, correct?
Mike: I suppose so. We used to go to the pub a lot while our wives were doing their wine-club thing. Less so after my second baby was born, obviously.
Juniper: And have you spoken to Elliot since Geneva's murder?
Mike: Nope. We packed up and moved away not long after. We all needed a fresh start and didn't like the thought of our kids being there.
Juniper: As his best friend, you didn't feel the need to catch up with him at all after the move?
Mike: Why would I? He's a murderer.

Juniper: Yes, there's a few interviews I see you gave in the year after her death where you made your views quite clear. If you don't mind, what evidence was discovered that leads you to believe he did it?

Mike: Well, for starters he has no alibi. We're all supposed to believe he just decided to wander around after leaving the pub that night. Bollocks, if you ask me. But also whoever strangled her did it with a piece of wire. That was premeditated. Plus her phone got nicked, her laptop too. They never found either of them. Her phone could suggest a mugging gone wrong, but her laptop? That was in her house. And it went missing. Means it was personal.

Juniper: No one else had access to Geneva's home that night?

Mike: Not that I know of.

Juniper: How did Elliot seem that evening while he was at the pub with you?

Mike: Antsy. Like there was something on his mind. I tried to talk to him about it but he wasn't really one for deep conversations.

Juniper: Did he mention Geneva at all?

Mike: Nah. They'd been on rocky ground for a while and everyone knew it. They barely ever spent time together.

Juniper: So, as far as you're concerned, Elliot and Geneva were having issues in their marriage. He left the pub and either spotted Geneva on the beach and killed her there, or killed her elsewhere and dumped her body on the beach and returned home?

Mike: I guess so, yeah.

Juniper: Why do you think he'd leave the body on the beach where it was sure to be found? Why not attempt to dispose of it?

Mike: How should I know? I'm not a killer. I don't know what went through his head. Maybe he panicked.

Juniper: You seem very certain that it was him. Considering he was your best friend.

Mike: It's not just me. Everyone thinks it was him.

Juniper: But you're the only person close to the case who felt the need to label him a murderer in numerous press interviews. In fact, in one interview you said you were 'sickened by the thought that you had ever spoken to him'. Out of curiosity, were you paid for those interviews?

Mike: That's none of your business! I talked to the press to protect my wife. If I hadn't done those interviews, they'd have hounded her for a comment and I knew she didn't want that.

Juniper: That's very noble of you. I wonder, if it came out that he was innocent . . .

Mike: He's not.

Juniper: But just hypothetically. *If* it came out that he was innocent, would you regret making those comments so publicly?

Mike: I . . . er . . .

Juniper: You are aware of the turmoil he's had to deal with since the murder, yes?

Mike: Well, yes . . .

Juniper: The fact that, amidst grieving for his wife, he's had to deal with being called a monster, has been forced out of his house, has had his life made a living hell . . .

Mike: Hey, I don't . . .

Juniper: All while knowing his supposed best friend has turned his back on him and has grabbed at any opportunity to make a quick buck by dragging his name through the mud to the press.

THIS ZOOM MEETING HAS COME TO AN END.

– Cut back to studio –

In case you hadn't gathered, that was Mike hanging up on our Zoom call. But while it may seem like I didn't get much out of that interview, I did manage to pull out one strand of information that I wasn't aware of before. Geneva's phone and laptop were missing. That's something I haven't seen mentioned in any of the articles covering this case. As Mike said, just the phone being missing could have suggested a mugging gone wrong. But both disappearing indicates there was something on those devices that the killer wanted, or perhaps something they didn't want the police finding. Presumably, since no arrest has ever been made, the phone and laptop have never been found. It's worth mentioning this to Elliot when I speak to him tomorrow. I'd be interested to know if his phone records ever got searched.

So, before we wrap up, let's take a look at the suspects so far. I think, even though the police never publicly added him to *their* list, that we can safely add Mike Crawford onto the list. So that means we are currently looking at:

– Elliot O'Connor
– Mike Crawford

Well, that's it from me today. Be sure to smash that 'like' button, leave your theories in the comments below and subscribe. You definitely do not want to miss the next instalment.

Chapter Four

Sunday, 19th June

Frankie

Frankie sits on Nadine's sofa, wishing that out of everything in Nadine's wardrobe she hadn't chosen to borrow a dress. It's too baggy around the chest, and the leather of the sofa sticks to her thighs and makes her feel both sweaty and cold all in one go. Or maybe the sweat she's breaking out into is from the anxiety coursing through her veins. Nadine has done her best to silence it, to assure her that just because Elliot is back, nothing has changed and their secrets are still all perfectly safe, but Frankie knows it's only a matter of time. The fact they thought they could get away with everything and just move on with their lives is laughable.

She glances at the clock. Eight minutes past one.

'Should we call her?' she says as Nadine sweeps over from the kitchen with a jug of iced water and gestures to her to put a coaster on the coffee table. One time, Frankie had forgotten and left a dark ring of condensation on the oak, and Nadine had gone so pale she looked as if she might faint.

Nadine is just about to answer her when the doorbell rings, and she flashes Frankie a look that says *I told you so. Just be patient.*

Frankie leans forward to pour three glasses of water while Nadine goes to answer the door. She pours slowly and deliberately, focusing on the way the light bounces off the liquid in an attempt to still her racing thoughts. Nadine returns a moment later with a sheepish-looking Zara trailing behind her.

'Hey,' Frankie says, pasting her friendliest, calmest smile onto her face. The last time she spoke to Zara was at the wake, and even though that was only two days ago, it feels like so much has happened since then. Ever since they saw Elliot moving back in, they had been wracking their brains for a way to get Zara to talk to them, but it turned out they didn't need to do anything. Just a couple of hours after spotting him, a text had come from Zara saying Elliot had spoken to her and she wasn't sure what to do, and now here they are.

The tension is thick as they all perch around the coffee table and glance at each other, wondering who should speak first. Nadine sucks in a breath, as if knowing the responsibility will eventually fall to her.

'Why don't you tell us what happened, Zara?' she says, picking up her glass and taking a sip.

Zara crosses her legs and swishes her hair over one shoulder. Even when noticeably agitated, she still manages to ooze cover-girl glamour.

'Nothing really happened,' she begins. 'He just came over to say hi. It just freaked me out a bit, actually talking to him after all this time.'

Frankie leans in. 'Did he say why he's come back?'

She shrugs. 'Just that it was time.'

A shiver runs down Frankie's spine at this. Time? Time for what?

'You shouldn't have spoken to him at all,' Nadine says, running a burgundy-painted fingernail along the rim of her glass. 'You should have ignored him and let us know straightaway.'

Zara narrows her eyebrows. 'I'm not twelve. I'm capable of speaking to someone without saying something I shouldn't. Besides' – she picks up her own glass and swishes the water around – 'he looks really sad. Broken. I couldn't just flat out ignore him.'

There is a pause, and Frankie and Nadine share a concerned look.

'Please don't tell me you still think he's innocent?' Nadine says.

'I didn't say that!'

'There was always something off about him, even when Geneva was alive. I'll bet he's even stranger now.'

'Yeah, well, Geneva can't exactly have been easy to live with.'

The room falls silent at this, Zara's words sinking in. They all know it's true. Geneva was a handful, to put it politely, and that was to the three women who were supposed to be her best friends. Frankie could only imagine what she must have been like with Elliot, behind closed doors. But it's one thing thinking it. It's quite another saying it out loud when Geneva is buried in a cemetery.

Eager to defuse the conversation, Frankie reaches over and places a hand gently on Zara's forearm. 'I think Nadine might be right. We need to be really careful around Elliot. I mean, don't you think it's a little coincidental that, just as he returns, this YouTuber starts snooping around?'

She notices Zara's confused expression at the same time as seeing Nadine's body tense in her peripheral vision. Her eyes flick between them, before landing on Nadine.

'You didn't tell her?'

Zara's brow creases. 'Tell me what?'

'I didn't want to worry her unnecessarily,' Nadine says, keeping her tone ever calm and collected despite the growing unease in the room.

'Worry me about what? I am here, you know?'

Frankie drops her head forward and starts massaging her temple. This is not going how she had hoped it would go. The last thing they need is to be butting heads amongst themselves.

'When I left the wake the other day, a woman approached me. She knew who I was, said she wanted to ask me a few questions about Geneva. She runs one of those true crime YouTube channels.'

Zara's eyes grow wide, the colour draining from her face. She stares at Nadine. 'And you didn't think I should know about this?'

Nadine sits back in her chair and smooths out her trousers. 'She's only posted one video about Geneva and it had barely any views.

Trust me, if I thought it was something you ought to be concerned about, I'd have told you.'

'Yeah, it's funny how you always want us to trust you, isn't it?'

'Well, have I let you down yet?'

The two of them continue sparring, but Frankie is no longer listening to them. Instead, she's focused on her phone where she's opened up the YouTube app and has navigated back to Juniper's channel. Her heart stammers.

'Two videos,' she murmurs under her breath, and Zara and Nadine both turn to look at her.

'What was that, Frankie?' Nadine says.

Frankie holds the phone up to face them. 'Not one video, two. She's posted another one.'

For a long while none of them says a thing. They just stare at the screen as if some gruesome horror might start crawling out of it like in *The Ring*.

'Oh, for heaven's sake,' Zara says eventually, snatching the phone out of Frankie's hand and hitting 'play' on the latest video. Juniper's voice once again spills out of the speakers. Only it's worse than last time. This time Juniper mentions them all by name.

Tingles, millions of tiny ants, start crawling their way along Frankie's skin as screenshots of Geneva's Instagram post flash onto the screen. She had suggested they all delete their social media profiles just after Geneva had been killed, but Nadine said it would just make them look like they had something to hide. It had made sense five years ago, but now, seeing their comments displayed on screen, like in one of those Netflix documentaries, she wishes she hadn't listened to her. In fact, there are many things Frankie wishes she had never listened to Nadine about.

And then Juniper says something that makes Frankie's throat constrict.

'Before I speak to him though, I thought it would be a good idea, for the sake of this deep-dive remaining impartial, to chat to someone who is absolutely sure of Elliot's guilt. Elliot's best friend Mike Crawford.'

Zara and Nadine gape at Frankie.

'That son of a bitch,' she says.

The air outdoors is crisp and cool, a stark contrast to the burning hot rage that's coursing through Frankie's core as she presses her phone to her ear. She's had to take a step outside after watching the video. She can't be having this conversation with her husband in front of her friends. Each ring of the phone grates at her patience a little more, and she finds herself clenching and unclenching her free fist as she paces the pavement.

Finally, the ringing stops and is replaced by a gruff clearing of the throat.

'Frank, hey, babe. How's things over there?'

'What the hell do you think you're playing at?' Frankie snaps, finding herself only infuriated further by his cheery, carefree greeting.

'Well, nice to hear from you too.' He doesn't sound in the least bit fazed by her jumping down his throat. He was obviously expecting this call.

'Why? Why would you give an interview to someone about Geneva without speaking to me first?'

'Hang on, let me get somewhere the kids can't hear.' There is the sound of shuffling on the other end of the line, then a door closing. 'OK. What were you ranting at me about again?'

'The interview on that YouTube channel?'

Mike lets out a sigh. 'I really didn't think it was that big a deal.'

'Not that big a deal?' Frankie has to stop herself from shouting at the top of her voice and alerting the other houses in the row. 'Mike, the whole point of moving to London was to get away from all this.'

'It was just one quick interview. If I'd known she was going to come at me like that, I'd never have done it.'

'Well, she had a point,' Frankie says, bracing herself for his defensiveness. 'You've always been so outspoken about Elliot. Even now. Why?'

'Why do you think?' His voice is definitely more hostile now, his usual jokey tone eliminated.

'I'm really not sure. It's like you want Geneva's murder to be all about you. You've got to be in the spotlight, even five years later. You can't just let it rest!'

The phone goes silent and Frankie feels a tinge of guilt at her words. She can't tell Mike why she's so angry at him for speaking to Juniper. She can't express to him how important it is that they don't stir things up and bring attention to themselves again. If he knew what she and the girls had done, he'd understand.

'You're right,' he says eventually. Frankie blinks, taken aback by how quickly he's yielded.

'What?'

'I can't let it rest. I trusted that man and he betrayed me. I was best man at his wedding. He's Albie's godfather, for Christ's sake. We had him round for dinners, in our house, around our kids. And all the while he was capable of murder. What if it hadn't been Geneva, huh? What if it had been our Callie he'd killed?'

Frankie's blood runs cold at that; the thought of her eldest daughter lying dead on a beach. Geneva's parents went through that, the unimaginable pain of losing a child. Frankie couldn't even look them in the eye at the funeral. Their grief was too much to bear to look at.

'The worst part is,' Mike continues, 'he's never paid for what he did. Not properly. So no, I won't stop speaking out. Why should he get to just disappear into the sunset and get away with what he did? Why should he be allowed to live peacefully? There was never any justice for Geneva, so it's up to us to make sure she isn't forgotten, and that no one forgets what a monster Elliot is.'

Frankie's mouth is too dry to say anything in response. The tinge of guilt has now morphed into full-blown shame. She perches on the low brick wall at the foot of Nadine's driveway and drops her head forward, wishing there was something she could say to Mike to help him understand why she's so desperate to move on from all of this.

'Frankie? You still there?' comes his voice, less angry this time and more like her usual carefree husband.

She swallows a few times in an attempt to lubricate her throat.

'Yes, I'm here,' she says eventually. 'I'm sorry. It's just weird being back here. So many memories, you know? It's bringing it all back.'

'Babe, when are you coming home? The kids miss you. We all miss you.'

An ache pulls at Frankie's heart. She's very rarely away from her family. As much as she likes to say that they'd all fall apart without her, it's really her who needs *them* to keep her grounded. She glances back at Nadine's house, picturing her and Zara inside waiting for her to return. Why is she even here? Nadine was right. This YouTube channel is a small blip on their journey to normality. Barely anyone knows it exists. Does she really need to be putting her life on hold and panicking the way she is?

'Tomorrow,' she says finally, standing up. 'I just need to wrap up a few things here with the girls and then I'll drive back in the morning. Put the kids on the phone for me.'

As she takes it in turn to speak to each of her children and then says her goodbyes to Mike, the worries that have been building up over the last couple of days seem to wash away, like the tide gradually making its journey back away from the beach. This is the right move. She can feel it in her bones. Once she's back in London with her kids, Geneva and Juniper and Elliot will all seem like a distant memory.

'Oof!' She lets out a grunt as her body impacts with someone. She'd been so focused on saying goodbye to Mike, she had taken a sharp turn towards Nadine's house without looking to make sure the pavement was clear first. Her phone flies out of her hand and bounces, then skids, along the ground.

'I'm . . . I'm so sorry,' she stammers as she bends to retrieve and inspect her phone. A long crack winds its way across the screen. She hisses through her teeth in frustration.

'It's fine.'

Frankie's stomach flips. She whips her eyes away from the crack and to the person she crashed into. Elliot is standing less than a metre away from her, staring at her phone, his brow creased in concern.

'Sorry about your phone. Is it insured?'

She opens her mouth to say something but her throat has

constricted, an invisible hand gripping and squeezing her windpipe. Upon noticing her lack of response, Elliot looks up at her, and his expression changes. Realisation. Understanding. He can tell how scared of him she is.

His head appears to shrink into his shoulders, turtle-like.

'I'll pay for a new screen,' he mutters. 'Just send me the bill.' And with that he shuffles past her and moves quickly towards his house.

Frankie watches after him, her body still gripped with fear, unable to move. Elliot coming round to their house for dinner feels like a lifetime ago. The Frankie from five years ago wouldn't have thought twice about passing him on the street or accidentally bumping into him. It would have been an insignificant moment of time to be forgotten forever. But back then she had no idea what he was capable of. Or what she was capable of.

Zara's words filter back into her mind.

'Geneva can't exactly have been easy to live with.'

No shit. Geneva O'Connor was one of those people who knew exactly how to get what she wanted, and how to manipulate everyone around her, but who, for some reason, was adored by each person she came into contact with. Frankie and the girls treated her like some kind of idol. They went where she wanted to go, did what she wanted to do, acted how she wanted them to act, and not once did any of them question it. Well, not until the end, anyway. It was just the way things were.

Perhaps that's why Frankie did as Geneva said all those years ago. She hadn't wanted to. If it hadn't been for Geneva opening that letter, she'd have kept her secret well and truly close to her chest. Or, if she was going to tell someone, it would at least have been one of her other, more trustworthy friends. But Geneva took that choice from her.

'You can't tell Mike,' Geneva had said. 'It will kill him.'

At the time, Frankie thought Geneva was looking out for her and advising her as a friend. Later, of course, it became clear that she had taken joy in knowing Frankie's secret, and encouraging her to keep it so. From that day, she had something on Frankie that she could tuck away, ready to whip out and use against her whenever it suited her. That's the kind of person Geneva was. That's why they all did what they did.

With Elliot now safely back in his house, Frankie glances back down at her broken phone and the family photo from when they all went to Legoland that serves as her background. The crack has snaked straight down the centre.

Right between her face and Mike's.

Chapter Five

Sunday, 19th June

Nadine

Nadine tucks a strand of her black hair behind her ear as she climbs out of her car, having collected tonight's dinner from her favourite seafood restaurant. They do offer delivery, and ordinarily Nadine would much prefer to have her guilty pleasure meals delivered to her door, but she needed to get out. Frankie has been sulking ever since her call with Mike, moping around the house with 'pissed off' written all over her face, and it's not a nice atmosphere there at the moment.

She needed a moment to breathe too. Since Juniper's second video went live, she's had to force herself to keep up the appearance of someone who isn't the least bit fazed by these latest developments. As Frankie and Zara got themselves all worked up, she sat calm, composed, as only she knows how. She didn't tell them that when she went to the bathroom she immediately stalked the internet for everything she could find on Miss Juniper Rose, only to be met with social media profiles set to the very highest of security settings, save for a public Instagram page which looks to have been created the same day she launched her channel. Nor did she reveal just how much her heart had stammered in her chest at the mention of the missing phone and laptop. No. Nadine did as Nadine does. Now though, in the privacy of her car, she can allow the trembling she's been forcing back to journey out to her fingertips.

She half wishes Frankie wasn't there tonight and that she could eat her takeaway in bed. She doesn't like sharing her space at the best of times. At least Frankie will be heading home in the morning. There is definitely a little sadness at that thought too – who knows how long it would be before they saw each other again? – but Nadine is mostly relieved. Relieved that Frankie has finally succumbed to Nadine's appeasing influence and doesn't seem to be freaking out quite as much anymore, and relieved that soon she would only need to keep an eye on Zara.

The drive to and from the restaurant has been enough to clear her head a little, and she focuses on the food she'll soon be devouring. The seafood mixed grill is to die for. The smell of it creeps out of the paper bag, drifting into her nostrils, and her mouth waters as she approaches her house. She instinctively reaches for her front door key, but then remembers she didn't bother to lock up because Frankie's there. They're going to eat seafood and curl up on the sofa with a blanket and a bottle of her finest red wine and watch trashy TV and forget all about everything that's happened over the past few days. Or at least, they're going to *try* to forget.

Once inside, Nadine slips off her heels, places them neatly on the shoe rack in the mudroom, and proceeds to the kitchen. Her stomach rumbles and she places a hand over it as if to quieten the unladylike sound.

'I wasn't sure if you wanted steamed vegetables or . . .' She trails off as she peers over the kitchen island to the living area and spots Frankie curled up on the sofa fast asleep. Her shoulders droop. Despite her eagerness to have her own space back, she had rather been looking forward to one last girls' night before Frankie leaves in the morning, but she's clearly exhausted and Nadine doesn't want to wake her.

She pulls out Frankie's meal from the bag and pops it in the oven to keep it warm, then steps lightly over to her sleeping friend. There is a wet patch gathering on the cushion where Frankie's mouth is hanging open, and Nadine resists the urge to rip it out from underneath her.

Instead, she picks up the soft white throw off the arm of the sofa and drapes it across Frankie.

The doorbell ringing makes her start. Her stomach is still growling. Apparently she isn't meant to eat this meal while it's still hot. Annoyed, she pads across to the hallway, glancing at her watch and wondering who on earth would be visiting her at this hour. When she opens the door, she's confused to see Andrew standing on her doorstep. She almost doesn't recognise him out of a suit; unlike at the office, he's opted for a pair of jeans and a pale-blue shirt with the sleeves rolled up, and somehow he looks even better than usual. He clocks her bewildered expression and his smile falters.

'I'm . . . guessing you forgot about our date?'

Nadine blanches, and she feels her cheeks flush. 'Andrew, I'm so sorry. Yes. Things have got . . .' She glances over her shoulder, where she can just about see Frankie's limp hand hanging over the edge of the sofa. 'A friend turned up and she needed my help. She's asleep on the sofa right now.'

'It's fine. Another time.' The disappointment is evident on his face as he starts to retreat back towards his car. Despite herself, Nadine feels it too.

'Wait,' she calls. His steps slow and he looks back expectantly. 'I just picked up a takeaway. There's plenty for an extra person if you wanted to join?'

To begin with, she thinks he's going to decline, she would if it were the other way around, but after a moment's hesitation, he smiles and makes his way into her hallway. He must immediately sense how she likes to keep her home, because he's quick to remove his shoes. She tries not to smirk at his Spongebob Squarepants socks.

'Wine?' she offers, plucking the bottle and two glasses from the island and carrying them into the second lounge where they won't have to worry about waking Frankie. 'Or are you more of a beer person?'

He takes one of the glasses. 'Wine is fine, thank you. Are you sure it's OK me being here with your friend staying?'

'Of course. Better than me watching her sleep all evening.' She realises a little too late how that probably came out, as if he's just something to pass the time until a better offer comes along, but it doesn't seem to bother him as she retrieves the seafood and starts arranging the containers on placemats.

'This is delicious,' he says, almost shyly, as he tucks into the lobster.

'It always is from Anchorage. Have you never been?'

He takes another sip of wine. 'Nope, I usually just frequent the kebab shop when I've had one too many.' He chuckles, but reddens at the same time. It's definitely different, sitting here wining and dining instead of making sarcastic digs at each other in the office.

'How long have you lived around here again?' Nadine asks, digging her fork into a piece of smoked salmon.

'I moved this way when I started at the firm, so coming up to seven years now, I guess. I'm not quite as bougie as you though, Miss Millionaire's Row. I'm on St Clair Road.'

'There's nothing wrong with liking nice things,' Nadine teases, with a smile.

He smiles back, and her stomach flutters. He really does look good. She knows exactly where she hopes this evening is heading, but she's not quite sure how to go about instigating it. It's been a long, long time. Still, Andrew doesn't seem to be in a rush for the evening to end. Once they finish the food, Nadine suggests he crack open another bottle of wine, and she feels herself gradually becoming more and more intoxicated. It's a good thing, though. It'll loosen the both of them up.

She eyes the empty plates and, after telling herself that under no circumstances would it be acceptable to tuck into Frankie's portion in the oven, she picks them up and takes them to the kitchen, where she proceeds to load the dishwasher. Andrew follows and, as she drops a dishwasher tablet into the compartment and straightens herself back up, she feels his eyes on her and turns round.

'My face is up here,' she says, smirking.

He flicks his gaze up to meet hers. 'What?'

'You were looking at my legs.'

'They were looking at me.'

They both laugh, though Nadine's gets caught up with the lump in her throat.

Sod it, she thinks. She's never been one to beat around the bush. Why bother now?

She swallows the lump, steps forward, slides her hands around his waist and presses her lips to his. And she wasn't wrong. He wants it just as much as she does.

When she jumps awake with a start it's still dark, the sky outside an early morning grey hue. She groans, rubs her eyes and presses the button on the side of her phone. It lights up, blinding her, and she's quick to shut it off again. She got enough of a glimpse, though, to know that it's just gone five o'clock, and there's not a whole lot of point in going back to sleep. Arching her back, she turns to look at Andrew, to take in his naked body one last time before they inevitably agree it's probably best for their work relationship that this doesn't happen again. But he isn't there. What is there however, is a note on the bedside table.

Nadine sits bolt upright in bed and snatches the note up.

This was fun. Had to shoot. See you at the office.

Teeth gritted, she screws the piece of paper into a ball in her hand. Son of a bitch. Nobody sneaks out in the morning on her. If anything, that's what *she* does to people.

Annoyance and embarrassment bubbling inside her, she hauls herself out of bed and trudges to her walk-in wardrobe. She'll have to choose an utterly stunning outfit for work today so that he curses himself for being such an idiot. Maybe her Dolce & Gabbana dress. It's a gorgeous, black tailored number with buttons running down the front, and it complements her figure perfectly.

Opening the double doors to her wardrobe quells her outrage at Andrew almost instantly. This is her favourite room in the house. A walk-in wardrobe was something she always dreamed about when she was a young girl, when the few clothes she owned were stuffed into a single drawer in her mother's dresser. They didn't have much, even though it was just the two of them, and Nadine always said she'd get a scholarship, a student loan, whatever was needed to ensure she'd be able to have a good career. A proper career. And that's exactly what she did. Of course, her mother managed to get herself inducted into high society in her own way. She finally married Nadine's stepfather, who just happened to be a self-made millionaire, and now anyone would think Mrs Howe had been born into royalty, with the way she acts. She has a spectacular knack for looking down on her daughter, even though Nadine's achieved more than her mother ever did.

Nadine reaches for her underwear drawer, but an odd niggle at the back of her brain makes her stop in her tracks. Straightening up, she studies the rails of colour-coordinated clothes, frowning. Something is off.

It takes her a few moments of scrutinising the contents of her wardrobe to figure out what's wrong. She steps towards the built-in shelving unit that lines one of the walls, housing her handbags, jewellery and shoes, and it's then that it hits her, stopping her in her tracks. All of her shoes are carefully displayed in the same way; one with the toe pointed towards the wall, and one facing the other way, just like in all the posh department stores. She likes storing them this way because she can see both the front of the shoe and also the red soles of her Louboutins. But one pair of heels, the ones with the peep toe, are both facing forwards, no red sole to be seen.

For a few seconds she can't move, can't even breathe. Her eyes shrink to slits as she tries to recall the last time she wore them. It was a good few months ago. She's sure she would never have put them back like that, but even if she had by accident, she'd have noticed it before today. A cold sinking dread falls over her.

Someone has been in here.

She flies over to the trunk that sits under the window, topped with a decorative plant and diffuser on a tray. Ripping the tray off the surface, she slides the trunk towards her, the bottom of it scraping against the floor. Her heart batters against her ribcage as she cranes forward and digs her nails under the edge of one of the floorboards. It creaks as it lifts, revealing the dark space below, framed with cobwebs.

They're still there, hidden in the depths, untouched.

Nadine slumps back onto her heels and sucks in a shaky breath, relieved tears gathering in her eyes. She looks back at the trunk, at the horrendous secret she's been harbouring for all of these years, and that simple movement causes the dam to break. The tears splash down onto her cheeks. That moment of panic, when she thought someone might have taken them, is like a plaster that's been ripped off. Where it had been holding in all the guilt and self-loathing from what she did five years ago, now it's all bleeding out over the floor. She hunches over and scrunches her fist against her mouth so as to muffle her pained sobs.

Once they subside, she takes a moment to gather her thoughts. She needs to be logical about this. She hasn't been found out. If someone had found them, they'd have taken them, and besides, there's no way anyone would even know to look under a secret loose floorboard hidden beneath a trunk of hats and scarves. And yet, she can't shake the feeling that someone has been in here snooping around. Straightening up and checking her reflection to make sure her eyes aren't too obviously puffy, she pads back downstairs. Frankie is still asleep on the sofa, right where Nadine left her, and the oven is still on, the takeaway from last night undoubtedly burned to a crisp now.

'Wake up,' Nadine says softly, jiggling Frankie's shoulder.

Frankie's eyes flick open with a start. 'No! Get off! Get off me!' Her arms flail wildly, and it's clear from the alarmed look on her face she's still half asleep and has completely forgotten where she is.

'Sorry, sorry!' Nadine says. 'It's just me.'

She waits for Frankie to stop attacking her and properly snap out of her dream before she says, 'I just need to ask you something.'

Frankie hauls herself up onto her elbows and rubs her eyes. 'What's the matter?'

'Nothing, I just . . . have you been in my wardrobe?'

'Your wardrobe?' Frankie's brow crinkles. 'No.'

A heavy sensation settles in Nadine's core. Chewing on her lip, she stands and moves towards the huge floor-to-ceiling windows that look out over the harbour. The moon, full and round, is casting a haunting glow across the water, its reflection rippling on the surface like a thousand ghostly hands. There's something unsettling about the way the light dances on the waves, like the sea itself is alive and breathing. A chill runs down Nadine's spine.

'Nadine? Are you OK?' Frankie says.

But she doesn't respond. She's too busy looking at the edge of the sliding door which has been left ever so slightly open, allowing a soft breeze to flow through the crack. Face stony, she pushes it closed and turns the key to lock it.

Chapter Six

Monday, 20th June

Zara

I have to go back to work. That's the first thought that enters Zara's mind when she wakes up. People often get the totally wrong idea about her. They see her boob job and the plump lips which she regularly injects with hyaluronic acid, and assume that all she cares about is her appearance and living it up at wild parties, but her business is her life. She needs to work. Craves it. And though she needed the time off to grieve for her mother, and come to terms with the gaping void she's left behind, she's starting to get antsy.

She spends half an hour sipping the cappuccino she always starts her day with; brewed fresh from her fancy Breville. It's the most used appliance in her kitchen and so she splashed out to get the best of the best. Once that's finished, she potters around the house attempting to distract herself. Ana will be in just before lunch, so there's really no need for her to make the bed or start a load of washing, but she's not sure what else to do. Besides, just because Ana is her cleaner doesn't mean she should have to pick up her dirty thongs from the bedroom floor.

When her phone flashes up with a message from Frankie asking if she wants to meet for a farewell drink, she practically leaps at the opportunity. Before Eleanor died, Zara never realised just how little social life she actually has, beyond that of the empty comments she receives on her daily Instagram posts, most of which are from total strangers. The only real people she ever spoke to were clients, employees and her mother. She hasn't really had friends since Geneva died, but she'd been keeping herself so busy at the clinic, she hadn't even noticed. Maybe it was a subconscious way of taking her mind off everything that's happened over the past five years.

The rain has finally started to let up for the first time since the funeral, the sun just peeking through the clouds, and as she's driven in a black cab towards the golf club she is reminded of just how beautiful Sandbanks is. She'd been so proud of herself when she moved here. The fact that she could afford one of these houses off her business income alone was enough to stick two fingers up at her dad, who she distinctly remembers telling her she'd never be anything more than a bartender flashing smiles for tips. God, she hates that man. There had been a tiny part of her that thought he might turn up at the funeral, but he lived up to his thoughtless reputation spectacularly.

When Zara arrives at the club, her feet are killing her, having been dropped at the end of the tree-lined driveway by a less than polite taxi driver and forced to walk the rest of the way in her heels. Still, she manages to paste a smile on her face for the obligatory #metime post on Instagram, tilting her head to just the right flattering angle so that her cheekbones are highlighted. She's spent years perfecting it. Selfie taken, posted and reshared to stories, she enters the club. Ordinarily, she'd make a beeline for the bar, but seeing Frankie hasn't yet arrived, she decides to wait for her elsewhere.

Meet you in the spa, she texts, before flashing a smile at the receptionist and making her way down the corridor that leads to the wellness rooms. Ordinarily, she goes to the spa at least once a week, but it's been three, what with all the preparations for the funeral, and she's feeling it. The smell of essential oils and eucalyptus reminds her of her clinic waiting room dotted with oil diffusers, and once again she finds herself eager to go back. Tomorrow, she decides. She'll go back tomorrow.

Her bikini is hanging up in her locker, freshly laundered as one of the perks of her premium membership, and as she slips into it she can already feel the stress of the last week starting to melt away. Maybe this is what she needed, instead of keeping herself holed up in her house, missing her mum and panicking about Elliot. A little TLC. She emerges from the changing rooms into the pool area, surrounded by floor-to-ceiling glass looking out onto the golf course, and steps into the warm water of the hydropool, lowering herself down until she's resting on the underwater beds. She's the only one here. Perfectly peaceful.

She's been in the pool a good twenty minutes, the rhythmic pulsation of the bubbles against her back sending her into a relaxed daydream, when Frankie's voice behind her makes her jump.

'I've been calling you!' she says, her voice laced with annoyance.

Zara blinks a few times, reorienting herself, before sitting up and turning in the water. Frankie is still fully dressed, though she's shoe-less as per the spa rules.

'Sorry, my phone's in the locker.'

'I couldn't get in. I don't have a membership card anymore, do I? I was expecting you to be at reception to admit me as a guest, or at least put my name on the list.'

Zara bites her lip. 'Sorry! I didn't think.'

'The only reason I got in is because Pete the manager happened to come out and he recognised me and was in a good mood.'

'Well, you're here now.' Zara pulls herself up out of the water and perches on the edge of the pool. 'Why don't you join me? We can chill out in the sauna for a bit. Sounds like you could do with a bit of relaxation yourself.'

Frankie raises an eyebrow at her. 'I would but I didn't exactly pack for a holiday. I don't have a swimming costume.'

Zara's head drops back. For a little while she had started to feel better, but Frankie is very much killing her vibe and bringing back the stress that the hydropool had done such a good job of alleviating. She hauls herself up and wraps a towel around herself.

'Fine, you go and get us some drinks. I just need to get changed.'

By the time she's dressed back into her white top, capri jeans and heels, and made her way back to the bar, Frankie has already drunk most of her lemonade. She's sitting at their old usual table, the one they used to sit at for their wine-club meets, cradling the near-empty glass in her hands, shoulders hunched. She gives her an odd look, as if she is attempting to send her a telepathic message, and her eyes dart to the side. Zara follows where she's peering over to and realises why she's looking so sheepish.

Elliot is sitting at one of the tables tucked away in the corner.

Before Zara can pretend she hasn't seen him, he catches her looking and offers her a wavering smile, lifting his hand slightly to give a half-wave. Zara hesitates, her compulsion to be friendly battling with her desire to get as far away from him as possible. She can see from the look on his face that he wants her to come over and chat, that desperate longing for things to go back to the way they used to be. Except things aren't the way they used to be.

Cringing slightly, she settles for a nod by way of acknowledgement and lowers her head as she shuffles past him, towards Frankie. She selects the chair that has its back to Elliot so that she doesn't have to deal with any awkward eye contact, but she needn't have bothered because the sound of his chair scraping back against the tiles echoes through the club, followed by the sound of the receptionist saying goodbye to him as he leaves. He's hurt she didn't talk to him.

Frankie's body seems to deflate as she breathes a sigh of relief.

'God,' she says. 'Talk about awkward. He didn't hang around getting back on the list.'

Zara leans back in her chair, guilt churning her insides. Of all the snooty members of this club, he probably thought Zara would be the one to not give him a hard time about coming back. But what else can she do?

'No Nadine?' she enquires, surprised not to see her with Frankie. She'd have thought Nadine would be watching the both of them like a hawk until Frankie was safely back in London and this YouTuber had stopped snooping around.

'She's had to go into work. Though I suspect she would have preferred to stay home and keep an eye on me.'

Great minds think alike.

Zara shifts in her seat, still getting used to this new awkwardness between them. 'I bet you'll be glad to get home to Mike and the kids.'

'Yeah, I will.' Frankie nods, though her voice sounds far off and unsure. 'It's been nice seeing everyone again. But I definitely don't want to hang around if Elliot is back. I still don't understand why he would return.'

Zara presses her lips together, heat travelling up her neck. Frankie immediately notices her pained expression, because her brow creases. 'You OK?'

She doesn't respond, just drops her gaze to her lap. Ever since she saw Elliot unloading the moving van, she's been desperate to talk to someone about him, but Nadine is out of the question. She'd jump down her throat so quickly she'd barely get two words out. Frankie is different though. Frankie was always the least highly strung of the group. And maybe the fact that she's leaving and they'll probably not see each other again until the next mutual wedding or funeral is a blessing; she can talk it over with her and then pretend like nothing ever happened. No awkwardness when they pass on the street. No constant fear that it's going to get brought up in casual conversation. She has to talk to someone. It's burning her up inside.

'I know we need to stay away from him,' she says eventually. 'I know he's dangerous, but . . . I knew him really well. Sometimes I wonder if he really was capable of hurting Geneva.'

For a moment Frankie just stares at her, the crease in her brow deepening.

'You still think he's innocent, don't you?'

Zara gives an uncertain shrug, and Frankie straightens in her chair. 'Tell me you don't still have feelings for him.'

Her voice echoes through the club and Zara shrinks, mortified. 'Shh!'

Luckily there's only one other couple, sitting near the window, whom she doesn't recognise, and after glancing up to see what the commotion was about they're quick to return to their conversation.

Frankie lowers her voice to a whisper. 'I thought you said you were over him?'

The heat has travelled past Zara's neck now and her whole face feels like it's on fire.

'I was. At least, I thought I was. You and Nadine kind of convinced me that he had killed Geneva and that I needed to forget about him. But, I don't know, seeing him here again, it's bringing it all back.'

'You haven't . . .' She lowers her voice. 'Tell me you haven't slept with him since he came back.'

'What? Are you crazy? No, of course I haven't.'

Zara swallows. She hasn't slept with Elliot since he came back to Millionaire's Row. But she's thought about it. Despite herself, despite seemingly everyone in the world telling her he's a murderer, she hasn't been able to stop thinking about it. The possibility of just one more night.

Their affair had taken her completely by surprise. She always knew she found him attractive, and she had a sneaking suspicion he felt the same way about her from the way he used to look at her, but she never in a million years would have thought it would ever lead to anything. But then he and Geneva started to have issues in their marriage and it just sort of . . . happened . . . as cliché as that sounds. There was one drunken night while Geneva was in London for the Soap Awards. Zara had already had a fair few glasses of wine when she saw him stumbling home, clearly having abandoned his car at the pub. She had gone over to check he was OK and when he slurred a barely audible sentence that contained the words 'you' and 'beautiful' and then leaned in for a kiss, she didn't stop him.

After that night, there was no going back. Every opportunity they had they were ripping each other's clothes off like a couple of horny teenagers. He never told her explicitly, but she got the feeling from him that he and Geneva rarely had sex. He was hungry for her, and she felt the same way about him. Occasionally, she'd allow herself to fantasise that he would one day decide to leave Geneva, that he'd had enough of her overbearing, manipulative behaviour and that he'd choose to be with Zara instead. She wasn't even sure if that was what she really wanted, but it felt good to think about it, even if that did make her a horrible friend. When Elliot eventually did decide that enough was enough and that it was Zara he wanted to be with, it was too late. Geneva was murdered and everyone decided Elliot was guilty.

It's been five years and Zara still can't quite wrap her head around it. It's even worse now that he's back in Sandbanks and she actually has to see him and converse with him. How the heck are you supposed to act around your ex-lover who had cheated on his wife with you before subsequently being suspected of her murder?

Frankie is still staring at her, mouth hanging open.

'Would you stop looking at me like that?'

This causes her to at least close her mouth, but the utter disbelief on her face is impossible to hide.

Eventually, Frankie shakes her head and exhales deeply with puffed-out cheeks.

'I get it. I do. It's hard coming to terms with someone not being who you thought they were.'

Tears gloss Zara's eyes. She swipes fiercely at them, unwilling to allow herself to cry.

'I still don't think we can trust Elliot, though,' Frankie says after a moment, releasing Zara's hand. 'He's still not a good guy. I mean, he did have an affair.'

Zara blinks. 'That doesn't make him a murderer, though. I had the affair, too. Does that make me a murderer? Who the hell are you to judge us, anyway?'

'You know that's not what I meant.' But it's too late. Zara can sense her skin getting hot under her blouse, her defensive streak spiking. Frankie's words have touched a nerve.

'Oh hell, I'm not articulating myself properly.' Frankie presses her fingers to her forehead. Before she can say anything further, the classic Samsung ringtone fills the bar. It takes a moment for Frankie to register that it's her phone that's ringing. She starts, pulls it out of her bag and frowns at the screen. Swiping up, she presses it to her ear.

'Hey, babe,' she says into the speaker, and Zara resists the urge to roll her eyes. Perfect Frankie and her perfect marriage, calling each other 'babe' and gushing about their six kids all the time. Though of course, Zara knows that's jealousy talking. She's unsure if she'll ever have what Frankie has, but if anyone deserves it, it's probably Frankie.

She's just about to start imagining what her life might have looked like had Elliot actually left Geneva for her, when Frankie's face drains of colour.

'Oh no . . .' Zara whispers. 'What's wrong?'

TRANSCRIPT

Video published 20/06/2022

Subscriber count: 2,913

Welcome back to *True Crime Over Wine*, where things are about to get interesting!

Let's begin with the interview I promised in yesterday's video. The one you've all been dying to hear. I've never had so many comments on a video . . . You all want to hear things from Elliot O'Connor's point of view. It's easy to see why. The man has not done a single interview since he left Sandbanks five years ago. Not one. So why is this channel different, you ask?

Well, originally he shut the door on me, too. He couldn't believe I'd actually found him. After all, he purposefully kept himself to himself so that he wouldn't start getting hounded again. But he eventually agreed to speak to me for a very simple reason . . . I don't think he's guilty. I really don't. And I think I'm the first person to say that to him. This channel and this series is the first beacon of hope he's had in years. That is why he's chosen to speak to me over the hundreds of press interviews he's been offered since Geneva was killed.

So, without further ado, here's the man himself . . .

– Cut to interview with Elliot O'Connor –

INTERVIEW FILMED AT 10.21 ON 20/06/2022

Juniper: OK, we're recording. Let's jump straight in. Can you describe what your relationship with Geneva was like?

Elliot: It was pretty good to begin with. I don't believe any relationship is perfect. Everyone has their flaws. Everyone argues, especially after being together for so long. But for most of our marriage we were good together. Great even.

Juniper: And how long were you married again?

Elliot: Nine years married. We were together two years before that.

Juniper: How did you two first meet?

Elliot: It was at the soap-awards party. I own a collection of nightclubs which are dotted all over the UK. Some of them are high-end clubs. You have to be on the list to get in. You can't just walk in off the street. Anyway, I often rent the spaces out to different companies, and those silly soap awards wanted somewhere for an after-party, so they used my club. She stole the room, as she always did wherever she went, and I couldn't stop looking at her. She must have noticed because at the end of the night she came over and gave me a kiss. Didn't even know my name at that point. I guess it just sort of carried on from there.

Juniper: Sorry, you referred to them as 'silly' soap awards. What do you mean by that?

Elliot: *sighs* I probably shouldn't have said that. That's actually one of the things we used to argue about. She never thought I took her career seriously enough.

Juniper: You didn't like her being an actress?

Elliot: Oh, I had no problem with her being an actress. I just can't stand those soaps. All the shouting and overacted drama. I tried to suggest she try a bit of theatre once, but she wouldn't have it.

Juniper: Not her scene?

Elliot: She wanted to be on TV. And she was getting the awards so there was no way she was stepping away. You know, one of the awards she got was 'Hottie of the Year'? She lorded that over everyone for months.

Juniper: That sort of brings me onto my next question. How would you describe Geneva? What was she like?

Elliot: Determined. Strong willed. She always had to be the best.

Juniper: She was popular though, wasn't she?

Elliot: Oh yeah, definitely popular. People always wanted to be friends with her. Or date her. I felt lucky as anything when we first got together. Couldn't believe she'd actually picked me.

Juniper: OK, let's fast-forward to the night she died. You said you and she were pretty good to begin with. So, not so good towards the end of her life?

Elliot: Um . . . no. We were arguing a lot. As I said, it was often about her career. She'd started doing some really heavy romantic scenes with her co-stars and I didn't like it.

Juniper: Were you concerned she was cheating on you?

Elliot: No, no. Well, not really. But it plays on your mind, you know? And then we argued about other things too. I wanted kids one day but she said it would ruin her figure. I wanted her at home more and she was always out with her friends.

Juniper: How long before her death would you say you'd been drifting?

Elliot: A few months, I guess.

Juniper: And what was your last interaction with her that night?

Elliot: She said she was going to her wine-club thing at Nadine Howe's house. I said I was going to the pub with Mike and that she shouldn't expect me home before midnight. I guess . . . she was a little quiet. I didn't really take any notice of it at the time, but looking back, I think there may have been something on her mind.

Juniper: Any idea what?

Elliot: Nope. Geneva was like a closed box with all her secrets locked away inside. You could never get anything out of her that she didn't want to share.

Juniper: Had she mentioned any fallings out with anyone? Anyone to make her feel scared or threatened at all?

Elliot: No. She didn't mention anything like that. I'd have told the police if she had. To be honest, I don't think she ever felt intimidated by anyone.

Juniper: How well do you remember that night?

Elliot: I remember it perfectly.

Juniper: Even though you were drinking with Mike at the pub?

Elliot: I have a pretty high tolerance for alcohol. I was tipsy, but certainly not enough to make any of the night hazy.

Juniper: And then you left the pub at just gone midnight, correct?

Elliot: About then, yeah.

Juniper: What did you do after you left?

Elliot: I just . . . walked around.

Juniper: You didn't drive to the pub?

Elliot: I left the car there. Didn't want to risk driving home when I'd had a bit to drink, you know?

Juniper: Why did you choose to walk around instead of going straight home?

Elliot: I just needed to think. There'd been so much hostility between me and Geneva and . . . honestly, I was considering asking her for a divorce.

Juniper: Yes, that's what I had heard. That actually brings me onto my final question. Before I ask it, please remember that, as I said before we started this interview, I need to cover all aspects and points of view of this story so that we can get a completely unbiased view of the events. OK?

Elliot: Yeah. Go on. Ask away. I have nothing to hide.

Juniper: If you did divorce Geneva, if she hadn't so tragically been killed, what would the financial situation be?

Elliot: *pause* We had a pretty airtight pre-nup. If we divorced, neither of us would be able to claim anything from the other. I'd have been fine. The clubs were our main source of income. She, however . . .

Juniper: Do you need a moment?

Elliot: No, it's fine. She blew most of her money. On what, I'm not entirely sure. But she was a reckless spender. Always buying things she couldn't afford. If we had divorced, she'd have been completely broke.

Juniper: Thank you for chatting with me, Elliot. That's all my questions for now.

– Cut back to studio –

OK, so one of the theories I've heard about why Elliot killed his wife is that she had discovered he was planning to divorce her and confronted him about it. Maybe she even threatened him. From what I know about her, she certainly wouldn't have wanted her extravagant lifestyle ripped away from her like that. They could have fought and *potentially* it could have ended in Elliot accidentally killing her, remembering that he had also had a few drinks that evening, even if he wasn't drunk, then dumping her body on the beach and taking her phone to make it look like a mugging gone wrong. But that still doesn't explain the missing laptop. Not only were the police unable to find it, but Elliot himself was the one who alerted them to it being missing. Why would he do that if his plan was to make it look like a mugging? It just doesn't make sense.

Let's switch gears for a moment. There's only so much evidence on this case available to the general public. It seems, for whatever reason, the police have decided to keep the details of their investigation mostly private. Many podcasters and YouTubers have criticised the police for this, saying that all information should be public knowledge, but it's actually fairly common for key details to stay under lock and key. So, we're going to have to fill in the gaps with what *is* readily available, and one of those things is the news coverage of the murder.

I've spent hours poring over the footage uploaded to YouTube. As predicted, the vast majority of coverage centres around Elliot. The news channels were just as eager as everyone else to paint him as the murdering husband, so they didn't really bother to film much else. It's all him covering his face and barging past reporters to get to his car. But there's some footage that features a few other people. Three other people, to be exact.

– Cut to news footage –

News reporter: It's a sad sight today at Sandbanks beach. Where this stretch of sand in Poole would ordinarily be bustling with excited families enjoying their holidays, today the mood is sombre. At six o'clock this morning a body was found by a local dog walker, and while the identity of the victim has yet to be revealed, police have confirmed that they suspect foul play and that this is an active murder investigation. Unsurprisingly, the residents of Sandbanks have been rocked by this revelation. You can see behind me some of them have gathered at the outskirts of the crime scene to pay their respects as the body is removed from the—

– Pause –

Let's stop it just there and zoom in a tad. Right there, behind the police line over on the right, are Geneva's three best friends; Nadine Howe, Zara Garcia and Frankie Crawford. Take a look at their faces. Now, obviously you can't use facial expressions to place guilt in a case like this, but what I think we can all agree is that there is definitely something off about those three women. The way they're all holding hands and leaning in to whisper to each other. And, call me crazy, but if you had just found out that your best friend had been murdered, wouldn't you cry? Yet, not one of her friends looks like they've shed a tear. Of course, it's not for me to say how someone should grieve in a situation like this – everyone behaves differently – but there's just something about their demeanour that makes me think they already knew she was dead. You should also keep in mind that they were the last people known to have seen Geneva alive, and that if one or all of them are guilty they could very well be covering for each other.

But wait! I hear you cry. *Every murderer needs a motive!*

Yes, yes they do. So did any of these three women have a reason for wanting Geneva dead? Well, it turns out, at least one of them may have.

Since I uploaded my first couple of videos, I've had quite a few of you sending in your theories, and one particular email caught my eye. Now, I've agreed that this person will remain anonymous, but according to this anonymous source, Geneva showed them a text message that she received from Frankie on 14th June, three days before she was murdered. It read, and I quote . . .

I swear to God, Geneva, if you tell Mike, you're dead to me.

Now, bear in mind that this is just from memory. This happened over five years ago and there is a chance this source may potentially have misremembered the exact wording of the message, but even if a word here or there is inaccurate, let's let the sentiment of that message really sink in. *If you tell Mike, you're dead to me.* Tell Mike what? What is it that she had on Frankie that would prompt her to send such a hateful message to someone who was supposedly one of her best friends? Was this secret enough to kill Geneva to stop her from telling Mike? The timing certainly adds up.

Of course, this is pure speculation and may not mean anything at all. But either way, I think Frankie definitely needs to go on our suspect list. So now we have:

—Elliot O'Connor
—Mike Crawford
—Frankie Crawford

Well, that's it from me today. Be sure to smash that 'like' button, leave your theories in the comments below and subscribe. I'd love for us to get to over two thousand subscribers by the time tomorrow's video goes live! We are just getting started.

Chapter Seven

Monday, 20th June

Nadine

Frankie's frantic text to Nadine telling her to come to the club as soon as she finishes work doesn't offer up any clues as to what's happened, but she knows it has to be something big for her to have not gone home. She forces her way through her meetings, trying hard not to let it show how desperate she is to get away. When today's client finally stops talking and says goodbye, she snatches her coat off her chair and makes a hasty start towards the door.

'Do you need to shoot straight off?' Andrew's voice stops her in her tracks. 'I was wondering if you wanted to go for a drink after work?'

Nadine gapes back at him, incredulous. Does he not remember disappearing on her this morning? Does he not see what an arsehole he was?

'I'd rather not,' she says simply.

He frowns, confusion etched across his face. He really doesn't get why she's pissed off. It's a shame. She thought Andrew might be someone she could actually start to really like. He makes her feel relaxed and uninhibited in a way she hasn't since she was a teenager, and she wanted to see more of him, even if that just looked like a few more nights of fantastic sex before they called it a day. But she won't be embarrassed the way she was this morning. If he thinks she's the sort of person he can get away with doing that to, he's got another think coming. Besides, everything has got so complicated all of a sudden.

'Nadine, do you have a moment?' Nadine's stomach flips as her boss, Alasdair, pokes his head out of his office. He rarely asks to see any of them in private. Any meetings are usually company-wide in the boardroom. She briefly panics that he's found out about her sleeping with a co-worker. But in the unlikely event that was true, he'd surely drag in Andrew to berate him, too?

'Now?' she says, painfully aware that Frankie is out there somewhere on a ledge, and Nadine is the one who will need to yet again talk her down.

'Unless you have something better to do?'

This clearly isn't really an optional conversation, so Nadine sucks in a breath and follows him into his office. He sits in his oversized leather chair and leans back, fingers brought to a steeple under his chin.

'You've been at the firm a long time now. How many years is it?'

'Seventeen. I started here as an intern at twenty-one,' she replies, swallowing hard to stop her voice from cracking. You don't show nerves in this job. Nerves are a sign of weakness.

'And you've done some amazing work for us in that time.'

Nadine braces herself, squeezing her legs together, waiting for the 'but'.

'I have some good news. How does senior partner sound to you?'

Her mouth drops open before she's able to stop it. She has to take a moment to be sure she's heard correctly. 'Oh, yes. Yes, that sounds amazing! Thank you.'

Nadine deals with a lot of actresses in her job, but for her ability to keep her composure she's sure she should be the one up for an Oscar. Instead of jumping up and down and squealing like she's desperate to, she offers her boss a grateful smile.

'I won't let you down.'

When she emerges from Alasdair's office, her hands are trembling and she feels as though she may faint. Senior partner. She's been working towards senior partner ever since she took the job here.

She was starting to think it might not happen, that one of the other, older lawyers at the firm might get it. None of the senior partners are female and none of them are under fifty. She's setting a company record.

Her phone buzzes in her hand, jolting her back to reality. Another text from Frankie.

'What was all that about?' Andrew asks, nodding towards Alasdair's office.

Ignoring him, she hurries out of the warmth of the office and into the breeze of the afternoon outside.

When she arrives at the club and passes through reception, it takes her a moment to spot Frankie and Zara. She had expected them to be hovering near the bar as usual, but as she moves through the luncheon lounge and scans the small groups of women, she spots them through the windows, sitting out on the deck by the pool. They're tucked away round the corner, as if terrified someone might spot them. As Nadine steps outside, the chill of the air hitting her as she does so, she spots Frankie's phone lying on her lap. She's staring at it intently while nursing a glass of wine. Zara is in the middle of topping up her glass when she spots Nadine.

'Nadine's here.' Zara's voice makes Frankie jolt up, and Nadine can see she's been crying. As she moves towards them a fresh wave of tears breaks free. Horrified, Nadine perches on the end of the sun lounger and pulls her into a hug.

'What happened?'

'Mike . . . h-hates . . . me . . .' she stammers in between gulps of air. She needs to explain further for Nadine to make any sense of what she's saying, but the tears have taken over her body and she descends into a trembling mess in Nadine's arms. She can tell now why they've chosen to sit out here. On a warm day the pool deck is the most popular area of the club. A combination of the sun glittering on the water's surface and the lush green of the golf courses in the distance can make it feel like another country, another world. But today, when the clouds above are threatening another downpour, the sun loungers are mostly abandoned. Private.

Even so, as Frankie cries, the feeling of eyes scrutinising them, of whispers circling them, is strong, but all Nadine can do is stroke her hair like a mother would a child while she weeps into her shoulder. She tries not to focus on the wet patch spreading on her designer suit jacket.

Eventually, Frankie calms herself enough to at least let Zara speak. 'That YouTuber; she posted a video and she said . . .' She pauses, obviously unsure of the most delicate way to phrase it.

Frankie wipes her streaming nose with a napkin. 'She told the world that I sent that threatening text to Geneva.'

Nadine's eyes widen and she finds herself uncharacteristically speechless. She knows exactly the text message Frankie's referring to. In fact, Nadine was there when Frankie sent it. She was the one who convinced Frankie that going round to Geneva's and having it out with her was a bad idea, that they needed to let it all blow over. But how anyone else could possibly have known about it has her stumped.

Frankie sniffs. 'I spoke to Mike on the phone before you got here. The conversation was short, but just long enough for him to ask what the hell I'd been talking about and for me to attempt an explanation and make some pathetic desperate apologies. It all took me by such surprise I didn't have any time to think about what I actually needed to say to him, and then it was too late. He told me if I couldn't be honest with him, not to come home. That he needed space. And then he hung up.' Her lip quivers as she finishes her sentence, making her voice tremble.

Frankie taps into her text thread with Mike and angles the screen to show Nadine. There are three messages begging him to let her explain, but he's ignored them all. Tears spill down Frankie's cheeks again and Nadine's heart aches for her friend.

'I have to ask,' she says after a moment, brow crinkled in concern. 'Is it not worth telling him? I mean, it's been so long. Surely it would be better, instead of having it weighing on your shoulders all the time?'

When Frankie brings her eyes up to meet hers, she can see they're bloodshot. 'I can't.'

Nadine stares at her, exasperated. She does understand why Frankie doesn't want to explain to Mike, but the frustration is rising up inside of her. She's put everything on the line to keep Frankie and Zara safe, to protect them from what they did, and all she asks is that they do as they're goddamned told. She doesn't need this shit. But she can't let them see how much she's starting to crack.

'OK then. If you're not going to tell him, you need to at least do as he asked,' she says finally, pressing the button on the side of Frankie's phone and plunging the screen into blackness. 'Give him some space; some time.'

'I should go home. I need to talk to him in person.'

'And say what? If you're not willing to tell him, what exactly are you planning on talking to him about? You need to wait until he's had a moment to calm down. If you go back now, it'll end up in a huge row. Do you want that in front of your kids? Is that really how you want to do this?'

Frankie buries her face in her arms, shoulders juddering as she sobs.

'I don't want to do this at all. I never thought this would come up again. The only person who could have dropped me into this mess is long gone.'

Nadine and Zara share a glance, and Frankie lifts her head just in time to catch it.

'When she found out, I thought I could trust her, that she'd be a friend,' she says. 'I never thought she'd start using it against me. Blackmailing me to do what she wanted. What kind of friend does that?'

Nadine doesn't even need to respond. She and Zara both know exactly what Frankie means. Geneva had something on each of them, a secret that only she knew. Secrets were power to Geneva. She wielded them like weapons. *You don't want to get on my bad side*, she used to say. *Not with what I know about you. I could end you with just a few words.*

And she has. Even from beyond the grave. Geneva has been dead for five years and here Frankie is, her world crumbling around her.

As they sit in thoughtful silence, something flashes across Frankie's face, a moment of panicked realisation. She looks up at Nadine, eyes wild.

'In the video she said something about an anonymous tip from an unverified source. It's got to be Elliot, right? Who else would she have shown a text like that to?' Her voice is getting shrill, attracting yet more attention, but the words still tumble out of her. 'Nadine, you have to do something! What if my secret comes out? Or Zara's?'

Nadine grabs her wrists and holds them steady, bringing her face close to Frankie's so that her perfume tickles her nose. When she speaks, her voice is low and foreboding. 'Frankie, you need to calm down and think about what you're saying. If someone were to overhear us, you don't want them to get the wrong idea.'

Trembling, Frankie nods, and Nadine feels her limbs relax under her grasp. But Frankie has a point. Nadine had been so caught up in Juniper's revelation of the threatening text that she hadn't even had a chance to think about how she came across this information in the first place.

An anonymous tip from an unverified source.

Frankie's right. The only people Geneva would have shown a text like that to, other than Elliot, are sitting out on this deck.

That familiar panic starts working its way up her core, churning her stomach and tightening around her chest, as she remembers the moment she got the feeling that someone had been in her wardrobe.

'I'll speak to the team at work,' she says after a moment. 'See if there's any chance of getting that YouTube channel shut down.'

As the words leave her mouth, a cheerful ding slices through the tension in the air. Frankie makes a desperate grab at her phone, clearly hoping it's Mike texting her back. But, of course, it's not her phone that went off. Her messages to Mike are still there, unread, no response.

Zara pulls her phone out of her pocket and taps at the screen.

'Fuck,' she whispers, and Nadine and Frankie both stare at her expectantly. She looks up at them and swallows hard. 'It's a message from her. She wants an interview.'

Hi, Zara, it's Juniper Rose from True Crime Over Wine. *Would you be available for an on-the-record chat any time this evening?*

Nadine reads the text message a fourth time, desperately trying to figure out how Juniper could have got Zara's number, and running various scenarios through her head.

'Does this mean I'm next?' Zara exclaims, her fingers tightening on the stem of her glass. 'Is she going to put me on the suspect list too?'

Nadine can see it in both of their eyes. Zara and Frankie are spiralling. They're regretting agreeing to keep quiet all those years ago, and journeying down a dangerous path. She has to rein things back in before it's too late.

'For goodness' sake,' she says, snatching Zara's phone from her hand and clicking on the options drop down next to Juniper's number. 'There. Blocked. Frankie, you do the same. Neither of you are going to say a word to her. This is all a drop in a bucket and the more we pander to her, the more guilty we look.'

Frankie gapes at her. 'A drop in a bucket? My marriage is over and you're calling that a drop in a bucket?'

'Your marriage is not over. Trust me, I deal with divorces every single day and you and Mike will work this out.' Even as she says the words, she's not so sure she believes them. People get divorced every day for far less. But if she says it with enough certainty, it might pacify Frankie somewhat.

Frankie drains the last of her wine and slumps back against the sun lounger. 'What the hell am I going to do?' she says, more to herself than to Nadine, but Nadine takes the opportunity to assert control nonetheless.

'You're going to stay with me for a few more days. Let Mike clear his head and calm down. We can figure out what you're going to say to him while he does that. Then you're going to talk and find a way forward. As for this YouTuber—'

Something in her peripheral vision snatches the words from her mouth. She leans back to get a better look through the window at reception. She hadn't been mistaken. There are only so many people who have that bright platinum hair around here, though Nadine has thus far not had the pleasure of seeing the nosy bitch in person as opposed to through the screen of her phone.

'Well, look who's here,' she says, and the girls follow her line of sight. Zara lets out a small yelp.

'She can't be a member here,' Frankie says. 'Is she hoping they'll just let her in?'

But as the words leave her mouth, the receptionist smiles at Juniper and hands her the guest sign-in book.

Nadine lowers her eyebrows. 'If she's on the guest list, that means she's meeting someone here.'

'Does that mean she's not here for us?'

The three women instinctively shimmy down their sun loungers so that they're mostly hidden from view as Juniper passes through reception and scans the luncheon lounge. Recognition flashes on her face and she smiles, and at the same time Nadine spots who she's meeting. Elliot is sitting at one of the tables in the corner, cup of tea in hand. He definitely wasn't there when Nadine had been looking for Frankie and Zara, so he must have arrived just moments before Juniper.

'They know each other. Really well by the looks of things,' Nadine murmurs, watching with interest as Juniper steps over to Elliot, leans over and places a small kiss on his cheek.

Chapter Eight

Monday, 20th June

Zara

Chills slink through Zara's body as she, Frankie and Nadine emerge from the golf club. They had had to wait until Elliot had gone to the bathroom and Juniper was buried deep into her phone before they could attempt sneaking out, and it all felt so wrong. Like they shouldn't have been there. As if it were they, not Juniper, who were the intruders.

'Want a lift?' Nadine says, hovering her hand over the handle of her sedan to unlock it.

'No, thank you. I could do with the fresh air.' That's not actually true at all. She wishes she had brought the car instead of taking a taxi, and foregone her opportunity to have a drink. Her head is pounding and she needs to get home to sleep this all off. But she doesn't relish the prospect of sitting in an enclosed space with her former friends when there is so much that needs to be said.

'OK. Make sure you text me if anything else happens. Anything at all, however small.'

Zara nods obediently as Nadine's phone starts ringing.

'It's work. I have to take this. Remember what I said!'

Nadine slides herself into the driver's seat, phone pressed to her ear, and Zara pulls her coat tighter around herself, preparing for the walk home. A hand resting on her shoulder makes her pause. She turns and Frankie smiles awkwardly back at her.

'Do you think it's worth talking to Elliot?' she says. 'You know, finding out what the situation is with him and Juniper? I mean, he'd talk to you, wouldn't he?'

Zara scowls, wishing she'd kept her and Elliot's affair hush-hush all those years ago. Nadine was right all along. It's far better if their secrets stay buried with Geneva.

'You want me to talk to someone you believe is a murderer? Alone?'

'Oh, no. Of course not.' A blush creeps over Frankie's cheeks, and she looks down at her shoes. 'You're absolutely right. Sorry. I wasn't thinking.'

They murmur a goodbye to each other and Zara begins walking down the driveway towards the gold-plated iron gates that serve as the club's entrance. She fully intends on calling a taxi once the girls have driven off. As she walks, she thinks about what Frankie said. The way she sneered 'he did have an affair', turning up her nose at the thought of Zara being Elliot's mistress, isn't sitting well with her. Pot, kettle, black is all she can think. She might have said something had it not been for the call from Mike distracting them. Although, if she's honest with herself, she probably wouldn't say anything. Confrontation has never sat well with her. It was always Geneva and Nadine who would send meals back at restaurants and get into arguments with inconsiderate drivers. Zara and Frankie were always the more timid of the group. She supposes that's why she always got on with Frankie the best.

Frankie has a point too. Elliot was quite clearly familiar with Juniper. It would be good to find out what he knows about her. Perhaps, if she did speak to him, she could find out if he was Juniper's mystery source. Or, if not, he might have some insight as to who it is.

The thought spins, propeller-like in her head, the whole time she's walking and again once she's in the taxi. Even as she passes Nadine's house, where Nadine's sedan is already parked up, and heads down her own driveway, she can't stop thinking about it. She's been trying to avoid Elliot ever since he arrived back. To actually be considering voluntarily talking to him is alien to her. She knows, too, that it's not really the prospect of him being a killer that's wracking her nerves. She's just not sure if she can trust herself around him. Even all these years later, even with all the suspicion that surrounds him, when he approached her the other day when she was taking her bins out, she felt the familiar flutter of attraction tugging at her insides.

A shiver runs down her spine as she passes through the front door. It always does these days. It's strange being in the house alone. It was far too big even for her, her mother and Eleanor's live-in carer. Now that she's alone here it feels unsettlingly enormous. Her eyes flick across the vast marble-adorned entrance hall with the many doors that lead out to the many rooms. For so long it had seemed the ultimate goal; being able to afford luxury like this. But what's the point of it all, really?

She massages her temple and turns her attention back to Elliot. When she opens her WhatsApp message stream with him, it sends a jolt of unsettling nostalgia through her. The most recent messages are from the year Geneva died. He had sent them just before he'd disappeared off the face of the planet.

Please talk to me Z. Everyone's turned on me. I don't know how much longer I'll be able to stick around here.

She had ignored it, and then he'd been gone.

A soft drumming starts in the pit of her stomach as she begins to type, fingers unsteady from a mix of danger and anticipation. Is she crazy to even consider talking to him? The possibilities of how this could all play out dance around her thoughts. Maybe he won't even want to talk to her. Maybe he'll be too hurt from the way she's been with him. She shakes her head and presses her thumb against the 'delete' key, watching her message erase letter by letter.

A good nap. That's what she needs. She curls herself up into a ball on the sofa and wraps her cashmere blanket around her; a fluffy cocoon to protect her from the world outside. But she can't sleep. Her mind is elsewhere now, not thinking about all the terrible things that could happen if she were to meet up with Elliot, but instead drifting back to before. His hands sliding down the small of her back. His breath on her neck. His chest heaving against hers. God, she'd fallen for him hard. Despite herself, she can't prevent her mind from bubbling with fantasies of what might have happened, where their lives might have taken them, had Geneva not been murdered.

Heartbeat increasing, she pulls out her phone again and retypes her message, tapping away quickly and hitting 'send' before she has a chance to change her mind.

Hey. I'm sorry for the way I was the other day. Do you fancy a catch-up?

A few moments later the double blue tick telling her he's read the message pops up. No going back now.

Zara has never felt so unsure of herself as she walks beside Elliot. Part of her is fizzing with excitement, the sense of déjà vu strong as they make their way down the cobbled street towards the nightclub that they had frequented so many times when they'd been sneaking around. It had been the ideal cover. Aside from being far enough outside of Sandbanks that they didn't have to worry about running into anyone they'd have known, it wasn't somewhere Geneva would ever have gone. Once she moved to Millionaire's Row, she was suddenly more country club than nightclub, despite the fact it's where the bulk of their money came from. Her income from *Copperdale Street* paled in comparison. Plus Elliot's employees were discreet and knew how to keep a secret, if only for the sake of keeping their jobs.

The other part of her, the more mature side, is acutely aware that the purpose of this evening is to deceive Elliot. To lull him into a false sense of security so that he might divulge some information about Juniper and how close she is to discovering their secrets that he might not have shared with anyone else. The thought makes her feel dirty, rotten, and she finds herself obsessing over her body language.

Is she standing too close to him? Not close enough? Does he think they're going to have sex tonight? Surely not, but then again, she has chosen to don her black strapless number that he always loved so much on her. Elliot has also dressed up, opting for a lavender shirt with the top button undone, showing just a hint of his tanned chest. The sight of him when she first laid eyes on him tonight had made Zara's heart skip one too many beats.

As they approach the nightclub, the air is filled with an intoxicating concoction of heavy bass music and the scent of kebabs and hot dogs wafting in from the street vendors. It makes her feel like she's at university again. That was always one of the reasons she loved coming here with Elliot, away from the airs and graces of the country club with its judgemental wives and onerous atmosphere. She could actually breathe here. When all the suspicion first erupted around Elliot, he had been forced to close a few of his smaller clubs, but to Zara's relief this one survived by the skin of its teeth. It was the first one he'd opened, his baby, the one that started it all, so it would have taken total bankruptcy before he gave up on it.

'So, how have you been? Really?' Elliot says – the first proper sentence he's dared utter to her since they met up at the train station.

'Fine.' Even as the stilted word leaves her mouth, she feels like an arse. She's the one who invited him out tonight. She may as well try to relax into it. 'Things have been a little rough since Mum died. I hadn't realised how much my life revolved around looking after her until I didn't have to do it anymore.'

'I wish I could have been there for you.' Elliot risks a glance her way and her stomach flips.

They approach the entrance to the nightclub, passing the queue of miniskirts and cigarette smoke, and the bouncer, an intimidatingly large man but with a friendly face, greets Elliot with a familiar pat on the back.

'Didn't know you'd be coming down tonight, boss!'

The cheerful manner with which he greets him is jarring. It's the first time Zara has witnessed anyone being even half decent towards Elliot since Geneva died. Perhaps it was only the residents of Sandbanks that held such deep-rooted hatred for him. Or maybe the bouncer was unaware of the allegations made towards his boss. Or, more likely, he cared more about keeping his job than about what Elliot may or may not have done.

'It's just a social visit. No business tonight,' Elliot says, before gesturing to Zara to head on in through the doors. As her stilettos touch the floor of the nightclub, the vibration of the heavy bass immediately pulses through her. They emerge onto the balcony overlooking the main dance floor, which is packed with sweaty bodies moving to the beat and highlighted every couple of seconds by the strobe lights.

Their first port of call is, of course, the bar, where the shaven-headed bartender is quick to recognise Elliot and hurry over to serve them.

'A pint of lager for me and . . . Sex on the Beach?' He raises an eyebrow at Zara and she can't help but smile back at him. He remembered her order.

'Please.'

She keeps her eyes fixed on the bartender as he prepares her cocktail, not daring to steal another glance Elliot's way. She knows she's playing a dangerous game. She knows she shouldn't trust him, but every time she meets his eye, that god-awful fluttering starts up in her stomach again.

Once their drinks are in their hands, they make their way through the swarms of jostling, gyrating dancers to their booth, separated off from the crowds, where they can just about hear each other over the music. It hadn't mattered so much that they could hear each other before. They didn't exactly come here to talk. Now, though, as Elliot's lips move and Zara struggles to decipher what he's saying, she has no choice but to shuffle closer to him and lean her head in towards his.

'What?' she says.

'I said I really have missed you, you know?'

Her blood simmers, warmth flowing through her.

'I thought you'd moved on,' she eventually replies, refusing to let her emotions and desires get in the way of what she's come here to do tonight. 'I saw you with that blonde-haired woman at the golf club? Juniper?'

'Are you spying on me?'

He lets out a laugh, and it momentarily causes Zara to feel stung. This is not a laughing matter, not for her at least. He must sense her slight annoyance because his face softens.

'We met at New Year's. I was a wreck, drinking way too much, and she didn't seem to realise who I was when we first started talking. It was nice not to have to talk about Geneva for a change. Anyway, we saw each other again a few times, and when I told her about my history she became really interested in true crime. Started her YouTube channel and she said she wanted to use it to reopen the case. To begin with, I didn't want it all dragged back up again, if I'm honest, but then she said she believed me. That she wanted to prove I was innocent. Well, that's the first time anyone's ever believed me so . . .' He trails off, realising his accidental dig at Zara.

She looks away, ashamed. If he is innocent, if he really was telling the truth all this time, she doesn't know how she'll ever be able to forgive herself.

'I'm going to be honest with you,' he continues, placing a hand on her shoulder, causing her to bring her gaze back to meet his. 'I have been seeing Juniper. I thought moving on was the right thing. I thought that's what you would have done. But seeing you, being here with you, it's made me realise . . . it's never stopped being you.'

Their eyes lock, and though Zara knows she should turn away, she can't. The suspense between them is deliciously, agonisingly intense. And then she forgets why she's here.

When Elliot's lips touch hers it's like they've never been apart. She knows she should stop, that this is all wrong, but she can't. She lifts her hand to graze his cheek, his stubble tickling her palm, and his hands wander her back in response. Electricity courses through her. While Elliot had been away, she'd convinced herself that she was over him, that everything that had happened with Geneva had wrecked their relationship beyond all repair, but subconsciously she had known from the second she saw him moving back into Millionaire's Row that she wouldn't be able to keep away from him. And apparently, he wouldn't be able to keep away from her either.

'We shouldn't do this,' she mutters, her words husky, lost to the music and the noise of the club. Elliot moves his mouth from hers to her neck and her breath hitches, her head tilts back, her eyes close.

No, they shouldn't do this. But then again, they should never have done it in the first place, and that never stopped them before.

TRANSCRIPT

Video published 21/06/2022

Subscriber count: 7,372

Welcome back to *True Crime Over Wine*. Well, what can I say? In just five days this channel has grown to over seven thousand of you, which I think is really a testament to how badly the public wants to see this case reach its just and honest resolution. I've been reading your comments and trying to respond to as many as possible, but it's so interesting to see just how many of you, who were initially convinced of Elliot O'Connor's guilt, have now started to question things for yourselves. I figured each day I would share an update on who seems to be the top suspect based on the comments, so let's take a look. The current list of suspects, in order of who you guys think is guilty or not, is as follows:

—Frankie Crawford, with an overwhelming majority.
—Mike and Frankie Crawford working together to cover it up coming in second, which is an interesting theory that I hadn't even considered.
—Elliot O'Connor coming in third.
—And Mike Crawford acting alone coming in as the least likely.

We've also had a few comments suggesting we need to look more closely into Geneva's other two friends, Zara and Nadine, which, I can assure you, I am doing. I haven't yet found a possible motive for either of them, but if I do, you will most certainly be the first to know.

Well, without further ado, let's get into the next interview, shall we? Unfortunately, my attempts to get an interview with any of Geneva's three friends have so far proved fruitless. You can decide for yourselves whether or not you think that comes across as suspicious. But I did manage to speak to Elliot O'Connor's parents. Now, I know what you may be thinking. It's his parents. Of course they're going to say he's innocent. There's not going to be anything surprising there. But, dear viewers, bear with me.

– Cut to Zoom interview footage with
Sue and Paul O'Connor –

INTERVIEW FILMED AT 09.45 ON 21/06/2022

Juniper: Thank you for agreeing to talk to me, Mr and Mrs O'Connor. I'm sure this has been a difficult time for you.

Paul: Yes, yes it has.

Sue: We're just grateful that you're doing this. We tried for so long to get people to listen to Elliot's side of the story but no one seemed to want to hear it.

Juniper: Well, I want to make it clear that while I do believe he's innocent, I have a duty to my viewers to cover this case in a completely impartial way. If evidence were to surface pointing towards Elliot's guilt, I'll have no choice but to share it. Do you understand?

Sue: Yes, we understand.

Juniper: OK. So, can you tell me a bit about your son?

Sue: He's, well, brilliant. I know we're biased but he's always surprised us.

Paul: Very entrepreneurial. I've no idea where he gets it from. I could never run a business of that scale. All those nightclubs became a bit of an empire, didn't they?

Juniper: They really have. Has his business been affected at all by the allegations made against him, do you know?

Paul: He says they haven't but it's obvious they have. He had to close half of them a couple of years ago. He told us it was because of all the stress, but honestly I think his revenue has taken a massive hit.

Sue: It's so unfair. All these, what do you call them, keyboard . . . keyboard?

Juniper: Keyboard warriors?

Sue: Yes! All these keyboard warriors don't realise that they're ruining someone's life!

Juniper: OK, let's take a step back. Before Geneva died, how often were you in touch with Elliot?

Sue: Not as much as we'd have liked. We live in the South of France so really only got to see them on special occasions. Christmas and anniversaries and the like.

Juniper: How did they seem when you did see them?

Sue: I didn't notice anything to suggest they were unhappy. Did you, Paul?

Paul: Not unhappy as such. Though there definitely was some tension after what happened with that girl.

Juniper: Sorry, what girl?

Sue: Nothing. Nothing. Paul, why did you have to bring that up?

Juniper: Anything you can tell me is really important. Even if you think you're protecting Elliot, the more full a picture I can get, the more likely I'll be able to help him.

Sue: It really has nothing to do with him and Geneva. It was such a long time ago.

Paul: Darling, remember we said we'd be completely honest with this.

Sue: *Long pause* There was a girl. At one of his nightclubs. It was a good ten years ago now. Elliot's always been so proud of the reputation his nightclubs have. They're safe. Not like those awful places where drinks get spiked and women get assaulted. He's always made sure to have the absolute best security and anyone causing even a little bit of trouble gets banned. Some of his nightclubs you can't even get into unless you're on a list.

Juniper: Yes, when I was doing my research I saw that. It's one of the reasons his nightclubs are so successful. You mentioned a girl?

Paul: She overdosed.

Sue: But as I said, it wasn't Elliot's fault. The slightest hint of drugs happening on his premises and he'd have had them out quick as a flash.

Paul: It was an accident. Terrible. He couldn't have known.

Juniper: I'm surprised I didn't know about this already. You'd have thought there would be news stories about it, given he's such a prominent name.

Sue: The family was well taken care of. They had no reason to cause a fuss.

Paul: Sue . . .

Juniper: Hold on a moment. Are you saying he paid the family to keep quiet about it?

Sue: Oh . . . well . . . er . . .

Paul: I think you've got more than enough for your YouTube channel, Miss Rose. If you'll excuse us, we need to be getting on.

– Cut back to studio –

Well, safe to say this scandal with the girl in the club has been well and truly covered up. I can't find any information on who she was or even reports of it happening in the first place. Clearly, Elliot was desperate to keep his reputation clean, and was willing to put a lot of money into it. I wish I could ask his parents more about it, but I have a sneaking suspicion they're not going to want to talk to me again in a hurry.

I have to say, this doesn't look good for Elliot. I mean, we know Geneva had something she was holding over Frankie, right? So maybe Frankie wasn't the only person she was using secrets against. Maybe she was using this to stop Elliot from divorcing her. I guess that's a motive for him. But it doesn't quite add up. If the reputation of his nightclubs was the most important thing to him, why would he risk it all by murdering his wife, even if it was to keep her quiet? It was obvious he'd be suspected. The husband always is. And as Mr and Mrs O'Connor said, his finances have gone downhill as a result of it. If he did kill Geneva to keep her quiet about this, he certainly didn't think it through properly. Of course, there is always a chance it wasn't planned, that it was a spur-of-the-moment killing. But that still doesn't explain why he'd have alerted the police to the missing laptop.

Another completely random theory is that maybe the family of the girl blamed him for what happened to her. Maybe they were sour for being offered money to keep schtum, and wanted to punish him. Or perhaps Geneva was the one to offer this girl's family the money, since she clearly liked to take control in situations like this. Maybe they wanted more money and she wouldn't give it to them, so they killed her knowing Elliot would most likely be the one to take the fall. This, I think, is a huge stretch, but I'm going to note it down anyway.

After my chat with Elliot's parents, I felt it was my duty, considering I have promised you all to remain totally unbiased, to look into his alibi a little further. I put this map and timeline together to help chart his movements that night, as well as what we know about Geneva's movements.

[Map displayed on screen]

It's time to visit the scene of the crime. I'm going to actually follow Elliot's movements from that night. I'm going to walk his steps. It's all very well speculating about what he could have done that night after he left the pub, but it's quite another to actually re-enact it.

– Cut back to footage outside the Cliff Poole Gastropub –

OK, and we're recording. I'm currently outside the Cliff Poole Gastropub. Thanks to CCTV we know that Elliot left Mike at the pub at five minutes past midnight and decided to walk instead of taking his car. We also know for a fact, thanks to his neighbour's Ring doorbell, that he arrived home at 00.46. So we're looking at roughly forty minutes of time unaccounted for. Now, before I came here, I referred back to the map I put together and cross-referenced with Google Maps, and the journey from the pub to the beach where Geneva's body was found is thirty-seven minutes by foot. That's assuming he went straight to the beach, which is unlikely given we've no evidence to indicate he knew she'd be there. But let's say he did, for the sake of argument. So, that has him arriving at the beach somewhere between 00.40 and 00.45.

Here we need to do a bit of guesswork, as it's not fully known whether Geneva was killed at the beach, or if she was killed elsewhere and moved. Though, do remember, Elliot left his car at the pub, so it's not like he was able to put her in the boot or anything like that. If he did kill her elsewhere and move her to the beach, he would have had to have carried her. So let's say, for the purpose of this exercise, Elliot spotted her wandering the beach on his way home. I'll check in with you again when I reach the beach.

– Cut –

Right, I've just arrived at the beach. Sorry if I'm a little bit breathless. I've just walked really quickly to get here, it only took me thirty-two minutes instead of the thirty-seven Google suggested. I want to make sure I do this in as short a time as possible, even though I think we can safely assume he probably wasn't walking that fast. So, we're Elliot, we've just passed the beach and seen Geneva. He goes over, they talk, it turns into an argument. Things get heated. I imagine that would eat up another good few minutes. Let's say five.

The coroner's report says the cause of death was strangulation. According to Google, it takes roughly seven to fourteen seconds for a victim of strangulation to pass out, and another two minutes or so for the victim to die. I'm going to set a timer on my phone for eight minutes to allow for Elliot to argue with her and kill her. Now, if we're looking at the timeline of the evening Geneva died, that takes us to, at the very earliest, 00:45.

– Cut –

Right, my timer has just gone off, so Geneva is now dead and we need to get home. Again, if you look on Google Maps, the walk from the beach to Elliot and Geneva's house is four minutes long, so I'm going to walk there as quickly as I can. In fact, I might even take it at a bit of a run, since he'd probably want to get away from the crime scene as fast as possible if he'd just killed his wife.

– Cut –

God, I'm out of breath. Right, I've just managed to run back to Elliot's house in three minutes. So, what time does that take us to on our timeline? 00.48. Holy crap, guys. That's two minutes after we know for a fact Elliot arrived home.

– Cut back to studio –

OK, I had to stop filming there because I was so out of breath from running and needed a chance to really look over the timings again. But I was right. Even though I was being super strict with how much time I allowed myself to follow in Elliot's footsteps, there just wasn't enough time. I purposely didn't give him much time for arguing with Geneva, or for panicking after he had killed her. I gave him no opportunity for dawdling on the walk to the beach. No opportunity for any detours. The fact is, Elliot *could* have killed Geneva that night, but it would have been nearly impossible for him to get home in the time that he did.

If anything has reassured me of his innocence, this is it.

I think that's enough for today. I do have another interview up my sleeve for tomorrow's video, but I think the people we all want to hear from right now are Geneva's friends, Frankie, Nadine and Zara. So, ladies, if you're watching this, please do respond to my messages. My audience is desperate to hear your side of things.

Let's revisit the suspect list, shall we? We currently have:

—Elliot O'Connor
—Mike Crawford

—Frankie Crawford
—Mystery girl's family?

Don't forget to leave your theories in the comments below and be sure to smash that 'like' button and subscribe.

Chapter Nine

Tuesday, 21st June

Frankie

Mike still isn't talking to Frankie, nearly twenty-four hours later. Her messages to him begging him to trust her remain unread. It's as if Juniper is attempting to wiggle her way in between every good thing Frankie has left, and she feels utterly powerless to stop it. There's no way to explain to him. Not without bringing all of her secrets out into the open, a gaping wound breaking free from its poorly sewn stitches.

This morning, she had jolted awake, her body drenched in sweat. She sat up, gasping for air, her heart thudding in her chest. It took a few moments for her to realise she was in Nadine's house, tucked up in bed, safe. But all morning the nightmare has been lingering in her mind like a thick fog. She used to suffer from this recurring nightmare all the time. Flashes and fragments of images that leave her feeling sick, terrified. But she hasn't had it for a few years, had managed to bury the memories so far down that they almost started to feel like she were an outsider watching a film. The anxiety she's been feeling as of late must have triggered it again.

At least Nadine's flustered flitting from room to room is somewhat of a distraction. Ordinarily, Nadine is a force to be reckoned with. Nothing ever seems to rattle her. Nothing, that is, except for her parents. From the moment she received the text from her father that they were 'in the area' and planning to 'pop down' for an out-of-the-blue visit in the afternoon, Nadine has been an unrecognisable whirlwind of stress. She'd messaged Zara asking if she could borrow Ana for the morning to help clean the house, which didn't sit well with Frankie. Ana is a person, not a tool to be passed from rich owner to rich owner. She wonders if she'd have been bothered by it five years ago, back when she herself was a part of this high society. Had she, too, looked down on everyone with less than her? Had moving away changed her? Softened her? It didn't really matter what she thought of it, though. Zara never responded to Nadine's request.

'You're getting yourself all worked up over nothing,' Frankie says as Nadine rushes in, glancing nervously at the time on her Fitbit and plumping the cushions on the sofa for the third time. 'The house is spotless as always. You wouldn't have it any other way.'

'It'll never be good enough for them. You know what they're like.'

Frankie can't argue because she knows it's true. Mr and Mrs Howe are like bloodhounds taking pleasure in sniffing out the slightest whiff of weakness in their only daughter. It isn't enough that she's a hugely successful solicitor, wealthy enough to live on one of the most expensive stretches of land in England. There's always something she hasn't achieved yet. When is she going to get married? Bless them with grandchildren? In the words of Mrs Howe, 'all the money in the world won't make you happy when you're old and alone'. Frankie hasn't actually seen Nadine's parents since she left Millionaire's Row, and though she wouldn't let it show for fear of making Nadine even more on edge, she's feeling nervous about the reunion too. If they could judge their own daughter so harshly, what on earth would they think of Frankie swapping her sprawling mansion for her small-in-comparison townhouse? Still, she had promised Nadine she'd join her and her parents on her yacht, despite the fact she's not a fan of being on the water. She always preferred to admire the boats from the comfort of steady dry land than to partake in going out onto them.

Cushions plumped, Nadine moves to the kitchen where she proceeds to arrange fleshy prawns on a bed of ice. Frankie joins her at the island and busies herself with slicing cucumbers for the salad, not wanting to get involved with the seafood. She hates the way the eyes seem to stare at her.

'I uh . . . I've invited someone else to lunch as well.' Nadine doesn't move her gaze from the prawns, rearranging them and tweaking their positioning as she speaks. 'My friend from work. Andrew.'

Frankie stops slicing and raises an eyebrow. 'Is there a man in Nadine Howe's life? And if there is, how am I only hearing about this now?'

'Well, in fairness he did come round Sunday night and you would have met him if you hadn't abandoned our girls' night in favour of falling asleep on the sofa.'

'And it's serious? I mean, enough for him to meet your parents?'

Nadine shoots her a loaded glance. 'I have no idea, honestly. I thought I liked him and then he shot off in the morning without saying goodbye and I was mad at him. With everything going on I've not even had a chance to process how I feel. But I can't face any more questions from my mother about why I can never seem to land a man.'

'Well, sounds like Andrew's a lucky man.' Frankie resumes slicing her cucumbers, quietly amused. 'He gets to suffer your mum's grilling instead of you.'

'Oh God, you're right,' Nadine says, pushing the seafood platter away from her and burying her head in her hands. 'Maybe I should tell him not to come.'

Frankie has to laugh. It's bizarre seeing Nadine so anxious. Finishing the salad, she collects up the bowl and places it in the fridge, subsequently retrieving a bottle of champagne.

'Here,' she says, flinching slightly as she pops the bottle. 'Have a glass of this. You need to chill yourself out. If they arrive while you're in this state you'll never live it down.'

It feels odd, her being the voice of reason while Nadine flaps, but good at the same time, bringing a sense of power of sorts. It's the first time she's felt any kind of power since she arrived back in Millionaire's Row, if she's honest with herself. Everything has spiralled since Eleanor's funeral, and she's felt totally out of control.

A pawn in someone else's game. If there's anything Nadine should be stressing out about right now, it's all this business with Juniper Rose, not her parents' opinion of her boyfriend or the plumpness of her cushions.

As if reading her mind, Nadine lets out a sigh. 'I'm sorry. I'm being such a self-obsessed bitch, worrying about my own issues. How are you doing after yesterday?'

Frankie shakes her head. 'He still doesn't want to speak to me. Not unless I tell him everything.'

'And that's really not an option?'

'No.' Frankie turns around and leans her back against the island, not wanting Nadine to see her face, how close she is to crying. 'This is one secret that needs to stay a secret.'

Her grip tightens on the counter and she hopes to God that Nadine isn't going to attempt to convince her again. She doesn't, perhaps because she knows all too well what it's like to have something dark you want so desperately to stay locked away.

'There's got to be a way to get that woman to move on,' Nadine says instead. 'I mean, there are thousands of other true crime cases she could film her ridiculous videos about.'

'What we need is for the police to suddenly find some missed evidence that will lead them to finally charge Elliot. He goes down, all our problems go away.'

They fall into thoughtful silence at this. She's right. If Elliot were to go down, not only would the YouTube videos stop, or at least stop looking into them, but their secrets would be safe once and for all.

'We've got a couple of hours until Mum and Dad arrive,' Nadine says eventually.

Frankie glances at her, unsure of what she's getting at.

Noting her confused expression, Nadine shrugs. 'Maybe we should try playing detective for a bit. If some random woman on YouTube can do it, why not us? We know the case better than anyone.'

Frankie sucks in a breath, a flutter of nervous excitement starting in her stomach. 'What do you suggest?'

'I've still got the spare key to Geneva's house, and Elliot's car wasn't on the drive when I looked out earlier.'

'That's trespassing!' Frankie lowers her voice to a whisper, as if worried someone could hear their plotting.

'Only if we get caught.'

They spend a good twenty minutes draining champagne as they talk themselves into it, out of it, into it and back out of it again. Nadine finally makes the decision for them by pointing out that all the while they stand around deliberating, Elliot is that much closer to returning home, and demanding they take advantage of the opportunity if only to distract herself from her parents' impending arrival. Frankie feigns hesitation, but she was always going to agree. People like her and Zara are the followers. The ones who do as they're told by the Nadines and Genevas of the world. That's why they did what they did five years ago. If Nadine hadn't taken charge that evening, things would have turned out completely differently, for better or for worse.

Now, outwardly fizzing with anticipation, Nadine glances at her phone and taps her fingernails against the countertop.

'Should we ask Zara if she wants to come with us?'

Frankie shakes her head. Zara has been blanking them all morning anyway, so the chances of her seeing the invite are slim. But even if she did, Frankie seriously doubts Zara would want to go snooping around in Elliot's house. Not knowing she still thinks he might be innocent.

Chapter Ten

Tuesday, 21st June

Nadine

It had sounded like a good plan when they were in the comfort of Nadine's kitchen. They'd be in and out of Elliot's house before anyone was any the wiser, and it would distract her for just long enough that she'd be able to greet her parents with the fresh enthusiasm they would expect of her. The more she and Frankie had discussed it, the more she fizzed with excitement. Now though, clutching the spare key that Geneva had provided her with years prior and trying to look as nonchalant as possible as they approach Elliot's driveway, she's second-guessing herself. Her perfect plan suddenly seems fraught with risk.

She's not even sure what they're going to be looking for once they're inside. It's not as if Elliot is going to have a signed confession just lying about the house. But maybe, all these years after Geneva's death, he's got sloppy. Some kind of hint as to just how bad their marriage was in the end, or maybe evidence of a motive the police have yet to uncover. If she's totally honest with herself, she's not really banking on finding anything of any real substance. She just wants a chance to see inside that house one more time, however morbid it might be. Would Elliot have redecorated in an effort to remove all traces of Geneva from the fibres of the building?

'I can't do this.' Frankie stops dead in her tracks as they approach the front door, staring at it wide-eyed and terrified, as if Geneva's ghost might open it at any second. 'What if we get caught? What if Elliot comes home?'

Nadine holds steady, keeping her composure. If she were on her own, she might abandon the plan too, but she can't let Frankie see how nervous she is. It had been her plan and she was the one who had convinced her to go along with it. Backing down now would make her seem weak-kneed and unreliable.

'It'll be fine. Even if he does come home, we can sneak out the back and onto the docks.'

'I don't think it's worth the risk. What if we don't find anything? What if we do find something and it's not enough to convict him?'

'Then we don't stop looking until we find enough. This has to end, Frankie. We can't go on like this, looking over our shoulders all the time.'

She's about to tell Frankie to go home if she's really that scared and leave the searching to her, when the sound of a car approaching causes them to shrink back behind the once perfectly trimmed, now overgrown hedges. Nadine peeks through the branches and follows the silver BMW with her eyes. It cruises past the house, not slowing in the slightest. It's not Elliot.

'We can't stand here arguing or we'll be seen,' Nadine hisses once it's passed. 'Let's just get inside.'

Despite her eagerness to appear composed and collected in front of Frankie, her hands tremble as she moves the key towards the lock. It takes her a good few attempts to get it to turn, and when it eventually does and they scurry inside, her stomach leaps into her throat. A frenzied beeping sounds, making her ears ring. The alarm. Of course, of course. How could she have not thought about him having an alarm on the door? All the houses in Millionaire's Row are alarmed.

The two of them make a beeline for the keypad on the wall. Nadine flips the plastic cover down, her breathing rapid and shallow.

'Can you remember what the code is?' Frankie shrieks, the sheer panic in her voice shattering Nadine's concentration. It was always

Elliot and Geneva's wedding anniversary. When was that? The 22nd of March? The 23rd?

Trying desperately to block both Frankie and the shrill, incessant beeping out, Nadine jabs her finger at four buttons – two, two, zero, three – then hits the enter button. A red error light winks back at her, taunting her.

'Damn it. I'm sure that was their wedding anniversary?'

Frankie does an agitated dance beside her, hopping from foot to foot. 'I thought it was that too. Shit! Elliot must have changed it. I knew we shouldn't have done this. We should go. Come on, let's get out of here before it's too late.'

'Frankie, would you shut up for a second and let me think?'

Nadine presses her fingers to her head, sucking in a deep steadying breath. She thinks back to Geneva and Elliot's fifth anniversary party, held in this very house. It had been an over-the-top extravaganza of an event, lavish and pretentious, just like Geneva. What date had it said on the invite?

She looks back up at the keypad and exhales through pursed lips as she taps the numbers again. Two, six, zero, three.

The house falls into silence, though the ringing is still going on in her ears, and she takes a moment to lean back against the wall. Frankie just stares at her, all colour drained from her face.

'Remind me never to ask you to come rob a bank with me,' Nadine says, smirking.

Key still gripped firmly in her hand, Nadine leads the way through the house. Elliot hasn't redecorated as she had suspected he might have done. In fact, it doesn't even look as though he's cleaned since he's been back. There is a thick blanket of dust on everything, save for the places where letters and bags have clearly been thrown down and disturbed it. As they pass through the hallway, a shiver runs down Nadine's spine. The photos of Geneva are still hung up on the walls. Smeary and hard to make out under the grime, but there. Why would he return, only to keep the house like this? Nadine had assumed his long-term plan was to do it up in preparation for putting it on the market, but maybe he can't bring himself to get rid of all the memories just yet. It's like stepping into some kind of ghoulish time machine.

She can practically picture Geneva stalking the landing upstairs, wondering why her friends are snooping around in her old home.

Shaking off the chills mounting in her body, she strides with purpose towards the staircase.

'Where do you want to look first?' Frankie murmurs as she follows closely behind. Her voice is tiny, mouse-like. She's obviously as freaked out as Nadine is.

'I'll look upstairs. In the master bedroom and the spare room they used to use for storage. You stay down here and search his office and the kitchen. Remember, it may not be obvious to begin with, but anything that links him to Geneva's death, you call me down straightaway.'

Frankie's eyes widen in horror. 'You want us to split up?'

'Think about it this way.' Nadine places a reassuring hand on Frankie's shoulder. 'We'll cover twice as much ground and you'll be able to get out of here that much quicker.'

She grimaces but doesn't argue, just watches after Nadine like a lost puppy as she ascends the stairs. Even after all these years, Nadine remembers the floorplan as vividly as if she were here just yesterday. Once on the landing, she makes a sharp left turn, into what used to be Geneva and Elliot's bedroom. A shudder works its way through her body. The bed is unmade, sheets strewn to one side, but she recognises the flamboyant palm-tree pattern amidst the creases. It's the set Geneva picked out, a day they went shopping in Bournemouth. He hasn't even purchased a new duvet cover. Nadine's nose crinkles at the stale smell of the room. It's making her itch.

Giving herself a shake, she moves methodically through the room, pulling open drawers and opening cupboards, trying her hardest not to disturb the dust too much for fear of him noticing. Everywhere she looks there are traces of Geneva. Her clothes hanging up in the wardrobe, her shoes tucked under the bed, her side table still filled with now unused knick-knacks: lip balm, hand cream, a small notebook. Nadine's breath hitches in her throat. A diary?

Stomach clenching, she reaches into the drawer and carefully pulls out the book. It's leather-bound and antique looking, though knowing Geneva she probably bought it in one of the department stores that boast a fabulous mass-produced 'vintage' line. Nadine allows the cover to flop open in her hand. It's wrong, of course it's wrong, but knowing that doesn't stop her. Geneva knew all of their secrets. It was only once she was gone, they realised how few of hers they knew in return.

It isn't a diary. It's an address book, the names and numbers of Geneva's contacts scrawled in messy handwriting. No wonder it was tucked away at the back of the drawer. All those details are kept on mobile phones nowadays.

The noise of the front door opening makes her drop both the book and the spare key. Crap. Elliot's home. How did she not hear his car pulling onto the driveway? She quickly closes the side table drawer and dashes to the bedroom door, but, as she reaches it, she remembers the address book. He'll definitely notice if it's just left on the floor.

'Shit,' she whispers, scurrying back to where she had dropped it. She picks it up and shoves it into her pocket, not wanting to take the extra few seconds to open and close the drawer again, before moving back to the landing.

Not even daring to breathe, she peers over the banister, down at the entrance hall where she and Frankie had been standing just five minutes earlier. She can't see him, but she can hear the rustling of him removing his coat. Would he come straight upstairs? Probably, if he wanted to get changed.

She's just about to inch her way over to the spare room when another sound makes her blood run cold. A voice. A woman's voice.

'Hey, it's me. I've let myself in. Want to make a start on clearing space for my things.'

Juniper. Juniper is in the house. And what does she mean by clearing space for her things?

Pulse quickening, Nadine leans further over the banister so that she can just about see Juniper's shadow dancing across the downstairs wall. She watches as it moves towards the kitchen. Now is quite possibly her only chance to get out without being caught.

'Hey, calm down,' Juniper continues, her voice carrying through the house. 'Don't get your knickers in a twist. I had to say something against you. People were commenting saying I was biased, overlooking any evidence against you because I want to clear your name.'

Fists clenched, Nadine pads down the stairs, praying none of the steps creak. As she nears the bottom, she cranes her neck to check that Juniper is safely tucked away in the kitchen, then scans the nearby doorways, searching for Frankie. Her eyes land on a flicker of movement behind the bookcase in Elliot's office. Frankie peeks out, and even from this distance Nadine can see her hyperventilating.

'Look, you don't have to worry, OK? I've got a plan all worked out. I've got some more information. I'll be putting more of a focus on Zara in tonight's episode.'

Nadine and Frankie gape at one another. Zara? What the hell has Juniper got on Zara? Nadine nods her head towards the front door, wordlessly telling Frankie they need to get out of here. They need to warn Zara. A bead of sweat works its way down her face as she presses herself against the wall and shuffles crab like towards the front door. Juniper can't see her from this angle, but if she comes back into the hallway from the kitchen, the game will be up. If Juniper realises they've effectively broken into Elliot's house, she'll have even more ammunition to use against them. Maybe it would even be enough to get the police interested in them as suspects again. This was too much of a risk, she can see that now. They have to move fast.

Frankie has taken the hint and is following Nadine's lead, edging out of the office and making her way along the opposite wall. Except that wall isn't a clear route like the one Nadine is navigating. Frankie's foot catches on the leg of the console table, and for one horrifying moment time seems to shift into slow motion as the vase that had been standing empty on its surface slides over the edge and topples towards the marble floor. Frankie's hands shoot out and grab the vase just before it lands. Nadine freezes, listening for any hint that Juniper might have heard them.

'What do you mean "don't touch anything"? I can't exactly move in with her stuff still in the wardrobe, can I?' she's saying down the phone. 'What are you talking about? Since when? Look, we'll talk about it when you get here.'

Looking as if she might be about to throw up, Frankie carefully places the vase back on the console table. Juniper sounds like she's getting ready to wrap up her phone call, and by the sounds of it, Elliot is on his way. They need to get out now. Nadine signals to Frankie to come over to her side of the hallway so that they can make a run for it through the door. She risks a glance in Juniper's direction, then scrambles over. Nadine twists the handle of the front door and winces as it squeaks, but there's no use in hanging around to see if Juniper's onto them or not. She pulls the door open, the chill from the outside air flooding in, and they shimmy through the gap and run.

Chapter Eleven

Tuesday, 21st June

Zara

Four messages. Zara has missed four messages when she eventually checks her phone at just gone lunchtime, waking from a deliciously deep sleep. She hasn't slept more than a couple of solid hours at a time since Eleanor died, and possibly even before that. Her night with Elliot though – the dancing, the kissing, the sex – was enough to sap any trace of energy.

Oh God, the sex.

What is she going to tell the others? Should she even tell them? Maybe it would be better to pretend this never happened, go back to awkwardly avoiding him and hoping their paths don't cross when she takes the bins out. No. It doesn't feel right. Not anymore. She'd done that because she'd been afraid of him. She'd treated him like a violent murderer just because everybody else had. But now, after spending the night tucked into the crook of his arm, watching the steady rise and fall of his chest as he slept, she's never felt safer. He didn't kill Geneva. He couldn't have. She'd known it in her heart of hearts before, had allowed her judgement to be clouded by what everyone else was saying, but last night has confirmed it.

The question is then, of course, who *did* kill Geneva?

That isn't her immediate concern, though. She lets out a small groan as she presses her hands to her eyes, wiping away the night, and looks around the room. It takes her a second to register that he's out on the balcony, bare-chested, wearing just his trousers from last night, and speaking on the phone to someone. After a moment he turns and steps back through the glass doors, and when he spots that Zara is awake, the smile he gives her makes her melt. He returns to the bed and she nuzzles back into his arm, enjoying his warmth.

'Hey, you,' she says, her voice husky from sleep.

'Hey, you.'

He shuffles back in the bed, sitting himself up with his back against the headboard, and Zara readjusts herself so that she's still in his arms.

'Everything OK?' she says, noting his slightly flustered face.

'Yeah. That was Juniper on the phone. I tried to tell her we needed to put a hold on things, but she didn't really want to hear it. I'll talk to her properly later though, I promise.'

Zara presses her lips together, trying not to think back to the last time they had a conversation like this, when he'd told her he was going to leave Geneva, and not long afterwards Geneva wound up dead.

'God, we had a lot to drink last night,' he says. 'I haven't felt hungover in a long time.'

A sinking feeling settles in Zara's chest. They had gone a little overboard with the cocktails last night. Was that the only reason he slept with her again? No. Everything he said to her, how it's always been her even after five years of not seeing each other, he said all of that long before he got drunk. This is real. They can't deny how they feel about each other any longer.

A thought occurs to her then, dark and exciting all at once. Geneva isn't here anymore, and he's putting an end to things with Juniper before they've even really started. The last time Zara and Elliot were together, they had to sneak around, their relationship tainted by secrets and lies. But they won't have to do that anymore. Sure, they'll be the talk of the town, the subject of all the gossip at the country club, and of course she'll have to deal with the judgement of Nadine and Frankie, but they could have a real shot this time. Be a real couple.

Her phone buzzes on the bedside table yet again, and Zara squeezes her eyes shut. She knows from the brief look at her phone when she woke up that at least two of the messages are from Frankie, undoubtedly wanting to talk about yesterday's awkward conversation, or perhaps wanting to complain about her marital issues. Why can't people just leave her alone? The constant interruption of messages pinging through is pulling her out of her fantasy, a dark cloud passing in front of the sunshine, and she likes it here. Here she can pretend that her being with Elliot is going to be easy. She doesn't have to face the reality of all the backlash they'll undoubtedly receive, when she's curled up in bed with him.

'Is it your friends messaging you?' Elliot says, running a finger down the back of her neck and along her spine. Her whole body fizzes.

'Frankie.'

'You should probably find out what she wants. It could be important.'

She sighs and begrudgingly rolls away from him to light up the screen once more. On second look at the unread messages, Zara sits up a little straighter. Nadine has been trying to reach her as well as Frankie. Maybe something really is wrong.

A stab of guilt hits her as she taps into the message, praying that nothing has happened to Frankie's kids. She'd never forgive herself if she'd been blanking her messages while her friend needed her.

Relief washes through her as she reads Nadine's message.

SOS. The parents are coming round this afternoon. Need all hands on deck. Meet us on my boat at 3?

'Everything OK?' Elliot asks, placing small kisses along her neck.

'Yeah, Nadine just wants me round this afternoon because her parents are visiting. She hates being alone with them.'

She glances through the window at the sky outside. Now that the rain that had plagued Sandbanks since the funeral has broken, the sun is finally peeping through the clouds. It would be a nice day for it, lounging out on Nadine's yacht with a glass of bubbles in one hand and a canapé in the other. She had planned on heading into the clinic this afternoon. Not to return to administering treatments. She figures they can cope without her at least until Monday. But some admin she couldn't deal with at home will have cropped up, and she wants to check on the place in general. Ease herself back into the world of work. Besides, her clients will be pleased to see her face.

Then again . . .

Elliot's lips against her skin send a tingle of pleasure through her, and she aches between the legs. Perhaps she should blow off both Nadine and work, and instead choose to spend the rest of the day right here with him. It's been a long time since she's had a lazy, self-indulgent day of sex and snoozing.

'You should go,' Elliot says, nodding encouragingly. 'I need to talk to Juniper properly anyway. Make sure she understands we're just going to be friends. I don't want to string her along, especially after everything she's done for me.'

Zara raises an eyebrow, suddenly remembering her original goal of going out with Elliot last night was not actually to sleep with him.

'Do you know what her plan is? Is she just going to do a certain number of videos or . . .?'

Elliot puffs out his cheeks. 'I think she's just planning on keeping going until the case is solved. I'm not really sure, to be honest. She seems certain she's going to be able to clear my name, but that just seems like a pipe dream at the moment.'

'I get why you want her to do these videos. Really, I do.' And she does. His whole life must just be constantly worrying about what people think, how they perceive him, what their reaction will be to him. She can't imagine living in fear of her car windows being smashed in or her house being vandalised. He is a scared shell of a person, and all because social media decided he was guilty. It's not fair.

'It's just . . .' She shuffles in the bed, suddenly too hot under the duvet. 'She's kind of messing with people's lives at the same time. Mike's not talking to Frankie after what Juniper said in her last video, and Frankie had nothing to do with Geneva's death. I'm just worried she's going to end up really hurting people with these accusations.'

Elliot nods thoughtfully, eyes fixed ahead of him. 'I guess I didn't really think about that side of things,' he says, voice low and despondent. He reaches out for her hand and gives it a gentle squeeze. 'I'll talk to her.'

The level of understanding he's showing, of selflessness, only makes Zara want to spend the day with him and blow everyone else off more. She nuzzles herself back into the crook of his arm, eager to savour a few more moments.

'I did tell her not to say anything against you, by the way.'

Her eyes flick up, throat constricting as he smiles down at her.

'Not that I think you've got anything to hide. But I just want you to know, when I was on the phone with her earlier I did specifically instruct her to leave you out of it. And I'll re-emphasise the point when I see her.'

Zara forces a thankful smile and looks away, unable to meet his eye.

Not got anything to hide? If only that were true.

The side gate to Nadine's garden is open, suggesting that her parents have arrived and she's already out on the yacht with them. Zara's skin still tingling from Elliot's touch, she makes her way through, stepping across the landscaped garden, with its oversized stone water fountains, and heads towards the jetty. She's careful to avoid the gaps between the wooden planks, having opted for a pair of strappy heeled sandals which she knows make her legs look amazing, especially when paired with her tight nude dress. Elliot's jaw had practically hit the floor when she'd emerged from her dressing room. He didn't look too shabby himself by the time they kissed each other goodbye. While she'd done her makeup, he'd had a shave and gelled his hair, making him look much more like the Elliot she remembers from before all this happened. If only they were a normal couple. He could have accompanied her to Nadine's yacht and the two of them together would have looked every inch a star couple.

The tension is already thick by the time she steps onto the yacht deck, and Zara can't tell if there's just been an argument between Nadine and her parents, or if it's just the usual atmosphere between them. Either is a distinct possibility.

Mrs Howe is the first to acknowledge her arrival.

'So lovely to see you, dear,' she says, hurrying to get up from her seat and plant a small kiss on Zara's cheek. Zara sits herself on the opposite side of the deck and helps herself to a glass of champagne. It's then that she notices an unexpected addition to their group.

'Hi,' she says, in an overly friendly tone, leaning forward to offer her hand to the sheepish-looking man sitting next to Nadine. 'I don't believe we've met. Zara Garcia.'

'Andrew Colt.' He gives her hand a strong shake, the kind businessmen always give, but something about the way he can't quite meet her eye catches her attention. She surveys him quietly as he reaches for a prawn.

'So . . .' Mr Howe begins, 'I hear Elliot O'Connor is back in town.'

Every person on the yacht visibly tenses, and Zara's stomach flips.

Nadine crosses her legs. 'Word spreads fast. He moved back on Sunday.'

'Why on earth he'd do that is beyond me.' Mrs Howe grimaces, shaking her head.

'No point in staying away when he's innocent.' All heads turn to Zara. She's being snippy, she knows that, but she can't help it. Finally deciding for sure that Elliot can be trusted is bringing out a protective streak in her she didn't know she had. Frankie glowers at her, clearly thinking back to the previous day's conversation.

'If he's innocent,' Nadine mutters under her breath. As if on cue, Zara's phone dings and she peers down at the message on her screen. It's from Elliot.

Having fun? I might go for a dip in the hot tub in a bit. Though I can't seem to find my swimming trunks. Oh well 😉

Heat travels across Zara's cheeks. She's quick to plunge the screen back into blackness, but not quick enough. Frankie is eyeing her suspiciously.

Zara turns to Nadine's parents, keen for a distraction.

'How have you been, Mr and Mrs Howe?'

'Oh, you know, same old, same old,' Mrs Howe says with a wave of her hand. 'I've been trying to convince this one to go back to work, but he's not having it.'

'Are you bored of him already?' Zara says with a smirk, and Nadine flinches. It was supposed to be a joke, but from Nadine's reaction she's guessing things aren't all rosy in the Howe household since Mr Howe retired. That's always the way with these people though. Suppressed resentment. Divorce is simply not an option, not when you're rubbing shoulders with your fellow elites and attempting to prove you have the best marriage, the best house, the best life.

'I told you,' Mr Howe says in a low tone. 'We'll have more time for travel now I'm retired.'

The silence that follows is deafening, and Zara feels compelled to start topping up her glass, even though she's barely had two sips, just to give herself something to do.

'So, Zara.' Mrs Howe forces a smile her way. 'How's everything at the clinic?'

'Good. We were featured in *Grazia* last month.'

'Yes, I saw. You've got some catching up to do, Nadine darling. I don't see the law firm being featured in any magazines.'

Nadine stares at her, incredulous. 'Law isn't quite as glamorous as plastic surgery.'

'Oh, I don't know. They're always doing those lists, aren't they? Top thirty women over thirty. You could get yourself on one of those if you applied yourself.'

'Nadine doesn't really have time to deal with silly journalists,' Andrew interjects. 'She deals with the biggest cases at the firm. I honestly don't know how she does it. Did she tell you she's been made senior partner?'

Nadine flashes him a thankful smile. *Kiss arse*, Zara thinks, though she does regret mentioning the article. She forgot the unspoken rule when it came to talking to Nadine's parents; never mention your successes because they'll always find a way to put Nadine down for not achieving it herself.

Mrs Howe frowns. 'I thought you already were a senior partner?'

'I was partner before, not senior partner.'

'Hm, I don't really understand what the difference is. Besides, it's not like you have any children to take up your time. I'm not sure how you can be quite so busy.'

And there it is. Every single time.

Mrs Howe, oblivious to the hurt on her daughter's face, or perhaps she just doesn't care, turns back to Zara. 'I did try to book an appointment at the clinic last week but they said you weren't there.'

Mrs Howe always books an appointment with Zara when she's in town. The public story is that she just pops in for vitamin infusions. Her penchant for Botox and fillers and lifts is something only Zara knows about. Luckily, she's amazing at her job, so any work Mrs Howe gets done looks perfectly natural. Mr Howe, on the other hand, has allowed himself to age gracefully, and it's working for him. He pulls off the silver fox look with ease. Zara always did think it unfair that men are so much better at ageing than women. For a while, they even get sexier the older they get. Still, if it weren't for the women of Sandbanks clinging desperately onto their youth, she probably wouldn't make the kind of money she does.

'I had to take some time off after Mum died.'

'Oh, of course, I'm so sorry we couldn't attend the funeral.'

As talk turns to Eleanor and all the wonderful things she did for the community, the sharpness in the atmosphere softens, but the undercurrent of thorniness is still there. It would be anyway; there's always an edge to the conversation when Mr and Mrs Howe are around, but it's even more so today, especially with the looks Frankie keeps giving Zara every time her phone buzzes.

The afternoon drags and eventually the sun starts to set, bathing the yacht deck in a pink glow that bounces off the surrounding water.

'Well,' Mrs Howe says as she stands up and sways, unsteady on her feet and not because of the gentle motion of the boat. 'Shall I open another bottle?'

'I should be heading off,' Zara says, placing her empty glass on the table, the picture of Elliot lounging naked in a hot tub still plastered across her mind. 'But it's been so lovely catching up with you both. Lovely to meet you too, Andrew.'

She plants a small kiss on each of their cheeks, before pulling her cashmere cardigan over her shoulders and making a start towards the jetty. As she's nearing the edge of Nadine's garden, a hand on her shoulder stops her. She turns to see Frankie looking back at her, her eyebrows drawn together in concern.

'Did you see our messages this morning?' she says.

Zara swallows. 'Uh-huh, not until late though. Sorry, I slept in.' Even though she can't bring herself to look directly at her, she can still sense herself buckling under Frankie's scrutiny.

'How come? Did you go anywhere nice last night?'

'Oh, you know . . .' Zara squirms, her attempt at coming up with an excuse falling flat. She should probably just tell Frankie to mind her own business. She knows it's just concern at the root of Frankie's questions though.

'You saw Elliot, didn't you?'

Zara hesitates, her immediate instinct to try to lie kicking in. But there's no point.

'Yes,' she says, trying to sound composed. 'As you suggested I should.'

'OK. And?'

'It was . . . fine.' Zara can tell the truth of what happened last night is plastered all over her face. 'He said he's going to ask Juniper to back off.'

Frankie's eyes narrow for a moment, before snapping open with realisation.

'You slept with him, didn't you?'

'Keep your voice down, will you?' Panicked, Zara flicks her gaze back to the yacht to make sure the Howes are not in listening distance. They're preoccupied, though, with Mrs Howe leaning a little too far over the edge of the boat and reeling off the colours of fish she can see in the water.

'You don't want to do this,' Frankie says, pulling Zara's attention back to her.

Zara shakes her head, disappointed in Frankie. Out of her two friends, she thought Frankie would be the one to give Elliot the benefit of the doubt.

'You don't know him like I do. He's not the monster you think he is—'

'—Nadine and I went into his house today.' The words tumble out of Frankie's mouth so fast, Zara has to take a few moments to properly process what she's said.

Becca Day

'What? Why?'

'We just wanted to see if there were any hints in there that would point towards him being the murderer. We need this case to be closed. We all do.'

'So you broke in?' She's trying to keep her composure, to not attract the attention of the people still on the boat, but she can't believe what she's hearing.

'We didn't break in exactly. Nadine still has her spare key.'

Zara scoffs at her, and Frankie's cheeks redden. She knows she's in the wrong.

'So?' Zara says after a moment. 'Did you find anything? Bloody knives stashed away? A lock of Geneva's hair? A signed confession?'

Frankie chews on her bottom lip. 'No.'

'Well, there's a surprise.' Rolling her eyes, Zara turns to leave, but Frankie pulls her back again.

'Wait, Zara. He's working with Juniper. Did you know she's moving in with him? She let herself into the house while we were there and we heard her talking to him on the phone. She said she's going to be putting more focus on you as a suspect in tonight's episode.'

A shiver runs down Zara's spine despite the warmth of the early evening.

'What?'

'I'm sorry. I really am but . . . I think he's using you. He's going to throw you under the bus.'

Zara swallows hard, attempting to slow her racing heart.

'He said . . . he told me he's going to break it off with her.'

'It didn't sound that way to us,' Frankie says, face pinched with remorse.

Tears prick at the corners of Zara's eyes and she blinks them back. 'I'll catch up with you later,' she says, turning sharply away and striding towards the side gate so that Frankie can't see how shaken she is. She can't keep doing this. Going back and forth all the time on whether or not to trust Elliot. No, she does trust him. Her gut says he's innocent. Frankie's just trying to put doubt in her mind because she thinks them getting together is a bad idea. Well, screw her.

110

But still, she thinks, as she emerges from the garden and joins Elliot on the driveway, he did tell her he'd told Juniper over the phone this morning that they were over. If what Frankie heard on the other end of the conversation is true, then that was a lie.

TRANSCRIPT

Video published 22/06/22

Subscriber count: 15,015

Welcome back to *True Crime Over Wine*. You guys have been absolutely amazing leaving all of your theories in the comments, and I'm getting loads through on social media, too. I'm trying desperately hard to reply to all of you but, as you can imagine, it's hard to keep up. This channel has grown so quickly, beyond anything I had ever imagined when I first decided to dig into this case. It just goes to show how badly everyone wants justice for Geneva.

Before we chat to today's guest, let's take a look at the suspect list and who you lovely subscribers think is guilty. We have:

—Frankie Crawford, still soaring ahead in the leader board.
—The mystery girl's family is pretty much tied with Mike and Frankie working together. We've also had lots of you hazarding guesses as to who could be related to her. Stay tuned until the end of the episode for a bombshell on that one!
—The theory that Mike and Frankie Crawford worked together is still coming in strong in joint second place.
—Elliot O'Connor coming in third.
—And Mike Crawford acting alone still coming in as the least likely.

So, let's move on to today's interview. I'm still struggling to get in touch with Frankie, Zara or Nadine. I've tried messaging them over and over and they've just blanked everything. I've also discovered in the process of poring through all the news footage and press interviews from five years ago that this isn't unusual behaviour for them. They didn't say anything to anyone about the murder back when it first happened either. I feel like not enough people called them out on it then. But I'm calling you out on it right now. Girls, if you're listening to this, your silence is just making you look more guilty. People want to hear your sides of the story. Please get in touch with me.

However, you'll be pleased to know I did manage to secure an interview with another of Geneva's friends. Now, Erica Richards wasn't a close friend as far as I can tell, not like Frankie, Zara and Nadine, but she was Geneva's co-star on *Copperdale Street*, and she contacted me specifically asking to be interviewed. I think you'll find what she has to say particularly interesting.

– Cut to Zoom interview footage with Erica Richards –

INTERVIEW FILMED AT 09.21 ON 22/06/2022

Juniper: Thanks for agreeing to talk to me, Erica.
Erica: Yeah, no worries.
Juniper: OK, so three people who are of particular interest in my investigation are Geneva's best friends. Do you know them?
Erica: I know of them. Like, I know who they are. I saw them mentioned on the news a few times back when it first happened, and Geneva spoke about them a few times. I've never talked to any of them, though.
Juniper: From the times Geneva mentioned them, what sort of impression did you get of them?
Erica: It's really hard to say. Obviously, I only got Geneva's side of the story. Like I said, I don't actually know them.
Juniper: No, but it's what Geneva said that I'm interested in. Did you ever get the impression that there were any issues between any of them?

Erica: Um . . .

Juniper: Yes?

Erica: Shit. Look, I don't want to throw anyone under the bus. Usually, whenever Geneva did talk about her friends it was just in passing, mentioning an outfit one of them had worn, that sort of thing. But there was this one time that's always stuck in my head.

Juniper: What did she say?

Erica: She came into work really pissed off. Like, on another level pissed. Couldn't even concentrate on her lines. The director kept having to pause and give her a break.

Juniper: And this was because of one of her friends?

Erica: Yeah. I went to ask if she was OK at lunch, and she started ranting about how she was supposed to have been her best friend and she double-crossed her and she's a bitch and all sorts of horrible things. I don't really want to repeat it all on camera. Geneva was really laying into her.

Juniper: Who? Which friend?

Erica: I can't remember a hundred per cent. It was such a long time ago and, honestly, I wasn't properly listening. But I think she was talking about the brunette. Zara, I think her name is?

Juniper: Zara? When did this happen?

Erica: That's the reason it's always played on my mind. This was the day before she died.

Juniper: What? And you didn't think you should mention it to the police?

Erica: Well, no. To be honest, I didn't think it was that big of a deal at the time. Geneva was a bit of a live wire. The smallest thing could set her off and you only had to look at her the wrong way for her to call you a bitch. It was a little out of the ordinary, but nothing to really alarm me. And then by the time I found out she was dead, the police had already ruled all three of her friends out as suspects and were focusing on her husband, so I kind of just let it rest. It's only when you started doing your videos that it made me look at that moment in a new light. That's why I wanted to come on here.

Juniper: Do you remember anything else from that day?

Erica: No, that's it. I'm sorry I can't be more helpful.

Juniper: OK, I think that's everything I need. Thanks again for reaching out.

– Cut back to studio –

Holy heck. OK, let's look at this objectively. It could be entirely coincidental. If this conversation between Geneva and Erica had happened any other time, I'm not sure I'd put so much weight on it. After all, what Erica said seems to be the general consensus. Geneva was easy to piss off. But the day before she died? Clearly something happened between her and Zara, and it just feels like way too much of a coincidence to not look more closely into this. I think we definitely need to add her to the suspect list, and if anyone knows any more about an argument between the two of them, please do get in touch via the email address in the video description. Zara, it would be amazing if we could hear directly from you.

Now, before we finish today's episode, I promised you I'd reveal a bombshell regarding the mystery girl, right? Well, I asked Elliot himself about it. He didn't want to do another full interview, in fact, I got the impression he was pretty upset with his parents for even mentioning this girl, but he did agree for the sake of transparency and clearing his name to tell me who this girl was. Her name was Rosa Castillo, and she and her sister were actually in the UK illegally. Elliot wouldn't tell me the details of how he 'took care of the family' after Rosa's death, but after doing a little – OK, a lot – of digging, I discovered that there is a certain maid living on Millionaire's Row named Ana Castillo. Ana was coincidentally given a work visa just one week after Rosa died. Who is her employer, you ask? Why, none other than Zara Garcia.

There's no obvious connections there in terms of how all of these things relate to Geneva's death, but Zara's name sure has cropped up a lot today, don't you think?

Let's take a look at the new suspect list, shall we?

—Elliot O'Connor
—Mike Crawford

—Frankie Crawford
—Mystery girl's family AKA Ana Castillo
—Zara Garcia

Don't forget to leave your theories in the comments below and be sure to smash that 'like' button and subscribe.

Chapter Twelve

Wednesday, 22nd June

Frankie

Frankie and Nadine had been in the middle of brunch at the club when the latest of Juniper's videos popped up on Nadine's phone notifications. They had only chosen to leave the house in an effort to clear their heads of the previous day's happenings: breaking into Elliot's house, overhearing Juniper's phone call, finding out Zara is quite literally sleeping with the enemy. Surprisingly, Nadine's parents had been the least stressful addition to the day. But this video sapped any chance they had of pretending that everything is still OK. As they leaned in over their salads to listen to the video, Frankie was sure everyone in the club was staring at them. They probably were.

Now, Frankie's eyes are fixed on her plate as she pushes lettuce leaves around with her fork. The weight of the world feels like it's crushing her. She wants to go home, curl up in Mike's arms, with her children jumping over them and squabbling for the remote. She wants to return to school runs and homework and wrestling the little ones into trollies at Tesco. Normality. The bland, dull life she's purposefully forged for herself, as far away from the drama of Millionaire's Row as possible. How did she end up being dragged back into it after all these years?

'We need to talk to Zara,' Nadine says, breaking the silence. The tension in the air is palpable. Frankie can tell Nadine is trying to hide her agitation, but the telltale signs of stress are there. The way she keeps tapping her foot under the table and straightening the already straight napkins, desperate to regain some command of the situation. 'We knew Juniper was going to go after her but . . .' She trails off, but she doesn't need to finish for Frankie to know what she was going to say.

Even though they were expecting today's video to be about Zara, nothing could have prepared them for something so . . . incriminating. Why hadn't she told them about an argument with Geneva, or, for that matter, this business with Ana?

Frankie nods thoughtfully, giving up on her salad and resting her chin in her hands. 'I suppose she hasn't responded to your message?'

They had asked Zara to join them for brunch and Nadine had texted her again after the video went live, but once again she's ignoring them. Frankie can tell what's going through Nadine's mind. Zara is becoming more and more of a loose cannon. A flaw in their deception. A risk.

Nadine checks her phone one more time.

'Nope.'

They'll have to go to her house then, but what kind of welcome they'll get is another matter entirely.

Frankie leans back in her chair. 'You don't think there's any way Juniper could find out what we did, do you?'

It's only a very slight movement, but Frankie notices it. Nadine's body tenses. Her expression tightens.

'Nadine?'

'Hmm? Oh. No, of course not.'

Frankie's eyes shrink to slits. 'What's the matter?'

She looks over at her, but Nadine's not quite meeting her eye. 'OK, I have to tell you something but you have to promise not to overreact. Do you remember I asked you if you'd been in my wardrobe?'

Frankie frowns, trying to think back over the previous few days. She does vaguely remember being asked something along those lines when she'd just woken up on the sofa.

'Kind of?'

'Well . . . when I told you both I'd sorted everything that night, that wasn't strictly true.'

The blood drains from Frankie's face. Suddenly, it's like the world is shrinking and distorting as she struggles to comprehend what Nadine is saying, as if she's trapped in a nightmare. She wants to pinch herself. Wake herself up. What is it about her friends, this dysfunctional group of women? Why is there always so much she doesn't know?

Our secrets keep us close, Geneva used to say. But Frankie thinks it's entirely the opposite. Their secrets are tearing them apart.

'What are you talking about?' she says sharply, and Nadine flinches, looking uncharacteristically unsure of herself. She glances around to check that no one is within listening distance, choosing her words carefully.

'I didn't get rid of . . . you know what. I hid them . . . under a floorboard in my wardrobe. I was sure they'd be safe. No one would ever think to look there, especially not under a floorboard. But then . . .' She shakes her head, eyes glassy. 'I don't know. I had a feeling earlier in the week that someone had been in there, snooping around.'

Frankie stares at her, stunned into silence. She wants to stick her fingers in her ears to block out the noise. It's all too much.

'I'm sorry. I should have told you.'

'You're damned right you should have!' Frankie grips the table, knuckles turning white. 'You told us to trust you. We can only do this if we're all in this together, that's what you said!'

'I know. I clearly wasn't thinking properly. But none of us were thinking straight that night, let's be honest.'

Frankie shakes her head, wishing she could go back in time and choose to never return to Millionaire's Row.

'We're going to have to tell Zara,' she says, standing up and pushing her salad away. 'Come on, let's go. No more secrets.'

Frankie's stomach is twisting itself into knots by the time they get there, her head pounding. Her sleep has been disturbed ever since she arrived back in Millionaire's Row and she feels as if she's been awake for days. She knows Nadine will be the one to steer the conversation with Zara, taking the lead as usual, but she isn't sure if she finds that a comforting thought or not. What is she going to say? Do?

At first they don't think Zara is going to answer the door, but after ringing the bell a second time they spot movement through the frosted glass window. When Zara opens the door, Frankie is momentarily stunned. She's never seen her look so rough. There are dark circles under her red-rimmed eyes and her hair doesn't look like it's even been brushed. Zara stares at them for a few seconds, allowing them to absorb her dishevelled appearance, then retreats inside, leaving the door open.

'Are you OK?' Frankie ventures, trying to sound normal as they hesitantly follow her in. She kicks off her shoes and Nadine does the same.

'Oh sure.' Zara, now in the living room, slumps back on her sofa with her feet up on the coffee table. 'Couldn't be better.'

Frankie and Nadine share a glance as they edge towards the sofa. The curtains are drawn, giving the living room a dark and dismal appearance to match Zara's mood.

'I'm guessing you saw the video then?' Nadine says.

Zara snorts, narrowing her eyes at Frankie. 'You got what you wanted, didn't you?'

'You think I wanted this?'

'You didn't want me with Elliot. You told me he was using me. Now you get to say "I told you so", right?'

'That's not fair!' Tears sting Frankie's eyes, and she swipes angrily at her face. 'We were only concerned for you.'

'Well, don't be. I'm fine. You two should worry about yourselves and your own secrets getting out.'

Frankie's stomach churns again. She's right. Juniper's YouTube channel is growing faster than any of them had been expecting, and the more eyes she gets on her videos, the more she seems to be able to dig. They had originally hoped she'd just give up after a while, but that's looking less and less likely.

'Zara, stop acting like a child!' Nadine snaps, moving to the curtains and whipping them open, making Frankie squint against the flood of sunlight. 'This is about all of us. All of us decided to keep that night a secret. If one of us goes down, we all do. There's no use in us turning on each other. We need to start being honest and talking.'

Frankie nods. Now she remembers why Nadine always takes charge. Because she's good at it.

She can see Zara faltering, seeing the sense in Nadine's words, but she's stubborn. She leans forward and shakes her head.

'I don't have the energy for this right now. I need time to process my feelings about Elliot. And I need to focus on getting myself back to work. I can't just let my life stop.'

'Well, if you want to really be able to focus on going back to work, we better get our stories straight,' Nadine says matter-of-factly. 'I'm going to make us some coffee, and then we're going to talk.'

A few moments later, Nadine places two steaming cups of coffee on the table and grasps a third in her hands. She perches on the oversized armchair and crosses her legs, sipping thoughtfully.

'Firstly,' she says, 'tell us about Elliot.'

Zara's body tenses.

'What about him?'

'When did it start back up between the two of you?'

She looks momentarily confused, then flicks her gaze to Frankie. 'You didn't tell her?'

Frankie shrugs. 'I didn't think it was my place to say.'

For the first time since they arrived, Zara offers her the briefest of smiles. Clearly she'd been expecting Frankie and Nadine to be gossiping behind her back, but Frankie was always the member of the group who least enjoyed spreading and listening to hearsay.

Zara sighs and rubs her face, before telling Nadine what she'd confessed to Frankie at the golf club, how she'd always doubted his guilt, and as she does so, Frankie gets the same nauseous feeling she did when she heard it for the first time.

Nadine says nothing once she's finished. She sits in silence as Frankie's heartbeat thrums in her ears, waiting to see what kind of reaction this revelation would garner. Eventually, Nadine lets out a long, slow breath through her teeth.

'Frankie won't say she told you so,' she says. 'But I will. You should have listened to us about Elliot. Nothing good came from you being with him five years ago, and nothing has changed.'

'Gee, thanks for the pep talk,' Zara sneers. But any of the fight that she'd normally have exerted at being talked down to like that has been sapped from her. She knows now that they're right.

A shudder travels down Frankie's spine as she remembers the venom in Geneva's voice when she had explained her plan to them; how Zara had somehow crossed her and she was going to make her pay. 'We're going to ruin her,' she had said. *We*. It wasn't even a question. It was an instruction. Frankie and Nadine were to go along with whatever cruelty Geneva had planned to destroy their friend. They didn't have a choice, as far as she was concerned. They just had to follow orders like the puppy dogs they had become. Except turning against Zara had been a step too far. Geneva hadn't been banking on them refusing to help her; the beginning of the end.

'What about Ana?' Nadine's voice snaps Frankie back to the present.

Zara shrugs helplessly. 'Geneva convinced me to take her on. I didn't know everything that had gone on at the club. I didn't need to know. She's a bloody good maid.'

That's definitely true; Ana certainly never took advantage of what she knew about Elliot, how easy it would be for her to destroy him. She works hard and is probably underpaid if Zara is honest with herself. Frankie grits her teeth, not wanting to say what everyone is thinking.

'Could Juniper be right? Could she have held a grudge against Geneva and Elliot for what happened to her sister?'

Nadine nods. 'She was working that day, wasn't she? Maybe she overheard what Geneva said to us about you and wanted to protect you?'

'No. Absolutely not.' Zara stands, shaking her head emphatically.

Sensing this conversation not going anywhere productive, Frankie is about to suggest they start writing down all the people who could have wanted Geneva dead, conduct their own little *True Crime Over Wine* episode, when a sharp banging on the door makes them all jump.

Zara sighs, letting her legs drop heavily from the table before standing up. 'If that's that YouTube bitch, you can talk to her.'

Both Frankie and Nadine lean towards the front door to listen in. When Zara opens the door and a man's voice sounds, Frankie stands up so quickly she's hit by a wave of light-headedness.

'Mike?' she says as she hurries to the door.

He buries his hands in his pockets when he spots her. 'Hey. I . . . uh . . . I went to Nadine's first but there was no answer.'

'Are the kids with you?' Frankie peers hopefully over his shoulder, hoping she might see five excitable sets of hands waving at her, plus Callie scowling in the background. She can't believe he's actually here. He looks rough – clearly he's foregone shaving over the past couple of days, but he's here.

'No. Mum's with them. I thought it would be a good idea for us to talk. In person.'

Dread settles into the pit of Frankie's stomach. Is he here to tell her he wants a divorce? No, surely not. Not because she refuses to tell him one secret.

Giving Zara a nervous smile, she steps out onto the front step and pulls the door closed behind her. She considers suggesting they go to Nadine's rather than standing and talking out in the middle of the open, but she can see he's already gearing himself up to talk.

'I need you to give me something. Anything.'

Frankie winces, wishing she could pull him to her. She hesitates. 'It's . . . it's not worth it.'

'What do you mean?'

'Whatever happened, it's gone and done. There's no use digging it all back up now.'

Mike scrunches his hands into fists. A vein pulses in his neck as he looks up to the sky. 'Well, you've got to tell me something, Frank. I'm going out of my mind imagining all the awful things it could be. I mean, what could have been bad enough that you had to threaten Geneva not to tell me? Did you cheat on me? Is that it?'

Tears building in her eyes, Frankie shakes her head, mouth opening and closing like a goldfish, wishing she could say something to put him at ease. He drops his eyes back to hers and steps forward. His hands grip on to her upper arms.

'You can tell me. Whatever it was, whatever you did, we can work it out. I won't be angry. But you have to tell me.'

She can feel herself relenting, her resolve weakening. Maybe it would be OK after all. Maybe Geneva was wrong when she said Mike would never be able to live with it. But as quickly as that thought enters her mind, so does the thought of her kids. Their faces.

'I'm so sorry.' She sobs, her body trembling under his grasp. 'I can't. It's not just you and me I have to think about.'

A flash of confusion crosses his face, but before he can say anything else his eye is drawn to movement on the pavement at the end of the driveway. Frankie follows Mike's gaze to where Elliot is standing.

'Don't,' she whispers to Mike, but it's too late. He's off, storming down the driveway.

'Why have you come back?' he snarls.

Frankie follows, nearly tripping over herself, her hand reaching for Mike's arm in a futile attempt to pull him back. An old couple strolling along the other side of the street stop to nosy in on the ruckus. There will undoubtedly be more onlookers soon. This can't happen. Not here. Not now.

Elliot hasn't said anything in response to Mike's outburst. He's just looking at his ex-best-friend, his face unreadable.

'I said, why the fuck have you come back?' This time Mike doesn't just shout, he reaches out his hands and shoves Elliot back. Elliot stumbles, his ankle twisting as it slides awkwardly off the edge of the pavement and into the road. 'Nobody wants you here. You should never have returned.'

'Mike, stop!' Frankie has to do something. This isn't her husband. He's always been angry at Elliot, sure, bitter that his best friend could do something so terrible, but he's not one to get into this kind of confrontation. This is the hurt and the upset from Frankie's secret that's causing all of this.

'You should just piss off back to whatever hellhole you disappeared into,' Mike continues, pushing Elliot again, harder this time. Still, Elliot doesn't fight back. Someone touches Frankie's arm and she lets out an involuntary gasp, whipping around to see Zara and Nadine standing behind her, eyes wide as they watch Mike rage at Elliot.

'Or better yet, why don't you do the world a favour and just top yourself!'

Frankie turns back to the chaos just in time to see Mike's fist impact with Elliot's nose. He spins, head snapping to one side, before crumbling to the ground. His head hits the road with a sickening thud.

'Hey! What the hell do you think you're doing?' A woman's voice cuts over the commotion. Fear shoots through Frankie, cold and sharp. Juniper.

The platinum-haired woman runs towards them, and Frankie's immediate instinct is to run, sprint in the opposite direction, but she knows she can't leave. Instead, she hurries over to Elliot, with Zara and Nadine following close behind. She reaches him seconds before Juniper, who drops to her knees next to him, her skirt hitching up as she does so to reveal an intricate rose tattoo on her thigh. Frankie lowers herself to the ground, too, and together they lean over to inspect him. He's awake, blinking rapidly, but there is a deep, red mark on the side of his head.

'Call an ambulance,' Juniper instructs, and Frankie, in total disbelief that she's taking orders from Juniper, of all people, pulls out her phone.

Chapter Thirteen

Thursday, 23rd June

Zara

At the clinic, Zara can't concentrate. She spends the day in a sort of trance, her mind locked on Elliot. She had been so sure, so convinced that what he had said that night was true, that it was finally their chance to be together. But he'd lied. He'd told her he had ended things with Juniper, but then she'd let herself into his house. And then they'd gone after Zara, even though he swore to her he'd told Juniper to back off. If Elliot cared about her, he wouldn't have let Juniper shine the torch of suspicion on her like that.

He's fine, apparently. Not that she'd specifically asked, but Frankie had sent her a message from the hospital updating her on his head wound, which turned out to be superficial. *They're keeping him in for observation*, she said. Zara just responded with a simple 'OK', because what else could she say? She's glad he wasn't seriously injured. But at the same time, she feels nothing but rage when she thinks about him, thinks about that video.

'Um.' Mia, the surgeon who's been holding the fort while she's been away, knocks tentatively on the door to her office. Even when Zara gestures for her to come in she doesn't, just hovers outside. 'Your last appointment has just called to cancel as well.'

Zara closes her eyes and presses her face into her hands. That's the third cancellation she's had today. She finally gets herself back to the clinic, finally readies herself to see her clients who have been waiting so patiently for her return, and now they're all cancelling. Just how far spread is this thing going to go? The last time she checked, the view count on the video calling her out as a potential suspect stood at 37,254, but the more time goes on, the quicker it seems to be growing. How many of those views are from residents of Sandbanks? She's not even going to be able to show her face at the club at this rate.

'You may as well go home, Mia. No point in you hanging around when we haven't got any clients.'

Mia shuffles from foot to foot. 'Are you sure? Do you need help closing up?'

'I'll be fine. You get yourself some rest. You deserve it.'

She gives Mia a grateful smile. She doesn't know what she'd have done this past week if Mia hadn't been so willing to take over the reins. Once Mia finishes collecting up her things and leaves, checking with Zara one final time that she doesn't need her for anything, the clinic is deathly quiet. Zara leans back in her chair and looks around her office. Framed awards and magazine cuttings decorate the walls. Her mum had been so proud of her for all she'd accomplished. She'd turn in her grave if she knew some YouTuber was threatening to tear it all down. Fleetingly, she wonders if there's any way she could threaten her to stop. It's what Geneva would have done. Or maybe she could pay her off, give her a sizeable sum in return for her backing off. But it's too risky. Threats and blackmail would just make her look more guilty, and if Juniper's moral code is high enough, she could just expose any attempts to shut her up to the world.

Sighing, she heaves herself up and starts working through the close-down procedures, making sure the clinic is ready and waiting for tomorrow's clients. That's assuming she has clients tomorrow. She runs through the calendar and decides to send an email to all who have booked, saying how she's thrilled to be back, thanking them for their patience, and reassuring them that it's business as usual. As she finishes up the email and hits 'send', a tapping at the main glass doors makes her jump. Mia must have forgotten something.

Fumbling with her keys, she heads towards the doors to let her back in. But it isn't Mia peering in through the glass. It's Elliot.

For a moment it's as if the clean, white, sterile building around her has crumbled to dust. Nerves spike the base of her stomach. She can't open the door. She mustn't let him in. But he's seen her. He knows she knows he's here. If she doesn't speak to him now, he'll only try to talk to her at home. Not engaging with him would just be delaying the inevitable.

'I didn't realise you were out of hospital,' she mumbles when she opens the door, trying to catch her breath. 'How are you feeling?'

'Fine. A little groggy.'

There's an odd expression on his face. Hurt? Anger? Maybe he's annoyed that she didn't come to the hospital to visit him, or respond to any of his many messages telling her he knew nothing about what Juniper was going to say in her video. She knows that's a lie. Whatever it is that's bothering him, it's as if it's seeping out of his skin. Where just a couple of days ago his presence made Zara tingle with excitement, now she's met with a sense of dread.

'You should go.' Her voice comes out barely a whisper.

Elliot's eyes narrow. 'Why won't you believe me? Why don't you ever believe me?'

As Elliot stares at her, a familiar nagging voice tugs at her and thoughts spiral through her mind. If he did actually kill Geneva, it explained why he'd got so cosy with Juniper. All part of a ploy to clear his name. Getting Zara to trust him again, seducing her, to throw her off the scent, while all the time he was trying to implicate her as his wife's murderer. As much as she doesn't want to believe it, it makes sense. Gripped somewhere between anger and fear, she takes a step back and attempts to push the door shut, but Elliot's hand shoots up and blocks it. He wedges his foot at the bottom.

'Zara, please, we need to talk.'

He's breathing heavily, his chest heaving under his shirt. He's got the sleeves rolled up in that casual way he does. Just a few days ago the sight would have made her weak at the knees, clamouring for him to take her in his muscular arms. But now they don't look sexy, they look dangerous. And deadly.

She's frozen to the spot, and he takes advantage, stepping into the waiting room and closing the door behind him. She scolds herself for not screaming out for help while it was open.

The door is glass, she thinks to herself. *Someone could see us.* The thought isn't much of a comfort though.

'Why would you talk to her about me? About Ana?' she spits, the fury she's felt since she watched Juniper's video bubbling over the fear.

'You don't understand.'

He moves towards her and she instinctively backs away.

'Don't come any closer!'

His mouth presses into a thin line. 'Look, I tried to stop her. I told her about Ana before we got back together, and as soon as I thought there was a chance for us, I told her I didn't want her putting any heat on you. But she wouldn't listen to me.'

'Bullshit! Everything you say is bullshit!' She's forced herself into a false sense of confidence now and she's running with it. 'You told me you'd broken it off with her.'

'That was the truth. I first told her I wanted to end things when I called her the morning after we spent the night together. I told her again in person later that day but she got really pissed off. Maybe that's why she went after you in the video, I don't know.'

She falters, looking away, not wanting to listen to him, not wanting to give him the chance to sway her again. 'Why did she have a key to your house?'

Elliot's brow creases. 'How did you know she had a key to my house?'

'Someone saw her letting herself in.' Heat rises in her cheeks. Even now, even though she's sure he's lying to her, she finds it wrong, unnatural, to lie to him. She can't drop Nadine and Frankie in it and let on that they'd been in his house when Juniper had been there.

He sighs, dropping his head forward. 'Because she was going to move in. I told you, when I met her at New Year's I was a mess. Having someone finally believe me after all these years felt good. Like I actually stood a chance. So when she said she wanted to take our relationship to the next level, I agreed. It was stupid fast but . . . I didn't see any reason not to. But you've got to believe me, as soon as I thought there might be a chance for us, I told her it couldn't happen anymore.'

The words he is saying sound somewhat believable, but Zara won't be sucked in again. She can't take the disappointment, the hurt.

'You need to leave,' she says, taking a step towards the door, but he blocks her path.

'Not until we've talked about this.'

There's something in his voice that makes her shudder. Heart rate increasing, she narrows her eyes.

'Move out of my way, Elliot.'

'I'm not going anywhere until we've had a proper conversation. I care about you too much to go home now.'

The realisation that he's not going to leave and isn't going to let her leave hits her like a ton of bricks. Panic and frustration rise in her core like vomit.

'I don't want to talk. I want you to go.'

'You've gone all these years letting me get on with it while my life was torn apart. You didn't once show an ounce of care or compassion even though you say you supposedly love me. Well, now's your chance to prove it to me.'

'Out of my way, Elliot!'

She thinks about Geneva, her last moments, how terrified she must have been when she realised that this time she couldn't blackmail her way out of it. That she was coming to her overdue, sticky end. Is this Zara's end? She should never have trusted Elliot, not when the murder is still unsolved, not until the killer was caught.

'I can't,' he says, tears brimming in his eyes. 'I've gone so long thinking I've got nothing left. You gave me hope the other night. Spending it with you, being with you, it's the first properly good thing that's happened to me in . . . I don't even know how long.'

He attempts to reach for her, to wrap his arms around her, but she pushes him away and turns on her heel. She makes a start for her office but Elliot is faster. He darts in front of her, blocking her way.

'Zara, for God's sake, talk to me!' He's shouting now, the charming, cool exterior cracking, and Zara flinches. She backs up, heart thudding in her ears, and edges deeper into the belly of the building. She doesn't want to move out of sight of the glass doors. It's the classic move in the horror movies that always ends up with the glamorous girl getting sliced open and strung up before the opening credits. But she has no choice. He's blocking any other option.

'Please, I'm begging you,' she says, her voice coming out vulnerable and weak, which she hates herself for. 'Just go. If you really care about me, you'll leave me alone.'

But he doesn't. He takes a step towards her, reaches for her hand. She snatches it away and storms towards the pre-op suites.

'Why won't you talk to me?' His voice, and his footsteps, follow her. Dull, rhythmic thuds.

'Because I'm fucking scared of you!' she screams. She lunges for the AUTHORISED PERSONNEL ONLY BEYOND THIS POINT door and tries to slam it shut, but it bounces off his palm as he follows her into the hallway.

'You don't have to be scared of me, Zara,' he says, his tone pleading. 'I'd never hurt you.'

But as the words leave his mouth, his body looms, filling the doorway, and once again she's trapped.

'Stay away!' She takes another tentative step back, but this time she trips. Her ankle twists, fire exploding in the joint, and her head is flying towards the corner of the supply cabinet and she can't stop it. Elliot's hands shoot out. He grabs her, yanks her up.

'Are you OK?'

Zara peers up at him, pleading, 'Please, just let me go.'

'You're really going to turn on me again?' His grip tightens on her wrist. His eyes darken. Was this it? Was this the last thing Geneva saw before she died? Terrified, Zara looks around wildly for an escape route, a way to get away from him, and her eyes land on the emergency exit.

She reaches her hand out, grappling with the items on top of the supply cabinet, and takes hold of the first thing she can – the surgical tray. Bracing herself, she flings it up towards his head with as much force as she can muster. As it impacts with his skull, he crumples, lets go of her wrist and grips on to the door frame to steady himself. In seconds she's out, not daring to look back to see if Elliot is coming for her. She bursts through the emergency exit and hoists herself over the railing. Her shoes touch the tarmac of the car park and she's running, gasping for breath as she puts as much distance between her and the clinic as possible.

As she reaches her car, she has a moment of blind panic when she thinks her key might still be in her office, but she digs her hand into her pocket and she feels it, a tiny little beacon of hope. She unlocks the car and throws herself in, revving the engine and powering off at top speed.

TRANSCRIPT

Video published 23/06/2022

Subscriber count: 26,746

Welcome back to *True Crime Over Wine* and the next instalment of the Geneva O'Connor case. Well, you did it. You managed to rocket this channel to over twenty-five thousand subscribers, and we're actually already on our way to 30k. I cannot thank you enough. Keep sending in your theories and suggestions. I'm loving the conversation that's going on around this case.

As always, let's review the suspects and who you guys think killed Geneva.

—Zara Garcia has shot into the lead with an overwhelming majority after yesterday's revelation that she argued with Geneva the day before she died. Well, just you wait. I have some crazy juicy titbits for you coming up in today's episode.
—For the first time since I started investigating this case, the second most likely according to you guys is all three friends working together: Zara, Frankie and Nadine. Now, I have to admit, I've considered this too, though we have yet to establish a potential motive for Nadine. That's not to say she wasn't involved, but, you know me, I try to keep my speculations based off of the facts in front of me.

—Elliot O'Connor is coming in third place.
—Ana Castillo, Zara's maid, is coming in tied fourth place with Mike
   Crawford, though honestly, very few of you actually think either
   of them had anything to do with it.

Right, let's move on to today's interview. Firstly, I want to publicly
apologise to Geneva's parents, Alan and Leslie. I've been trying to
contact them since I started this case for a comment and they've
ignored me, and I might have pushed my luck a little bit yesterday
when I went to their house and asked if they'd give me an interview.
This, understandably, caused a lot of upset for both of Geneva's
parents, who are still having to deal with not only their only daughter's
death, but the fact that her killer is still walking free five years later.
It's not surprising that they don't want to talk about it. To attempt to
interview them was tactless and wrong, and I went too far.

So, I didn't manage to interview them, and to begin with I was
worried I wouldn't have anything new to share in today's episode.
But, I'm pleased to say, that is not the case. Now, I don't know if
you remember I had an anonymous source who said Geneva had
told them about the threatening text message Frankie had sent to
her. Well, after the revelation about Zara yesterday, I got back into
contact with that anonymous source. This person is actually friends
with Zara on Facebook, and I asked them if I could take a look at her
profile, since obviously she wouldn't accept a friend request from me.
I actually thought they might say no, but they didn't. As you might
expect, I've been basically non-stop stalking her social media pages.
It turns out, she has had a fair bit of tragedy in her life, too. Her older
sister Lou killed herself in 2016, just one year before Geneva was
murdered. Now, on first glance, this doesn't seem to suggest much.
It's just incredibly unlucky to have two such tragic incidents occur
in such a short space of time. But something did stick out as odd to
me as I was browsing through Zara's timeline.

Zara is quite outspoken on social media. She's the type of person
to post photos of her food, outfits of the day, Zara is 'feeling grateful'
and all of those kinds of posts. In fact, if I was a creepy stalker, I
could pretty much find out exactly where she is at any given moment

because she updates about her life so much, even going so far as to 'check in' at the various venues she's at and sharing her running route on her stories. Now, in 2016, which is when her sister died, she had been consistently updating her social media at least four times a day, and then when Lou passed away these updates abruptly stopped. If it was anyone else, I wouldn't necessarily think this was strange. If you're grieving then social media probably isn't going to be your top priority. But I've compared this period of her life with her social pages from this year.

Zara's mother passed away earlier in the month and, even though – if her photos are anything to go by – she was way closer to her mum than her sister, she has never stopped updating her social platforms. She's been posting details about the wake, thanking everyone for their kind messages, sharing updates on how much money has been donated in her mother's name to various charities, posting memories and photos of the two of them. But when Lou died, she went totally silent. Why? What's the difference between when her sister died and her mum died? Why did she act so uncharacteristically back then?

Lou's boyfriend at the time of her death was tagged in a couple of group photos, so it was pretty easy to find his profile and track down an email address. I have to say, I thought I was clutching at straws with this one, but just on the off chance, I decided to contact him to see if he knew anything about Lou and Zara's relationship. And, oh boy, buckle your seat belts, kids, we're in for a wild ride.

– Cut to Zoom interview footage with Stephen Pollard –

INTERVIEW FILMED AT 10.45 ON 23/06/2022

Juniper: Right, we're recording. Thanks so much for agreeing to this interview.
Stephen: Yeah, it's all good.
Juniper: So, I wanted to ask you a little bit about your girlfriend Lou. I'm sorry for your loss.
Stephen: Thanks. It's been a long time but I still miss her.
Juniper: I can imagine. It's a terrible way to lose someone.

Stephen: Yeah, and so pointless.

Juniper: Just take your time. If anything is too raw or too much for you, we can pause the recording. I specifically wanted to ask you about Lou's relationship with her sister, Zara.

Stephen: *Exhales deeply* Right, before we get into this, I just want to say that I've kept my mouth shut about this for all this time because I didn't want to hurt Lou's mum. Eleanor was a really lovely woman. She was always so good and welcoming to me and she was so broken by Lou's death, I just couldn't do it to her. But now . . . now I feel like I owe it to Lou to let everyone know the truth about what happened.

Juniper: What do you mean?

Stephen: Lou and Zara were always pretty close. I mean, it was a typical sister relationship from what I could see. I think there was a little bit of competitiveness there, but nothing that would strike me as odd.

Juniper: OK . . .

Stephen: Zara wasn't the issue. The issue was her friend, the one who died.

Juniper: What? Geneva?

Stephen: Yeah. Ah shit . . . Sorry, I don't even know how to word this. I don't want to talk crap about a dead girl, you know? But it's the right thing to do.

Juniper: Of course, take your time.

Stephen: OK . . . Basically, the reason Lou killed herself was because a video got out. It was . . . um . . .

Juniper: Intimate?

Stephen: Yeah. Yeah, you could say that. It was a video that she and I filmed . . . in private. It wasn't ever supposed to be seen by anyone. It was just for us, you know? A bit of fun. Anyway, the video got out somehow. By the time we realised what had happened, it was all over the internet. Lou was a teacher and a load of her students got wind of it and shared it. You know how these kinds of things escalate. We got it taken down, of course. We even got the police involved, but the video had been uploaded from an anonymous account using a fake email address so they couldn't figure out who posted it. But by then it was too late anyway. It had already been shared so much and turned into all sorts of memes, it didn't matter that the original video had been taken down. It was everywhere. When her boss at the school found out, he said he had no choice but to let her go. All she'd ever wanted was to work with teenagers, to give them a good start in life, you know? Everything got taken away from her.

Juniper: I'm so sorry. That's absolutely horrendous.

Stephen: Yeah. She was just completely broken. It didn't matter what any of us said or did. I think she blamed me, too. I was the one who suggested making the video in the first place.

Juniper: I'm a little confused though. What does all this have to do with Geneva O'Connor?

Stephen: Oh, come on. You seem smart. Have a wild guess.

Juniper: Wait, are you telling me Geneva was the one who shared the video?

Stephen: Bingo.

Juniper: How do you know that?

Stephen: I know because Zara told me. At Lou's funeral, she was really distressed. Like, really, really distressed. More than you would expect. She couldn't even make it through the vicar welcoming everyone. It's like she saw the coffin and just flipped out, ran off outside. Eleanor was in no state to go after her so I went out to check if she was OK and I found her just sort of staring at the empty grave where Lou was to be buried. She was in a kind of haze. I don't even think she realised she was actually talking to me. But she was just saying that it was all her fault, over and over again. I told her not to be so silly, that she had nothing to do with it, and that's when she told me. Geneva was the one who shared the video. Then it was like she suddenly woke up and realised what she had said. She begged me not to tell anyone, that it wouldn't help Lou now and all it would do is destroy Eleanor even more. Eleanor loved Geneva. It would have broken her heart to know she'd done that to her daughter.

Juniper: But why? Why would Geneva do such a thing?

Stephen: Your guess is as good as mine. I didn't know her all that well, but from what I can tell she made a habit of finding things out about people and then using it against them. I don't know what Lou did to piss her off, but it was clearly enough for Geneva to want to ruin her life. And she did it.

Juniper: God, I'm going to need some time to process this. Did you see much of Zara or Eleanor after Lou died?

Stephen: Not really. I visited a couple of times but I could tell it was upsetting Eleanor, me hanging around. I thought it was best to just leave them to move on with their lives.

Juniper: What about when Geneva was killed?

Stephen: I heard about it. I think most people did. And, I've got to admit, I was glad. She was such an awful person. I didn't think she deserved to live when Lou is dead because of her.

Juniper: Did it occur to you that Zara might have had something to do with Geneva's death? Revenge for what happened to Lou?

Stephen: Of course it did. But, like I said, I didn't want to hurt Eleanor more than she already had been. By that point she was ill, really ill from what I'd heard. I couldn't start interfering, telling the police what happened with Lou. Zara would have been arrested and that probably would have been enough to finish Eleanor off. Now that she's gone though . . . I just feel like I owe it to Lou to share what happened. All these people saying what a tragedy it was that Geneva was killed like that, how awful it is, laying flowers on the beach all the time. It sickens me, to be honest. She doesn't deserve to be grieved. Lou does.

Juniper: Thank you so much for talking to me, Stephen. I hope you can start to move on.

– Cut back to studio –

I have to admit, after we hung up the call, I sat for about two hours trying to wrap my head around all this. I mean, the fact she would actually go through with something like this is just . . . well . . . it's disgusting, honestly. It makes me sick.

Zara is looking worse and worse the more we find out. We knew she'd argued with Geneva, but this? If ever we were looking for a motive, this is it.

Of course, Stephen shares this motive. I mean, he said himself in his interview that he was glad Geneva was dead, that she didn't deserve to live when Lou was dead because of her. You could really tell how much hatred he holds for Geneva, even now, all these years later. But I don't think he'd have told me everything he did if he had killed Geneva. He wouldn't shine a spotlight on himself like that, publicly announcing his motive when no one was looking at him in the first place. He probably wouldn't have even agreed to speak to me if he was guilty. So, I don't know about you, but I'm inclined to believe him when he says the only reason he kept quiet until now was to save Lou's mum from more hurt.

It really does keep on coming back to Zara. No wonder she went quiet on social media after Lou died. The guilt she must have felt, that it was her own best friend who did this to her sister, must have been absolutely crippling.

The question I obviously had after talking to Stephen is what could Lou have possibly done to Geneva to make her want to ruin her life? Zara clearly knew about whatever it was. I asked my anonymous source, to see if they knew anything about what had gone on between Zara and Geneva. Once again, I've promised to keep this person's identity confidential, and I am going to preface this with the disclaimer that what they shared with me is very much an alleged claim. They were not willing to share with me how they obtained this information, whether or not they have any proof or why they have chosen to wait until now to reveal this information, so just bear that in mind. But allegedly, Zara and Elliot were having an affair.

God, let's just let that sink in for a moment.

So, according to this source, Geneva caught on to the fact that Elliot was cheating on her. They said, and I quote:

'Geneva had photos that proved Elliot was doing the dirty on her. These photos were taken through the window of Zara's house. Though the curtains are drawn, you can clearly see Elliot's outline in these photos. The woman he is kissing matches Zara's height and build.' End quote.

So, let's review. According to Geneva's co-star Erica Richards, Geneva was ranting about Zara the day before she died, saying that she'd double-crossed her. According to Stephen Pollard, Lou's boyfriend at the time of her death, Geneva was the one who shared the sex tape that ultimately ended in Lou's suicide. And now, according to my anonymous source, Zara was having an affair with Geneva's husband Elliot.

I've tried reaching out to Elliot for comment on this but he seems to have gone MIA. The messages I've sent him today haven't been read at all. I wish Zara would agree to an interview. My head is spinning and I have so many questions for her. But something tells me I'm not going to hear from her now.

I don't think we're going to get anywhere from me just sitting here and thinking. I need to do some more digging, try to establish Geneva's reasoning for sharing Lou's sex tape and try again to make contact with Zara. Before I sign off, let's take a look at the suspect list again:

—Elliot O'Connor
—Mike Crawford
—Frankie Crawford
—Ana Castillo
—Zara Garcia

And now, I suppose we should also add on Stephen Pollard.

Don't forget to leave your theories in the comments below and be sure to smash that 'like' button and subscribe. I'll see you again tomorrow.

Chapter Fourteen

Thursday, 23rd June

Nadine

Despite Nadine's determination to stop everyone from losing their heads – to make sure no one does or says anything that will destroy the web of lies she's built – she knows she's lost her handle on things. Zara is still barely speaking to them, even after they were proven right about Elliot and Juniper, and now she's walking on eggshells around Frankie too. Since Mike went home, knuckles bloody from his run-in with Elliot, she's been in a foul mood. Nadine feels like shaking her. She understands that all of this is hard on Frankie's marriage, but she needs to look at the bigger picture. Her relationship with Mike is just one tiny piece of the tower that's going to come crashing down if they don't take control, and fast. She no longer trusts either of her friends not to screw everything up.

As she watches Frankie skulking around the kitchen, opening the fridge and staring mindlessly into it as if all her answers lie behind a packet of cheese, her thoughts shift to Juniper.

Juniper, Juniper, Juniper. All she ever thinks about these days is Juniper. The source of their troubles. There has to be some way to stop her from releasing these videos. She's tried doing some digging of her own again, even though she already knew all Juniper's social profiles were set to private. She's even spoken to a few friends at work, asked if there's any kind of legal angle they can take, perhaps going down the defamation route, but it seems if they were to attempt anything of the sort, they'd likely not win, and even if they did, it would result in a highly publicised court case. Precisely the opposite of what she needs.

A frantic banging on the door cuts through the silence of the house, making both her and Frankie jump. They eye each other nervously, before Nadine heads to the hallway. The sight of Zara standing on her doorstep in her work clothes, hair in disarray, mascara streaked down her cheeks, makes her breath catch in her throat.

'What happened?'

Without even giving her a chance to talk, Nadine ushers her in, keen to get her out of the sight of any potential passers-by. As she places a hand on Zara's back, she can feel her trembling through her shirt.

'Elliot attacked me,' she says as they move into the living area. 'At the clinic.'

Frankie rushes over when she sees the state of her.

'What? I thought he was in hospital!'

'He discharged himself.' Zara as good as collapses onto the sofa while Nadine and Frankie sit either side of her. 'He kept saying he wanted to talk and he wouldn't leave. Wouldn't let me leave. I was so scared.'

She hunches forward and buries her face in her hands. Nadine signals to Frankie to put the kettle on. She wonders if she should go and get Zara one of the sleeping pills she keeps stashed in her bathroom to calm her down.

'I can't live like this anymore,' Zara mumbles, her words muffled by her palms. 'I can't cope with all the secrets and the lies and the fear.'

Nadine strokes her back. 'I know. We're all stressed right now. You just need to give me a few more days. I promise you I'll work this out. Get us back to normal.'

'We should turn ourselves in,' Zara says suddenly. 'We should tell the police everything we know.'

Frankie freezes, kettle held in mid-air. 'You're not serious?'

'Why not?' Zara's head jolts up. 'Then all the lies would finally be over. And maybe if we told the police everything, it would help them solve the case. They could arrest Elliot and put him away for good.'

Nadine stares at Zara. 'We're not telling anyone anything,' she says sternly. As much as she's been concerned about her friends' reliability over the past few days, that was nothing compared to the dread that's now working its way through her at the thought of Zara opening her big, Botox-infused mouth and ruining everything. Not when her life is going so well, when she's finally about to be made senior partner. She dares her parents to look down on her once they see her new pay cheque. She'll be making more money than her mother could dream of.

'I . . . uh . . . I hate to add to the stress . . .' Frankie is looking down at her phone, all colour washed from her face. She lifts it up and angles the screen towards them. 'I set it to notify me if a new video was published.'

They watch the video in stunned silence. Then, as it nears the end, Zara descends into a howl. Not a normal cry, but a primal, desperate wail of anguish. Frankie is quick to wrap her arms around Zara, to pull her close to her and rock her, mother-like, as Zara sobs into her shoulder. Nadine, meanwhile, can do nothing but stare at her. What she wants to do, what she really, really wishes she could do right now, is to slap her hard across the face.

How could she do this to them? How could she not have told them about Lou when she knew how much they all have riding on this?

'Zara,' she says, once her bawling has quietened enough for her voice to be heard. 'You need to tell us everything. No more secrets. I can't protect you if I don't know everything.'

Zara sits up, wiping her snotty nose with her sleeve, but she doesn't speak.

'Why did Geneva share that video?' Still Zara refuses to answer, and Nadine feels the rage building inside her, working its way up her throat, tearing away at her composure. 'Tell us!' she shouts, making Zara jump.

'Nadine! Stop!' Frankie gapes at her, clearly as shocked at her outburst as Nadine is herself.

'She . . . she . . .' Zara's stuttering response comes out between hiccupping gulps for breath. 'She found a pair of Elliot's boxers. They were stuffed down the side of my sofa. She confronted me about them and . . .' She buries her face into her hands. 'I told her I had no idea how they got there. I swore to her I'd never even had Elliot in the house. I didn't think. If I'd known she was going to think Lou was the one having the affair and go after her I'd have never . . .'

Her explanation comes to a halt as she descends into yet more fits of tears. Nadine thinks back to how Zara had been after Lou died, the way she turned in on herself, threw herself into her business, and it suddenly all makes sense. She'd allowed Geneva to think Lou was the one sleeping with her husband, and Geneva destroyed her.

Unable to stomach listening to Zara's cries, Nadine moves to the kitchen and pours her a glass of water. She places it down on the coffee table in front of Zara a little too hard, so that it splashes over the edge of the glass and drips off the coaster, but even that's not enough to distract her.

Zara takes a sip of the water and her sobs ease slightly.

'I don't understand how anyone could have known about the photos of you and Elliot,' Frankie says, shaking her head. 'I mean, we're the only people you told. Who the hell is this anonymous source Juniper keeps talking to?'

'Maybe she showed someone the pictures before she died?' Nadine suggests. 'Although, that doesn't sound like Geneva. She'd have wanted to keep them to herself until she confronted Zara.'

'And there was no time between her confronting Zara at wine club and her getting killed for her to be able to share them with anyone. Not unless she met someone on the way to the beach.'

'I still don't think she'd have shown anyone, though.'

Zara mutters something, snapping Frankie and Nadine out of their conversation. Frankie had almost forgotten she was there, she'd gone so quiet.

Nadine cocks her head to the side. 'What?'

'It has to be the killer,' she says quietly, bringing her bloodshot eyes up to meet theirs. 'That's the only thing that makes sense, right? Someone had to have found the photos on her phone before . . . before we stole it.'

Chapter Fifteen

Five Years Ago

Frankie

'You did tell Geneva it was here and not the club, didn't you?' Zara asks, bringing another bottle of wine into the living room to top up everyone's glasses.

'Yes. In fact, she's the one who said it was my turn to host, when we were chatting about it on Instagram.'

Frankie can see the annoyance in Nadine's body language, the way she's sitting stiff and stilted. She can't abide lateness. Once, Frankie forgot all about wine club and didn't turn up at all, instead getting sucked into a reality show on TV while her phone was on charge upstairs. When she eventually went to retrieve it, she had a stream of angry text messages, and she had to face the dreaded Nadine silent treatment for about a week afterwards.

The doorbell rings and Frankie smiles. 'There, that must be her now.'

She goes to answer the door, even though it's Nadine's house, because she knows if Nadine answers it, she'll jump straight down Geneva's throat for being late.

It is Geneva standing on the doorstep, but immediately Frankie knows something is wrong. Alarm bells go off in her head. Geneva's got that look in her eyes, the one you always hoped you'd never be on the receiving end of. It's radiating off her. Like she's out to kill.

'Sorry I'm late.' She forces a smile and grits her teeth.

'It's fine. We were starting to get worried. It's nearly eleven. Are you OK?'

Geneva doesn't reply, just steps through the doorway and slowly makes her way along the hallway, like a cat stalking its prey. Frankie wants to remind her to take her shoes off or Nadine will throw a fit, but something tells her she shouldn't. Instead, she watches as Geneva turns off the hallway and into the living area.

'Zara,' she calls in a strange, sing-song voice. 'Come chat to me upstairs, will you, hun?'

The look on Zara's face is as if she's just been called to her execution. Frankie and Nadine exchange a concerned glance. They've all seen Geneva act like this before. Once, not long after Frankie had first moved to Millionaire's Row, one of the other women on the street had accused Geneva of flirting with her husband. She even went on Twitter to publicly shame her, tagging the producers of *Copperdale Street*. Frankie never did find out exactly what Geneva did to that woman, but she and her husband moved away not long after. Another time, an old classmate from Geneva's school posted a picture on Instagram of Geneva as a teenager, from back when she was slightly awkward with braces and glasses, before she glammed herself up in preparation for her eventual rise to B-list fame. The picture went viral around the same time she won the Hottie of the Year award, and for a long time that photo was displayed alongside her award acceptance photo in the newspapers. Geneva, in retaliation, decided to out that girl as bisexual to her extremely Catholic parents.

There's only one thing Frankie can think of that Zara could have done to deserve that look. Has Geneva somehow figured out that Zara's been sleeping with Elliot? Frankie can't see how – the only people who know are she and Nadine, and both of them know better than to drop Zara in it – but Geneva has a particular knack for finding things out. Frankie shudders at the thought.

The urge to attempt to listen in is almost unbearable as Frankie and Nadine sit in awkward silence, awaiting the return of their friends. It's not long before Geneva and Zara's muffled voices rise in both volume and urgency, and then Frankie's sure she can hear Zara crying. She stands, ready to interfere, when the sound of a door being flung open echoes through the house and Zara comes running down the stairs.

'What's the matter?' Frankie says, shocked to see that Zara's mascara has smeared down her cheeks.

Zara doesn't respond. She flies past Frankie, not even glancing her way, and out of the house. When Frankie looks back up to the top of the stairs, she sees Geneva watching from the balcony with a smirk on her face.

'What did you say to her?'

'Only what she needed to hear,' Geneva says simply, floating down the stairs as if she has not a care in the world.

Nadine emerges from the living room, glass of wine in hand. 'What's going on?'

'What's going on' – Geneva reaches the bottom of the stairs and plucks the glass of wine Nadine is holding from her grasp, downing what's left of the wine – 'is that Zara is no longer a part of this group.'

Frankie and Nadine exchange a nervous glance. 'Excuse me?'

'You don't need to know all the details. All you need to know is that she's crossed me. And she's going to pay. We're going to ruin her.'

'Hang on a minute.' Nadine takes her glass back from Geneva, and Frankie has to marvel at her balls. If Geneva had taken her wine, she'd have just gone and got herself another glass. 'You can't just say something cryptic like that. What has Zara actually done?'

Geneva's eyes narrow, and Frankie notices they're a little bloodshot. She suspects that mouthful of Nadine's wine may not have been her first alcoholic drink this evening.

'It's a secret,' Geneva says, her lips quirking up at the corners. Frankie can tell Nadine is on the verge of asking her if it's to do with the affair, but they both know better. If Geneva doesn't know, the last thing they need to do is give her more ammunition, and if she does know, Frankie's unsure what she'd do to them for not informing her.

She can't not speak up though. 'Geneva, you can't expect us to just turn on Zara.'

When Geneva turns to look at her, chills slink down Frankie's spine. 'I thought you were my friends,' she says.

'We are. But . . . we're Zara's friends too.'

Geneva lets out a half-laugh, rolling her eyes. 'Zara is a whore. A self-centred, disgusting whore who, apparently, doesn't give a shit about the people she calls friends. If you want to take her side, fine, but know that she'll eventually cross you too. She doesn't care about any of us, not really.'

'Take her side? What are you talking about?' Nadine cuts in. 'How can we take anyone's side when we have no idea what's going on?'

'Look, it's quite simple, girls. And think carefully about how much I've done for both of you before you answer this. How many secrets I've kept for you both. It's her or me.'

Geneva's words hang in the air like poisonous gas. Frankie looks over to Nadine and can see she's thinking the same thing as her. Of everything Geneva has just said to them, one particular part has stuck out. *Think carefully about how many secrets I've kept for you both.*

Geneva had made a similar thinly veiled threat a few months before. She and Frankie were supposed to be having a lunch and spa date at the club, but Mike surprised her with a trip to the cinema while the kids were in school. It had been so long since they'd had a proper date, Frankie didn't think twice about blowing off Geneva. She didn't even properly blow her off. She just rescheduled – saying they could crack open a bottle of wine at her place in the evening instead. But the next morning, it was obvious Geneva was pissed off. She'd come over to Frankie's with some bullshit about how friends should take priority over husbands because, at the end of the day, friends are the ones who know all of each other's dirty little secrets. It was so obvious that she was referring to what she had found out about Frankie a few months prior, even though it was Geneva who had convinced her not to say anything to Mike. That ended up in a huge row, though thankfully all the kids were still asleep and dead to the world. After Geneva was gone, Frankie had sent her a text message telling her that if she ever told Mike, she'd be dead to her. Perhaps a little extreme, but she was so overcome with anger. What kind of friend does that? Uses secrets against you like that?

After their falling-out, though, everything seemed to go back to normal. Geneva acted like her threat had just been a big joke, assured

Frankie that she'd never really turn on her like that. But now here she is, doing it again.

'Screw you, Geneva.' Nadine is the first one to break the silence, and Frankie's stomach clenches as the words leave her mouth. 'You don't get to hold shit over us. We're not your puppets.'

Geneva digests Nadine's words, then tilts her head to Frankie. 'What about you?' she says, her voice sickly smooth.

Body tensing, Frankie holds her breath and nods. 'Nadine's right. You can't blackmail us.'

It takes a long, long time for Geneva to finally react to Frankie's words. When she does, it's not the outrage that Frankie's expecting. Instead, a serene smile crosses her lips. It's unnerving.

'Have it your way,' she says, before flicking her hair over her shoulder and sauntering out of the house.

'Shit, shit, shit.' Frankie's head pounds as she searches her living room, flinging cushions off the sofa and digging her hands down the edges. She got back from the failure of wine club and relieved her babysitter just after 11 p.m. She and Nadine both agreed they should just let Geneva sleep on whatever had got her all worked up, and they'd talk to both her and Zara tomorrow. Frankie had got home with the intention of going straight to bed.

'Mum?' Callie's voice behind her makes her jump.

'Oh, darling! You scared me. What are you doing up?'

Callie's face is washed out, pale. She's not been sleeping well lately, too busy lying awake and stressing about her GCSEs. Frankie wishes she could take them for her.

'Are you OK?' Callie asks.

'Yes, I'm fine. I just can't find my stupid phone. I must have left it at Nadine's.'

Callie nods her head towards the console table. 'It's there.'

'Oh!' Frankie blinks, taken aback. She was sure she'd looked there already. The run-in with Geneva must have really frazzled her nerves. 'Thanks, darling. What are you going to do with your old mum, eh?'

Callie doesn't laugh. 'OK, well, 'night then,' she says.

'Goodnight, sweetheart.'

As Callie turns and heads back up the stairs, Frankie's heart aches. As her oldest child, she's always felt that she and Callie have a special bond. But these past few months she's become moody, withdrawn, and Frankie isn't quite sure how to reach her. She slumps down on the sofa, mind whirring. She can't be bothered with this drama between Geneva and Zara. Whatever's happened between them is nothing to do with her. She has her family to worry about, her kids to focus on. Not playground spats between grown women.

Rubbing her temples, she stands up and goes to retrieve her phone from the console table. As she does so, it starts to ring. Nadine.

Sighing, she swipes to answer it. 'Nadine?'

'Look, I'm really worried about Zara,' Nadine says. 'She's not answering her phone. I knocked at the door to check if she was OK and Ana said she's not come home yet.'

'She's probably out clearing her head.'

'Maybe. But I think we should probably see if we can find her. She'd had a lot to drink by the time she left and she was really upset. You know what Geneva's like.'

Frankie purses her lips, her bed upstairs calling to her. Of course, she knows Nadine is right. Nadine is always right. But she's already sent the sitter home and she can't exactly call her straight back. She casts a weary eye at the spot where Callie had been standing. Callie's old enough to be left with the kids for ten minutes or so. If she's quiet, all six of them will be none the wiser. Besides, Mike should be back from the pub soon.

'OK, I'm putting my shoes on now.'

The evening is warm as Frankie and Nadine trudge down the street, scanning the landscape for any sign of Zara. The peninsula they live on is a huge circle, so they can either wander down along the docks or up along the beach. They opt for the docks. As they reach the northern point of the peninsula and prepare themselves to start walking back down alongside the beach, they finally spot Zara, sat on one of the benches, shoulders juddering.

'Zara, we were worried about you.' Frankie hurries over and puts her arm around her friend.

'Geneva's going to ruin me,' Zara says, sobbing.

'No, she's not. She's just making empty threats. She wouldn't actually do that.'

'You don't understand.' Zara shakes her head, causing tears to splash down onto her thighs. 'She knows about the affair. She's not kidding around. She has pictures on her phone. And she knows . . . something else. Something that will ruin everything for me.'

So it is the affair. But what else could she possibly have on her? How many awful things has Zara done? Frankie can tell from Nadine's expression she's desperate to pry more, but Frankie just wants some sleep.

'Come on, let's get you home.' She holds out her hand and helps Zara to her feet, which isn't an easy task as she's wearing her signature stilettos and is unsteady from all the alcohol she's consumed. 'We'll talk to Geneva in the morning. I'm sure this isn't as bad as you think it is.'

Zara continues to cry but she doesn't fight Frankie as she leads her away from the bench. Arms linked to provide each other with support, they start making their way back towards their houses, this time opting for the beach route.

'What's that over there?' Nadine says, craning her neck to look over towards the ocean. Frankie can see what she means. There's a strange darkening on the sand, like some kind of long log, perhaps something that's washed up on the shore. But it's so dark it's difficult to make it out.

Nadine lets out a gasp. 'Oh my god . . . I think . . . I think it's a person.'

Frankie's heart skips a beat. She squints, trying to make sense of what she's seeing, then covers her mouth in horror. Nadine is right. It's a person lying on the sand.

Frankie swerves on the pavement, letting go of Zara's arm, adrenaline surging through her as she bounds towards the water. As she gets closer, she can make out more of the person; curled hair, a tight-fitting white dress, heels.

'Geneva, can you hear me?' She falls to her knees beside her and is about to grab her, shake her, do CPR, anything, when hands pull her back.

'Wait!' Nadine holds Frankie still. 'Look at her. Look at her, Frankie. She's dead.'

Tears fill Frankie's eyes and she blinks them away, trying to focus on Geneva's face. It's ghostly pale in the moonlight. Her eyes are wide open, frozen with shock and fear. A thin metal wire is wrapped around her neck, cutting into her skin. She is completely still.

'We have to do something. Call an ambulance! Maybe there's still a chance!'

She sees Zara fumbling for her phone, but Nadine snatches it off of her.

'Hold on! Can you just . . . can you just let me think for a minute!'

Frankie gapes at her, not believing what she's seeing. What is there to think about? Their friend is lying dead on the ground in front of them.

Nadine presses her fingers to her head, and Frankie can see they're shaking.

'Zara . . . tell me you didn't do this,' she says eventually.

Zara's jaw drops open and she starts shaking her head wildly.

'What? No! I didn't! How could you even think that?' Her words gradually become more shrill as she gets more upset, her chest heaving as she hyperventilates.

Nadine raises a silencing hand. 'OK, OK. I believe you.' She pauses, allows Zara to calm herself a little. 'But the police won't. You know that, right? This is going to come back on us. We all argued with her tonight. She was going to spill all of our secrets.'

Zara lifts her fingers to her head, grips her hair. 'Oh God . . . the photos on Geneva's phone. The police will see them. It wasn't just photos of me either. Apparently there's proof of all of our secrets on there. It's like a little library she's compiled ready to use when she needs it.'

'So, what do you propose we do?' Frankie snaps. Her head is spinning. She feels like she's going crazy.

'We need to take her phone. Get rid of anything that could point towards any of us having a motive.' Nadine says it with such calm and composure that Frankie suddenly finds herself terrified of her.

'You can't be serious!'

'Frankie, she's dead, for Christ's sake! We can't do anything about that, can we? But should our lives stop? There'll be a trial, it will be publicised, maybe we'll even end up in prison. Can you bear letting your kids go through that?'

Frankie's breath hitches in her throat at the mention of her kids. She gives herself a shake, swallows the lump in her throat, and stares at Zara.

'You can't honestly be considering going through with this?'

Zara hasn't taken her eyes off Geneva's body. She shakes her head, looking as if she's about to throw up. 'I can't do it to my mum, Frank. You know she's not been well and that's only going to get worse. Me going to prison would finish her off. I have to be there for her.'

Unable to bear looking at her friends, Frankie turns away. She watches the gentle to and fro of the tide, the water bubbling and foaming over the rocks. It looks so peaceful. A stark contrast to what's going on just metres away from it.

'We have to make a decision now, before someone sees us here.' Nadine's words pull her back. 'We can only do this if we all agree never to speak of this night ever again. Let's take a vote.'

'I vote we do it,' Zara says, pulling her sleeves down over her hands.

Nadine nods. 'Me too.'

'You know she'll have had a backup, right? Geneva's not stupid. If there's evidence on her phone, there'll be evidence somewhere else too. Probably on her laptop.'

Frankie had hoped that pointing this out would make her friends see sense, see how ludicrous this plan is, but Nadine just says, 'You're right. I'll take her keys and go and get her laptop too. But we'll have to hurry. I don't know how long Elliot will stay at the pub for.'

Frankie watches in dismay as Nadine, slipping on her wool gloves, rummages in Geneva's pocket. She retrieves the keys and phone, then closes her fingers tight around them.

'We never speak about this. Ever. Understand?'

'Never,' Zara repeats. They turn their heads to Frankie and look at her expectantly.

Arguments fill Frankie's mouth, but they die away as she thinks of her kids. If she goes to prison, some of them will be adults by the time she's free. Can she really risk it?

'OK,' she says eventually, and Zara's shoulders droop as she lets out a heavy breath.

Nadine makes a start back up towards the road. 'Come on, let's go.'

'Wait. Are we not even going to call the police? Tell someone she's here?'

'We need to distance ourselves from this as much as possible. We were never here.' Nadine glances back in Geneva's direction, but shakes her head, unable to actually look at her body. 'Someone will find her in a few hours. Let's get home and pretend this never happened. Leave the phone and laptop to me. I'll get rid of them.'

Chapter Sixteen

Thursday, 23rd June

Frankie

'So, the only people who had access to Geneva's phone, who knew what was on there, was us,' Zara continues. 'The only other person who could have gotten hold of it between her leaving wine club and being murdered is the killer, right?'

Frankie shakes her head. 'That doesn't make any sense either. They murdered her and then decided to scroll through her phone? And then just decided to leave it there with the body?'

'Well, how else do you explain this mystery source having those photos?'

Frankie's eyes flick to Nadine and she raises her eyebrows. Understanding, Nadine puffs out her cheeks, exhaling slowly.

'I have to confess something.'

Zara stares open-mouthed at her as Nadine explains how she hid the phone and laptop under her floorboard, about the day she thought someone had broken in. Frankie can't quite read Zara's expression. It's somewhere between shell shock and full-on rage. She doesn't blame her. Even hearing it for a second time, that sense of betrayal gurgles in her stomach again.

'But I really didn't think it was anything to worry about,' Nadine says as she reaches the end of her story. 'The phone and laptop are still there, safely under the floorboard. I checked the other day.'

With this, Zara stands so suddenly she nearly loses her balance. Shaking it off, she storms towards the front door.

'Where are you going?' Nadine calls after her.

'Show us.'

They filter, unspeaking, over to Nadine's house and up the stairs. The pounding of their footsteps echoes the thudding of Frankie's heart. As Nadine leads the way into her wardrobe and starts removing objects from the trunk, a cold sweat breaks out on Frankie's forehead. As the floorboard lifts, she and Zara lean in, holding their breath.

For a few seconds, Nadine looks as if someone has pressed pause on her. She just stares, lifeless, into the hole in the floor. Then she slumps back onto her heels, fingers still gripping the floorboard so hard it looks like it might snap. Frankie doesn't even need to look.

'They're gone,' Nadine whispers.

Zara lets out a sort of strangled cry beside her. Her breathing starts growing shallow and rapid. 'What? I thought you said you checked they were still there?'

'I did!'

Holding on to the door frame in an attempt to steady herself, Frankie squeezes the bridge of her nose.

'This can't be happening,' she mutters under her breath.

Before she knows what's going on, Nadine has snapped back into life and is bustling past the both of them. She storms over to the desk on the far side of her bedroom and rips a sheet of paper out of the drawer.

Frankie steps gingerly over to her, her legs like jelly. 'What are you doing?'

'None of this makes any sense. I need to figure this all out.'

She pops the top off a black marker and draws a horizontal line across the centre of the paper.

'I thought someone had been in here on Monday morning.' She scribbles the date and 'break-in?' above the left-hand side of the line. Blowing a stray strand of hair out of her face, she looks up at them, fiery determination in her eyes. 'And today's video was the first time Juniper mentioned the photos, right?'

There are a few moments of fumbling as Frankie locates the video on her phone. 'Yep. She mentioned the anonymous source on Monday, but nothing that specifically hinted to her having access to the phone and laptop until today.'

Nadine returns to the paper, this time writing today's date and 'photos' in the middle of the line. Frankie can see what she's doing now. It's a timeline.

'So maybe whoever took them, the person we have to assume is the anonymous source, came in on Monday morning, or perhaps Sunday' – she circles it twice – 'but couldn't find them. That's why, when I checked, they were still there. So then that means they returned and actually found them sometime between Monday and now. Let's see, when were we both out of the house? Yesterday. We went and had brunch at the club and then went to Zara's.' She writes the date and 'stole phone and laptop' in between the other two dates.

'OK . . .' Frankie rests a hand on the desk as she cranes her neck to see the paper. 'But did you notice anything weird yesterday? Any signs of forced entry?'

'That's just it. No. After I thought someone had been in here, I've been double-checking the doors are locked. Whoever took them had to have had a key.'

'Who else has a key except for us?'

'No one.' Nadine shakes her head. 'That's why this doesn't make any sense.'

Frankie squeezes her eyes shut. A sharp pain is piercing through her forehead, as if someone is driving a nail into her skull.

Zara starts to pace the bedroom. 'Who the hell would have thought to look under a floorboard, anyway? It's absurd!'

'Tell me about it. The only thing I can think of is that someone must have overheard me when I told you at the golf club, Frankie.'

'There was no one near us.' Frankie shakes her head. 'There's no way.'

But as the words leave her mouth, a thought, a ridiculous idea, stirs at the back of her mind. She thinks back to those cheesy spy movies Mike always watches with the kids, that she's been subjected to on one too many occasions.

'Where's your coat?' she says, hurrying back to the wardrobe.

Without even waiting for an answer she runs her hands along the outerwear hanging up on the railings, perfectly organised by colour and thickness. She finds the coat Nadine had been wearing that day in the golf club and checks every pocket, every button, every seam. Nothing. What else had Nadine been wearing that day? Think. Think.

Her bag. Her black bag that she always carries with her wherever she goes. She spins, a wave of light-headedness hitting her as she does so, and locks eyes on the Louis Vuitton. She performs the same checks that she did on the coat, running her fingers along the edges. As her hand touches the bottom of the bag, her stomach lurches. She turns the bag upside down, the contents spilling out onto the floor.

'What the heck are you doing?'

'Shh!' Frankie holds up her hand, gesturing for Nadine not to come any closer. Pressing her lips together, she tugs on the tiny black box that's stuck onto the leather. After a couple of attempts, it pops off into the palm of her hand. She's never seen one before, but she knows exactly what it is. A listening device. Quite a cheap one by the looks of it, probably ordered off some online spy toy shop, but it's clearly done its job. She drops it to the floor, picks up one of Nadine's stilettos, and slams the heel down onto the box.

'Whoever's been feeding Juniper information has been listening all this time,' she says, and both Zara and Nadine's eyes widen. 'Someone is messing with us.'

The three of them have been sitting staring at the timeline in silence for what feels like hours. They've dedicated the right-hand side of the page to listing out people who could potentially be Juniper's anonymous source. The obvious option, highlighted right at the top of the page, is Juniper herself. Maybe there is no anonymous source and she's just sharing the information she's gleaned from the phone, laptop and listening device. But there's still the question of how she would manage to get into Nadine's house without there being any signs of forced entry.

Underneath Juniper's name are the rest of the people who have a spare key; Frankie and Zara, Nadine's parents, and the window cleaner who comes every other month. None of whom are likely suspects. They've hit a maddening dead end.

Nadine opens her mouth to say something, but before she gets a chance, Frankie's phone starts to ring. She peers down at the number on the screen and swears under her breath.

'It's Mike. I'm going to have to take this.'

She forces herself to sound breezy as she shuts herself in the dining room and answers the phone. This is the first time Mike has reached out to her since his run-in with Elliot.

'Hey, what's up?' she says, fingers tightening on the phone.

'You need to come home right now. Callie's in hospital.'

The Mercedes skids to a halt in the car park of St Amelia's hospital, and Frankie scrambles out and towards the entrance so fast she nearly breaks her ankle tripping over the edge of the pavement. From what she managed to get from Mike over the phone, Callie collapsed and the doctors believe it's due to her having not eaten enough. Apparently, she's stable, they've given her fluids and they're currently just keeping her for observation, but the panic is whirling inside Frankie even so. She knew Callie was looking thin. She should never have stayed in Sandbanks for so long.

She makes her way through the maze of corridors, frantically scanning the direction boards for the 'Orange Zone' that Mike said they were in. When she eventually bursts onto the ward, she immediately sees her mother sitting in the hallway, surrounded by five of her children. They all bound towards her as they spot her.

'Mummy! Mum! Mummy! We've missed you!'

As she's enveloped by their hugs, with the teenagers Albie and Kayla lingering on the outside so as not to look too overly happy to see their mum, warmth spreads through Frankie. This is where she belongs, with her kids. Not drinking endless bottles of wine at the club. It isn't her anymore.

Once she's covered the youngest three in kisses and given Albie and Kayla a loving squeeze, despite their protests, she looks solemnly over to her mum.

'Where's Callie?'

'She's in there. Room four. Mike's in there with her.' Her mother nods her head towards the door and gives her a reassuring smile. 'She'll be fine, love.'

'Thank you so much for watching the kids.'

'Oh, it's my pleasure, you know that. I'm going to take them back to the house, get some dinner in them. They wanted to stay to see you, but I don't think the hospital staff are too keen on them all being here.'

'Of course.' Frankie eyes the receptionist, who is indeed watching them like a hawk, her mouth pulled into a disapproving line. 'I'll see you later, kids.'

'Are you coming home, Mummy?' Pippa, her youngest asks, burying her face into Frankie's sleeve.

'Yes, sweetheart. I just need to make sure Callie's OK first.'

It takes her mother a while to prise Pippa off of her arm, but once they're gone she sucks in a deep breath and heads to Room 4. Her chest tightens as her eyes land on Callie, lying in the hospital bed with a cannula in the back of her hand. Mike, who had been looking down at the floor, jolts his head up as she enters.

'Hey,' he says. 'She's just fallen asleep.'

Blinking back the tears, she moves to sit in the other chair, next to Callie's bed. 'How is she?'

'She's fine. Apparently, she'll be good to go later on today. They just want to check her blood pressure again when she wakes up.'

'Did they say anything about . . .' the word lodges itself in her throat, but she forces it out '. . . an eating disorder?'

'It was mentioned, though they didn't use that term. They checked her weight and said it was slightly below average but nothing to be majorly concerned about. They reckon it was just a fainting spell caused by low blood sugar where she's been forgetting to eat. They did give me this, though.' He hands Frankie a leaflet entitled 'How To Help Your Child Eat Well & Be Well'. 'As if we have any input on what she eats now she's at uni.'

Frankie sighs. 'Maybe she should move back home so that we can keep an eye on her.'

'Honestly, I'm not sure that's the best environment for her right now.' Mike's face is stony, his hands clasped together in his lap so tight that his fingers are going white. 'She can tell something's up with us, Frank. I've been trying to keep things normal at home, telling the kids you're just catching up with friends, but she's not a kid anymore. She outright asked me if we'd had an argument. In fact, she asked if we were getting a divorce.'

Frankie's eyebrows draw together. 'Why would she think that?'

'Why do you think? You've been gone for days with no explanation. And, I'll admit, I've probably not been in the best mood since that video came out.'

Guilt worms its way through Frankie's insides, wrapping its way around her and squeezing. She's so tired of feeling guilty. Not just for leaving her family over the past few days, but for everything. Getting rid of Geneva's phone and laptop. Not notifying the police when they found her body. Sending her that horrible text. And of course, what she's hidden from Mike. She suddenly finds herself thinking about Zara, about what she said in Nadine's living room.

'I can't live like this anymore.'

Zara had wanted to come clean, to finally stop with all the lies. Maybe she was onto something.

'OK.' Frankie closes her eyes, not quite believing what she's about to say. 'I'll tell you what Geneva knew about. I'll tell you my secret.'

Chapter Seventeen

Friday, 24th June

Zara

'Hey, how's Callie?' Zara, having just finished her baguette when Frankie walked into the club, stands and pulls her into a hug. Once they separate, Nadine does the same.

'Good. In fact, everything's really good.' Frankie sits down opposite them, and Zara has to admit there is an energy to her that there hasn't been over the past few days, and more colour in her cheeks. 'Mike's come back with me. Once Callie was discharged, we agreed we all needed a holiday. Some family time, you know?'

'So, all six of your kids are here? In Sandbanks?' Nadine says, not bothering to hide the dismay in her voice.

Frankie laughs. 'Relax. I'm not going to bring them all to yours. We've checked into a hotel near the beach. That way they can have some fun and I can figure things out with Mike but I'm still here until . . . well, until we figure this Juniper thing out.'

As Nadine visibly relaxes, Zara leans in across the table. 'So, you and Mike are OK?'

'I think we're going to be.' Frankie nods. 'I told him.'

For a moment, it's as if everything has been put on mute. The bartender clinking glasses, the receptionist answering the phone, the old couple having a chat over at one of the other tables, all of it goes silent. Frankie can clearly see the horror on both Zara and Nadine's faces, because she's quick to add, 'My secret. Not yours. I didn't tell him anything about that night. Just . . . just what Geneva had on me.'

'And he was OK when you told him?' Zara desperately wants to ask her if there's anything more to it than what they're already aware of. After all, they know all of her dark, dirty secrets now. There's nothing left for them to discover about her. It's about time she got to know some of their skeletons, too. But she knows better than to ask.

'Yeah. I mean . . . he was shocked. And upset. But we talked for a really long time, and he was just happy that it was finally out in the open, that I wasn't lying to him about it anymore.'

At this, she turns to look Zara directly in the eye. 'I think you should go to the police about Elliot attacking you yesterday. Show them the CCTV footage from the clinic. Tell them about your affair too, that Geneva found out about it.'

'What?' Zara shakes her head, aghast. She hunches her shoulders and flicks her eyes around the luncheon room. It's like the second Frankie mentioned Elliot, she suddenly had the overwhelming sense of being watched.

'You said you wanted all the secrets and lies to be over, right?' Frankie continues. 'We need to start being a bit more honest. Even if we can't tell them what we did that night, we can at least start telling them a little of what we know. If you tell them what Elliot did, they might have enough to question him again. Maybe they'll be able to figure out who's messing with us. And if he did kill Geneva . . . Well, it's like you said. This will all be over.'

There is something in what Frankie's saying that makes Zara feel a little lighter. She had said she wanted to go to the police, but Nadine had shut her down so quickly she'd dismissed the idea. Maybe she just needed someone to tell her it would be OK.

She glances over at Nadine, expecting to see her readying herself to interject, but even she is looking thoughtful.

'Maybe Frankie's right,' she says eventually. 'Maybe you should tell them what happened with Elliot. But if you are going to go to the police, we need to make sure we've got our stories straight. And you need to be absolutely certain that you're not going to accidentally spill the beans about what we did that night. If you do, we'll all be going to prison.'

Yes. Finally, they're going to do something instead of just blindly waiting for a miracle. Zara sits back in her chair and crosses her legs. 'Anyone fancy the sauna?'

If ever there was a good place to have a private discussion, the sauna is it. It's small, only suitable for maybe four people at a time, so whenever someone enters the pool area and sees the three of them sitting on the wooden benches, they opt for the steam room instead. Zara breathes in deeply, enjoying the warmth as Nadine goes over the details one last time. If she's going to go to the police, she needs to promise to only speak about what happened yesterday at the clinic. She can share the CCTV footage to show them how he attacked her, and she can divulge that she had previously had an affair with him, suggesting that if Geneva had found out, it could be a possible motive for him murdering her. She is not to say anything about the photos, or about the fact that Geneva had been planning to ruin her as a result of finding out about the affair. And, of course, she mustn't say anything about being on the beach that night. Their story stays the same as it has done for the past five years; after wine club at Nadine's house, they all went home.

'Nadine, it's fine. We've been over this four times now. I know what to say.'

'You need to be absolutely sure you're not going to slip up,' Nadine says, leaning forward and gripping onto her bench.

'I am.'

'Right, if that's settled, can we get out of here?' Frankie fans herself with her hand, puffing out her cheeks. No longer a regular here, it's easy to tell she's not used to the heat of the sauna. She's flustered, her cheeks bright red, and her breathing is shallow.

'Ugh, you two do know how to interrupt the zen,' Zara says, closing her eyes and tilting her head back. 'Go on, I'll be out in a minute.'

Frankie practically falls out of the sauna and Nadine follows her. *Just five more minutes*, Zara thinks. If she's going to go to the police and relive the whole terrifying experience with Elliot, she needs to be in the right frame of mind. Nothing wrong with a little calm before the storm.

After probably more like ten minutes, she stretches her legs out in front of her and rolls her shoulders. She doesn't really want to leave, but even she is starting to get a little overheated. Taking one more deep, centring breath, she goes to push open the sauna door.

But it doesn't open.

'What the . . .' She tries again, this time with more force. The door shakes but doesn't budge. It's as if something is pinning it closed from the other side. Her heart stutters.

Clenching her jaw, she places one foot on the bench and hoists herself up so that she can peer through the porthole window at the top of the door. As she lifts herself her breath is snatched away. It's stiflingly hot near the top of the room compared to lower down. She cranes her neck to see what could possibly be blocking the door, but the angle is all wrong. All she can see is that the pool area is empty. Frankie and Nadine have left, she realises with a sickening lurch, and there's no one else here.

Unable to bear the heat a moment longer she jumps back down, lowering herself back to a more comfortable temperature. But it's still so hot. Panic rises up inside her like a tidal wave, consuming her.

'Help!' she calls out. 'I'm stuck in the sauna!'

Her chest tightens and her breathing comes quick and fast. She grabs the handle and shakes it, back and forth, back and forth, her whole body trembling from the effort, but it still doesn't open. As the panic increases, so, seemingly, does the temperature.

'HELP!' Her scream is so loud it tears at her vocal cords. Her eyes feel like they're about to well up but no tears form. Everything is dry. Her mouth feels like sandpaper.

Letting out one more strangled cry, she drops herself down to the floor. It's not a big room, there's only just enough space for her whole body, but it's the least hot place to be. She squeezes her eyes shut and tries to drag air into her lungs.

Inhale. Exhale. Inhale. Exhale.

But it seems the more she breathes the drier her mouth is becoming. She doesn't know how long she's been in here exactly, but it must have been at least forty-five minutes before she realised she was trapped. She needs water. Her body is screaming out for it. She's never felt thirst like it.

'Please . . .' she whimpers, her ability to scream out lessening the hotter and more dehydrated she becomes. 'Help me.'

The world around her swirls. The lines between the planks of wood that make up the benches twist and mutate, multiply before her very eyes. She blinks, willing herself not to pass out. If she does, that's the end. But it's too late. The blackness is already engulfing her, smothering her.

The Todd Lane Show

First aired 26/06/2022

Todd: Hello. Good evening. How are you? Welcome to *The Todd Lane Show*. Coming up tonight, meet the vet who has over thirty rescue dogs in her home, hear from the ex-prisoner who's been touring the country raising awareness for brain damage victims, and what would you do if your boyfriend left you for your daughter? All of that's to come, but first, 17th June marked five years since the murder of *Copperdale Street* actress Geneva O'Connor made headlines across the nation. Specifically, this case drew major attention due to the lack of arrests made, and to this day, this murder is still unsolved. I have here with me today YouTuber Juniper Rose who decided to resurface the case on the five-year anniversary, and has been conducting her own personal investigation. Thank you for coming on the show, Juniper.

Juniper: Thank you for having me.

Todd: Now, your videos have really taken on a life of their own over the past week, haven't they? I mean, you've gone from a few hundred followers to . . . I think when we checked this morning you were nearing the fifty thousand mark.

Juniper: They really have. I think it just goes to show how desperate everyone is for the truth and that the general public will not accept failure on the police's part. You know? If they're not going to solve this thing, if they're not going to find justice for Geneva, then we need to do it ourselves.

Todd: Why did you decide to start making these videos in the first place? Why this case?

Juniper: Well, I've been making videos about different true crime cases for the last couple of years but they never really took off. I've always wanted to cover the Geneva O'Connor story. I actually live not far away from where it happened. I'm about fifteen minutes away by car. So many YouTubers have covered this case, reeling off the facts that are readily available on the internet and then giving their opinion, but I wanted to do something different and really do a proper investigation. So, being so close, I'm able to visit the location Geneva was found, walk the streets that suspects walked, talk to the key people involved in the case.

Todd: Indeed. These videos really are becoming more of a docuseries, I'd say.

Juniper: Exactly.

Todd: Did the police say anything regarding your investigation when you first started?

Juniper: I tried speaking to them but to no avail. Basically, after a certain amount of time, the investigative effort on difficult-to-solve cases stops, unless there's new information which then enables a fresh investigative effort. In my opinion, I'd already uncovered more than enough to warrant that by my second video, but unfortunately it isn't my call.

Todd: And, you've taken the rather controversial stance that you don't believe the widely accepted theory that Geneva was killed by her husband Elliot, is that correct?

Juniper: Right. I think he was an easy target. I don't think there was enough investigation into Geneva's friends. I think the police failed on this case in many ways, not just by allowing it to go cold.

Todd: Speaking of Geneva's friends, we have them here with us tonight. I believe this is the first time ever since the murder occurred that they've agreed to publicly speak out on the matter, is that right?

Juniper: Yes, it's taken a lot of time and convincing for them to even speak to me off the record, so this is a really exciting step.

Todd: Indeed. Before we welcome them on, though, can you tell us a little bit about the past week? I know you had to take a break from uploading the videos over the last couple of days.

Juniper: That's right. The day after I released my last video, there was an incident at the country club Geneva used to attend and that her friends still attend. Apparently, someone locked Zara, who's one of Geneva's friends, in the sauna in the spa. By the time Frankie and Nadine, the other two friends, got her out she was unconscious from the heat and dehydration. I chose to pause my investigation out of respect for her ordeal and to allow her to fully recover, but when I was asked to come on this show, I did reach out to them and ask if they would be willing to come on and talk.

Todd: It's hard to imagine being locked in a sauna. We'll be finding out all about that right after this break. We'll be speaking with Zara Garcia, Frankie Crawford and Nadine Howe, and getting their point of view on the events that took place five years ago. Don't go anywhere.

– Ad break –

Todd: Welcome back. Before the break we spoke to YouTuber Juniper Rose about her independent investigation into the Geneva O'Connor murder case. Now we're also joined by Geneva's old friends Nadine Howe, Zara Garcia and Frankie Crawford. Welcome, ladies.

(Awkward silence)

Todd: OK. So, tell me, what has it been like having this case re-examined in such a public way all these years after it actually occurred?

(Pause)

Nadine: Well, truthfully Todd, it's been hell.

Todd: Care to elaborate?

Nadine: When something tragic happens, when someone dies who you're close to, it can take a really long time to grieve. To move on. Especially when the circumstances surrounding their death are particularly difficult. But that's what we've been trying to do for five years. Grieve for our friend and move on. It's not been easy but we've all gradually started to figure out what life looks like after Geneva. This has all brought it rushing back.

Todd: It must be especially difficult seeing as Juniper here has been quite vocally pointing the finger at you ladies, too – in particular Frankie and Zara.

Nadine: If anything could make this situation more difficult, that's it, yes. Being wrongfully named and shamed.

Juniper: Can I just cut in real quick?

Todd: Of course.

Juniper: I just want to say that I'm not pointing my finger at anyone. Not yet. I've made it very clear since I started these videos that the whole purpose is to uncover the truth. My audience are drawing their own conclusions from the evidence I'm presenting to them. It's not, as you seem to think it is, some kind of witch-hunt.

Nadine: I think it's pretty obvious that your 'audience' are going to be swayed by whatever you say though, isn't it?

Todd: OK, let's keep this friendly. I do have to ask though, Nadine, if Elliot O'Connor is innocent, as Juniper seems to think he is, isn't it a good thing that she's causing people to look at this case again? Surely you don't want an innocent man going down for something he didn't do? Surely you want justice for your friend?

Nadine: Of course we do. But serving justice isn't the job of some inexperienced, wannabe detective on YouTube. There are people whose actual job it is to find the culprit in these situations.

Juniper: And yet an inexperienced, wannabe detective seems to be doing a better job than the police.

Nadine: Look, if Elliot is innocent then that just goes to show how dangerous these kinds of videos can be. The whole reason he had to move away from Sandbanks was because YouTubers and podcasters and people on social media decided he was guilty. If everyone had just left it to the police, he'd never have gone through everything he did. These kinds of videos and speculation without all the facts can ruin innocent people's lives.

Todd: OK, fair point. So, let's talk about the facts then. In one of Juniper's earlier videos, she mentioned a text message that Frankie sent to Geneva just before she died. Can we get that message up on the screen please?

– Text message shows on screen –

Todd: What caused this message?

Nadine: Frankie was just . . .

Todd: Thank you, Nadine, we've heard a lot from you today. I wonder if Frankie herself could answer this question?

(Pause)

Frankie: *clears throat* Um . . . Geneva had found out something about me. A secret. She liked to keep secrets so that she could use them against you if you ever disagreed with her or you ever crossed her.

Todd: And you thought she was prepared to spill this secret of yours?

Frankie: I . . . I wasn't really sure. I didn't think she would, but she was always a little . . . unpredictable. When I sent that text, it was more out of initial panic. We made up afterwards. She actually laughed it off.

Todd: So, in the name of getting the facts out there rather than wild speculation, can I ask what the secret was?

(Long pause)

Nadine: It's private. You have no right to ask questions like that.

Todd: You don't have to share anything you're not willing to. I just know a lot of people watching tonight would appreciate the honesty.

Frankie: It's OK, Nadine. *takes a deep breath* I told my husband and daughter already last week and we're working through it together as a family. I took a paternity test for my eldest daughter which showed that she is not my husband's biological child. Geneva caught me opening the results, read the letter over my shoulder. That's why I got so . . . emotional when she tried to use it against me. It doesn't just affect me. It affects my whole family.

(Long pause)

Todd: Well, thank you for your candour, Frankie. I'm sure that must have been really difficult to talk about. *clears throat* Er . . . Zara. You look well recovered after your incident in the sauna. Can you tell us what happened there?

(Pause)

Todd: Zara?

Zara: Hm? Oh, sorry. What was the question again?

Todd: Could you tell us about what happened in the sauna?

Zara: Somebody locked me in. They'd pushed a lounge chair up against the door which pinned it closed.

Todd: That must have been absolutely terrifying. Do you have any idea who could have done that or why?

Zara: Yes. Elliot O'Connor did it.

Juniper: What?

Todd: I'm sorry, you know this for sure?

Zara: Absolutely. He had attacked me the day before at my clinic and I only just escaped. Later, in the sauna, the girls and I had been discussing going to the police about him. He locked me in there to stop me from doing so.

Juniper: Hang on. Do you actually have any proof that Elliot did it?

Zara: I don't need proof.

Todd: Juniper does have a point. Especially as we've been talking about not making wild, public accusations. Was there any CCTV in the spa?

Nadine: There was. We looked at it with the police and whoever blocked the door seemed to know exactly where the cameras were. They had a hood that shielded their face whenever they were facing towards the camera.

Juniper: So . . . no. You don't have a shred of evidence. I mean, for all we know it could have been one of you two who locked her in there.

Nadine: Now hold on a second . . .

Juniper: In fact, it's really convenient that you two went back to the sauna and got her out just in time. Maybe the three of you concocted the plan together to frame Elliot. Maybe this is just another attempt to throw the spotlight off yourselves.

(Nadine stands)

Todd: OK, I think that's just about all we've got time for. We're going to take another short break. Next up, ever thought about adopting a dog? How about thirty-two? Stay right where you are.

Chapter Eighteen

Sunday, 26th June

Nadine

'That sneaky, conniving . . .' As Nadine emerges into the green room of the TV studio, closely followed by Frankie and Zara, she throws her phone down on the sofa with such force it bounces back towards her and skids along the floor. 'She set that interview up! Like he'd have asked you to share your secret on live television. She must have told him to go down that route.'

Frankie lowers herself down onto the sofa, rubbing her face with her hand.

'It was always going to come out,' she says, her words void of emotion. 'Better it comes from me and we can stop looking like we've always got something to hide.'

'Do you need to call Mike? Will he have been watching the show?'

Frankie shakes her head. 'I spoke to both him and Callie last night. I warned them that this would probably come out if I went on the show, that Callie would likely have to go back to university knowing her friends may well have seen it. They both said exactly what we said when we got Juniper's message. Mike told me that it's time to stop hiding in the shadows, time to start telling the truth.'

Nadine nods, pleased that Frankie now has Mike on side to help keep her from spiralling. Yesterday, when Juniper's request that they join her on the show had first come through, she'd seen it as an opportunity. The main thing that Juniper kept circling back to again and again was that they were refusing to comment, that it was making them look more guilty by staying silent. She thought it would be the chance they needed to get their side of the story across. Now, though, she's wondering if they did the right thing. Frankie looks more truthful than she did an hour ago, but now she's officially got a motive in the world's eyes.

As this thought crosses her mind, she notices that Zara hasn't said a word, and is standing in the corner of the room, arms crossed, with a face like thunder. Frankie must notice it too, because she frowns and says, 'Are you OK?'

'Just hearing you talk about the paternity test again. It reminded me how pissed off it made me the first time.'

Nadine scrunches up her nose in confusion. 'What are you talking about?'

But Zara's attention is locked on Frankie. 'I wanted to say something back then, but you were so pathetic, crying about Geneva reading that letter and acting "oh, woe is me". I kept quiet back then but ever since Juniper's videos left a little dent in your marriage, I've found it harder and harder to bite my tongue.'

'Bite your tongue about what?' Frankie crosses her arms. 'If you've got something to say to me, go for it.'

'OK, I will.' Zara copies Frankie's defensive stance, making them look like two fighters in a ring. 'You always judged me so harshly for sleeping with Elliot. You made me feel like shit for breaking up his and Geneva's marriage, but you did exactly the same. In fact, no, you're worse than me because there's kids involved in your situation.'

The colour in Frankie's face has completely washed away, and her eyes darken. 'Zara, you don't know the full story.'

'Well, come on then.' Zara suddenly snaps to life. 'Tell us. Tell us how Mrs Perfect Marriage can think it's her place to look down on others when she's just as bad.'

'All right, stop it.' Nadine takes a step between them and raises a warning hand to Zara. 'This is exactly what Juniper wants. She's hoping we'll turn against each other. We're not as strong if we're not united.'

A snort erupts from Zara's nose. 'Listen to you. Stronger together. What a load of bullshit. We haven't been united since Geneva died. Probably not even before then. This isn't a friendship. It never was. It was a relationship of convenience and it fell apart as soon as she died. Don't kid yourself otherwise.'

Nadine presses her lips together, stung by Zara's words. She moves towards her and places a hand on each of her arms, feeling her tense beneath her palms. 'Look, I know you're lashing out at us because you're stressed, scared, hurt. But we're not the ones you need to be directing your anger towards. We need to put the focus on the person who's doing this to us.'

Tears prick at Zara's eyes. 'But what can we do about her? It's free speech, right?'

'I don't mean Juniper. She's just a symptom. We need to address the root cause. The killer. The one who's still out there, watching this all unfold and thinking they're the smartest person in the world for getting away with it.'

'Elliot?' Frankie says, gingerly coming to join them.

'Maybe. But there has been another person niggling at me.'

'Who?' Zara and Frankie say in unison.

Nadine takes a deep breath, the very thought of what she's about to say causing her mouth to fill with a sickly metallic taste. She's been mulling over this possibility ever since Zara told them about the photos, but she hasn't wanted to properly entertain the idea. Now, though, she has no choice.

'The night that I thought someone had been snooping around in my wardrobe. It was the night Andrew stayed.'

Both girls gape at her, their eyes like saucers.

'I'm not saying it's him,' she continues, an unfamiliar tremor sounding in her voice. 'I mean, there's no motive there. As far as I know he didn't even know Geneva. But I can't shake the thought. It's been driving me insane. If he somehow knew I had the phone and laptop hidden in my house somewhere, that was his opportunity. And he disappeared in the morning. Didn't even stay for a cup of coffee.'

As she finishes, the room falls into silence, the only sound the *tick, tick, ticking* of the nearby clock. Then, as if a spell has been broken, Zara starts to laugh. It echoes around the room, bouncing off the walls.

'You've got to be kidding me,' she says through fits of laughter. 'This whole situation is just ridiculous. Who's next? The two old ladies down the club? The freaking lawn mower?'

She laughs and laughs, each chuckle grating at Nadine's ears. Zara has officially lost it. The pressure is too much for her. Which means she's a loose cannon.

Frankie, meanwhile, remains quiet, thoughtful.

'You should never have kept them,' she murmurs eventually. Her words bring Zara's laughter to an abrupt halt.

'She's right. Why *did* you keep them?'

'I . . . I . . .' Nadine shakes her head, unsure of what to say. She hadn't been expecting them to turn on her. She'd thought they would latch on to her Andrew theory and the three of them would come up with a plan for how to test her suspicions.

'I don't know why I kept them,' she says truthfully. Because she doesn't know. Not really. She had thought about disposing of them, grinding the parts under the heel of her stilettos and feeding the broken pieces to the belly of the ocean, but there had been a nagging voice inside her that told her she should keep them. 'I suppose . . . I thought there might be evidence on them. I didn't think I should just destroy it.'

'No . . .' Zara's eyes shrink into slits. 'That's not why you kept them. You kept them because you wanted the dirt that Geneva had on us.'

'That's not true. I never looked at it, I swear. I had no idea what either of your secrets were.'

'But that's the only logical explanation!' Zara's voice is rising in pitch, and Nadine is desperate to quieten her. They're alone in the green room, but there's no telling who's outside. The studio is littered with employees, not to mention Juniper herself is somewhere in the building. 'You knew our secrets were on there and you thought you better keep hold of them just in case you needed to use them against us one day. Was it because you were scared we wouldn't be able to keep quiet about that night? Was it your insurance?'

'No!' She says it with conviction, but as the denial leaves her lips, she questions herself, if only for a second. Was that part of the reason she wanted to keep them? She had been worried that Frankie and Zara wouldn't be up to keeping what they did under wraps. Maybe there was a small, subconscious part of her that thought the secrets on Geneva's devices may one day come in handy.

Zara sneers, her nose scrunching up with disgust. She turns and storms out of the green room, slamming the door behind her. Nadine looks to Frankie, pleading. Zara is past having a reasonable conversation. She's too caught up in the emotion of the situation. But Frankie is different, more level headed.

'You're just as bad as Geneva,' Frankie says in a low, despondent voice. Then, without another word, she follows Zara out into the hallway and leaves Nadine alone.

Chapter Nineteen

Sunday, 26th June

Frankie

When she had returned to the hotel after leaving the television studio, and seen Mike throwing little Pippa into the pool and heard her laughter and caught a glimpse of Callie sunning herself on one of the lounge chairs, Frankie had descended into tears. Real, burning tears of guilt and humiliation. She didn't even care that people stared as she made her way, sobbing and hiccupping, over to the pool edge. They probably already knew why she was crying anyway. If they hadn't seen Juniper's videos before, they were much more likely to have seen *The Todd Lane Show*.

Mike had ushered her and the kids to the hotel room where they could have some privacy, and there she continued to bawl, with her younger kids watching her as if some alien had taken over their usually calm and composed mother. Eventually, Frankie calmed enough to head on down to the restaurant for dinner, but even then she could only pick at her linguine. She noticed Callie didn't eat much either, even though both she and Mike have been watching her food intake like a couple of hawks since they returned from the hospital.

Now, Frankie sits curled up on the sofa, buried into Mike's arms, as they watch Pippa, Effie and Louis snuffle in their sleep. Kayla and

Albie are in the other room with Callie, and Frankie's sure she can hear the TV on through the wall, but she hasn't the energy to get up and tell them to go to bed.

'We should just go home,' Frankie mutters, wiping her wet cheeks with her cardigan sleeve.

Mike shifts beside her. 'I thought you wanted to hang around while this all got sorted out? You know, be there for the girls?'

'Yeah, that was when I thought we still had a friendship to salvage.'

'Ah, come on.' Mike squeezes her shoulder and she nuzzles closer into him. 'It's a tough situation. People say things they don't mean.'

Tears threaten to spill once more. Mike is being too kind to her. She doesn't deserve it. Maybe it was he, not her friends, who she should have been confiding in this whole time.

'Nadine said something after the show.'

'What did she say?'

'She said she thought the person dishing dirt on us to Juniper might be the guy she's seeing.'

Mike looks down at her. 'What do you think?'

'I don't know. I don't see how it can be.' Her eyes instinctively flick towards the wardrobe, which only holds their suitcases that they couldn't be bothered to unpack. She wishes she could tell Mike what she's thinking, but that would involve telling him about the phone and the laptop, which would mean admitting what they did. It's bothered her ever since she left the TV studio, though. Even if Andrew had slept with Nadine in order to gain access to Geneva's devices as part of a warped plan to make them look guilty instead of him, how would he have known to look in the wardrobe in the first place?

Another thought enters her mind, dark and dangerous. Heart racing, she pulls herself out of Mike's warm embrace and heads to the bathroom.

'You OK?' he says.

'Yep, I'll be right back.'

Once the door is firmly closed, she pulls her phone out from her back pocket, navigates past the group chat she's been using with Zara and Nadine, and opens up a new thread with just Zara.

* * *

'I've been thinking about it all night,' Frankie says as she takes a long sip of coffee. This is her fourth cup already and she's starting to get jittery, her leg bouncing on the footrest of Zara's breakfast bar stool. Her head is spinning. 'You know what Nadine is like for keeping control of a situation. Maybe she's just using this Andrew theory to cover her tracks.'

'I don't know, Frankie,' Zara says. 'I mean, I know I've been saying a lot about her recently but this is something else. You really think she's the one sharing our secrets?'

'It makes sense, doesn't it? She's the only one who knew where the laptop and phone were hidden, and do you think it's just a coincidence that you and I have had our secrets spilled and she hasn't? Geneva must have had dirt on her too, that's why Nadine wanted to take them in the first place. Why haven't her skeletons come out? Maybe she planted the listening device on her bag because she knew we were getting close.'

'But if she wanted to do this to us, why wait until now? There have been plenty of YouTubers she could have buddied up with. Why wait five years?'

Frankie falls into silence, though her brain still whirrs. This is what had stumped her, too, as she lay awake turning theories over and over in her mind last night.

'Maybe she didn't want to do it while Eleanor was still alive.'

Zara flinches. 'She did love Mum. Everyone did.'

'And all this started straight after the funeral.'

Puffing out her cheeks, Zara slumps against the breakfast bar. 'But if she's the one doing this to us, does that mean . . .'

'That she killed Geneva? Maybe. She was alone between us leaving the house that night and us going to find you. Who knows what she did in that time?'

It's a ludicrous theory, but then again, perhaps not as ludicrous as she had initially thought. Nadine is the one who wanted to get rid of anything that would give her a motive. Nadine is the one who's been pulling the strings since Geneva died, stepping neatly into the role of group leader, telling them what they should say and when. Is it really that much of a stretch?

'We need to find out what Geneva had on her,' Zara says softly.

'There's no way. We've got no idea where the phone and laptop are now, and even if we did, I'm not staying with her anymore. But I do think we need to keep an eye on her, and be sneaky about it.'

Zara shakes her head. 'This is not how I expected this to all play out.'

Me neither, Frankie thinks. *Me neither.*

Making like a couple of private investigators in heels, Frankie and Zara pull up around the corner of Nadine's office and watch. Nadine hasn't spoken to them since their disagreement at the studio yesterday, and Frankie wants to see what she'll do when she finishes work. Where she'll go. Probably home, but she's not sure what else they can do. A last-minute stake-out seems their best option at the moment.

She leans her head back on the headrest and taps her fingers on the steering wheel, her fingers itching for one of her stashed cigarettes. There's still an air of awkwardness between her and Zara, though it has been somewhat disguised by their mutual concern about Nadine.

'I didn't cheat on Mike,' she says, not daring to take her eyes away from the office building.

Zara stiffens beside her. 'But I thought you said Callie wasn't Mike's?'

The memories spark in Frankie's mind again, her recurring nightmare flooding back to her even though she's wide awake. She's thought about telling Zara so many times, but she couldn't live with herself knowing she'd told someone else before she told Mike.

She squeezes her eyes shut, remembering the awful sensation of being totally out of control. One arm flopped over someone's shoulders. The other groping the wall to steady herself. Crashing into the chest of drawers. Rolling off the bed. The thumping of the music reverberating around the house as she could do nothing but lie and groan. Blacking out and waking up not quite sure what had happened, or who it had happened with, but knowing that something was wrong. Then taking the pregnancy test and knowing for sure. Twenty-one years old, not even sure if she wanted kids, and her life had been decided for her.

Now, sitting next to Zara, she's wondering if it's finally time to tell her. Now that Mike and Callie know. She sucks in a deep breath and gives herself a shake. 'Fuck it,' she says, reaching over to the glove compartment and retrieving her cigarettes. She pops one between her lips and lights it before offering one to Zara. Before she can accept it, however, Frankie's eye gets drawn back out to the office building.

'Shit, get down!' Abandoning her plan to tell Zara what happened, she shimmies down in her seat, pulling Zara down with her, and fumbles to flick the cigarette out of the car window before she sets fire to herself.

Nadine walks out of the entrance doors so quickly they almost miss her, but instead of heading towards the car park as Frankie expects, she takes a sharp turn and starts making her way along the exterior wall of the building. And she's not alone. Andrew is hot on her heels, breaking into a half-run to keep up with her angry strides. Keeping pressed against her seat, Frankie's eyes follow them as they move to the back of the building and disappear through a wooden gate. The bin store.

'What the hell,' Zara murmurs beside her.

Frankie sits herself back up and opens the driver's door as quietly as possible. 'Come on.'

They copy Nadine's route, keeping their footsteps light. Frankie gets a sickening wave of déjà vu from when they were sneaking around inside Elliot's house, but this time she's determined not to mess things up. She'd been blindly following Nadine that time. Now, Zara is following her.

They don't go all the way to the gate, just get close enough that they can just about hear Nadine's voice. She's attempting to whisper, but the anger in her voice is making it louder than she probably intends.

'I mean it,' she's saying. 'You keep your mouth shut, do you understand? They can never know. No one can ever know.'

'Nadine, I have no idea what you're talking about. Why won't you believe me?' Andrew's reply comes. 'I thought we were friends.'

Sensing their conversation might be coming to an end, Frankie turns quickly and signals to Zara that they need to leave. They hurry back to the car, throw themselves back in and Frankie pulls off from their stake-out spot, nearly revving the engine in her fluster. Her hands tighten on the wheel as they drive away, her chest heaving.

'Shit,' Zara says, her voice shaking. 'What do you reckon that was all about?'

Frankie shakes her head, unable to form a coherent response. Her brain is stuck on one thought. It had been Nadine all right in that alleyway, but it sounded awfully, harrowingly, like Geneva.

TRANSCRIPT

Video published 27/06/2022

Subscriber count: 68,196

Welcome back to *True Crime Over Wine*. Firstly, if you're not following me on Instagram, make sure you head over and do that. I posted a celebration pic last night with some giant foil balloons celebrating hitting the 50k mark, and already that feels out of date because just look where we are now. Over 68,000 of you want to see justice for Geneva O'Connor. Thank you so much for the outpouring of support I received after appearing on *The Todd Lane Show*, and for those of you who found me from that episode, please do subscribe and stick around. Before we jump into today's episode, let's have a quick word from our sponsor.

– Sponsor Ad break –

Thank you so much to GG Smoothies for sponsoring today's video – giving your body the horsepower it needs. Before we hop into today's interview, let's go over the current suspect list.

—Zara Garcia is still well in the lead, with what happened to her sister and her affair with Elliot sitting high on the potential motive list.
—Frankie Crawford is just about coming in second after it was

revealed on *The Todd Lane Show* that Geneva was threatening to tell Mike about the paternity test. However, in a slight turn of events, a fair few of you in the comments section have jumped to Frankie's defence, saying her honesty yesterday suggests she's not trying to hide anything. Others are saying she only shared what she did to try to make herself *look* innocent. I'd say the split on this one is about fifty–fifty.

—The theory that the three of them worked together is creeping up the list, only just behind Frankie, although I suspect after today's episode this theory may move up even higher.

—Mike Crawford is actually no longer in last place after yesterday's show, with some suggesting maybe he killed Geneva because he knew about the paternity test and was worried his daughter would find out.

—Elliot O'Connor is coming in fifth place.

—Ana Castillo, Zara's maid, is coming in sixth, joint with Stephen Pollard, Lou's ex-boyfriend.

Now, one of the things that's popped up time and time again is that we've heard very little from or about Nadine Howe. Ordinarily, I'd say that hints at her innocence, but in this particular case, I think it might be the opposite. We know one thing for sure, right? That Geneva liked to find out the secrets of all those close to her so that she could basically hold them ransom. So we have to assume she had something on Nadine too. Not hearing much about her during this investigation just makes me think that Nadine is better at covering her tracks than her friends, which makes her very capable when it comes to . . . oh, I don't know . . . covering up a crime? It's also worth noting that she's been very much leading the other two when it's come to them responding to any kind of questioning about this case. I don't know if you saw yesterday's *Todd Lane* episode, but she wouldn't even let Frankie or Zara speak until he specifically asked that they be allowed to answer questions. I definitely get the vibe that she's pulling the strings in this situation.

Anyway, I decided it was time I dug a little deeper into the life of Nadine Howe, which actually was much harder than I'd been anticipating. Of the three friends, there is the least information about her online. She's a hot-shot lawyer and so her social media is all set to private. I've looked at all the information I can find online about her until my eyes felt like they were going to bleed, and I honestly thought I'd hit a brick wall with this particular line of investigation. But then, finally, I had a breakthrough.

This morning, literally about two hours ago, an email landed in my inbox from a woman who will remain anonymous, and she has given me permission to read it out to you with the proviso that I redact certain personal details. I'm going to bring the email up on the screen so you can see it as I read it.

– Email displays on screen –

From: ████████████████████
To: juniperroseYT@gmail.com

Dear Miss Rose,

I hope this email finds you well. I've been watching your YouTube videos and I believe I have some information, but I don't want to be interviewed on your channel or have any of our details shared online. I'm hoping you can still use this information without us having to be any more involved.

When I first started watching your videos, one of the names you mentioned stood out to me – Nadine Howe – but I couldn't remember exactly where I'd heard it before. I figured it out today, though. My mum, ████████████████, divorced my dad seven years ago. When I saw Nadine appear on *The Todd Lane Show* I remembered where I had heard her name before – she was my mum's divorce lawyer. Mum has since passed away and I've got all of her paperwork and documents stashed away in my home office, so out of curiosity, just to see if I was right, I looked through everything, and I was, but something really strange stuck out to me. Mum paid three amounts for Nadine's representation. A deposit of ███████████████ and the final balance of ██████████████████ was paid directly to the firm using sort code ████████ and account number ████████. But there's a third payment of ████████ which seems to have been paid to Nadine herself, using sort code ████████ and account number ████████. Does this seem right to you? Mum was quite old at the time, easily confused when it came to dealing with paperwork and legal jargon. I don't think she'd have known if something was amiss when it came to paying for her lawyer. It may be nothing, and sorry if this is a total waste of your time, but it just seems really odd to me. I can't imagine a law firm requiring the deposit to be paid directly to the solicitor. I've attached screenshots of all the paperwork and bank statements, but as I said, I really don't want this stuff plastered over the internet, so please use it with caution. I'm happy to speak to the law firm too if we think there's been some kind of gross misconduct here.

Regards,

████████████

This is it. This is Nadine's motive. If she did what this person is suggesting she did, fraudulently took money from an elderly client, and Geneva somehow knew about it – because, let's remember, Geneva always had dirt on everyone – then this is one hell of a reason to want her dead. This isn't just a secret about an affair or a covered-up overdose. This could ruin her. She could go to prison.

Now, ordinarily, I'd try to contact Nadine for comment when I discover something like this. Not that I think she'd actually talk to me. And, to be honest, I didn't want to give her the chance to use her skills as a lawyer to talk her way out of it. But due to the nature of this allegation and the fact that it involves a large company, I decided it was best to send the evidence that was supplied to me in this email directly to the law firm and I also chose to hand it in to the police. As yet, I don't know what the result will be, but for now I want to stress that this is an unverified allegation. Until we get word from the police that criminal activity has taken place, I don't want to speculate too wildly.

However, I think we have enough here to at least put her onto our suspect list. So, now we have . . .

—Elliot O'Connor
—Mikc Crawford
—Frankie Crawford
—Ana Castillo
—Zara Garcia
—Stephen Pollard
—Nadine Howe

Don't forget to leave your theories in the comments below, be sure to smash that 'like' button and subscribe, and I will see you tomorrow, when hopefully I will be able to update you on this allegation. See you then.

Chapter Twenty

Monday, 27th June

Nadine

Nadine sits in the dark, her curtains drawn, blocking any hint of sunlight that dares to seep through the windows. She's been sitting on her sofa, knees pulled up to her chin, ever since she arrived home from the police station an hour ago. And she's not planning on moving any time soon.

It had all happened so quickly. The heavy knocking on the door had nearly made her slip in the shower, and as she hurried down the stairs in a dressing gown and with her hair thrown up in a towel, head still fuzzy from the heat of the shower, she'd been expecting to see Frankie and Zara standing on her doorstep. Now, looking back, she almost wants to laugh about how embarrassed she'd been that the police had caught her at such an indiscreet moment. She also can't help but wonder why the others didn't think to warn her. Frankie has her phone set to notify her every time Juniper releases a new video. She'd have known about it and could have at least given her half an hour's heads up.

Nadine presses her forehead against her knees, willing her head to stop pounding. Honesty had been her only option in her police interview. They had all the evidence right there. The bank statements, the confirmation that the payment was made directly to her, the email trail between her and her client. There was no point in denying what she did. Her secret is officially out there, along with Frankie and Zara's. All their worst fears have come true, her house of cards has well and truly crumbled. It's like Geneva never died at all.

It had been a moment of drunken vulnerability when she told Geneva what she had done. When she first moved to Millionaire's Row at the tender age of twenty-two, Geneva was her first friend. The one to welcome her to the world of the elite. But what she had done to get here, stealing that money from her elderly client, weighed heavy on her heart. Too heavy. Under the fog of false confidence that the third bottle of wine brought, she thought she could trust Geneva. She thought it would help, getting it off her chest. What a joke.

The trill of the doorbell slices through the silence in the room, and Nadine winces. Who could it be now? Frankie? Zara? Juniper? Maybe some of her subscribers who have come to graffiti on her driveway and leave dead birds on her windscreen. Is this how it all started for Elliot? This waiting for something bad to happen? She's been allowed to come home for now, though has been expressly warned to stay local as the police will want to speak to her again, but she's wondering if she'd have been better off being locked in a cell while they figure out what to do with her. At least in a cell she'd be safe from whatever nastiness the world will now want to inflict upon her.

She ignores the doorbell, wishing the dark cave that she's made for herself could be soundproof too, completely blocking out the outside world.

The sound of the letterbox opening sends a spark of fear shooting through her, and visions of home-made bombs being dropped onto her welcome mat fill her mind.

'Nadine? I know you're in there.'

Andrew. It's Andrew at the door. The tone of his voice sends a shiver down her spine. Gone is the friendly warmth they've always had between each other. Even when she accused him of being Juniper's source and he was pleading his innocence, he still never lost that air of amiability. But now he has. Now it's been replaced by anger.

'I don't want to talk,' she eventually calls back, her heart racing.

'Well, that's too bad. I'm not leaving until we do. I can stand out here and shout through your letterbox if you want. I'm sure people would love to come and see what all the commotion is about.'

Nadine's mouth tightens. She's not sure why she still cares what anyone will think when she's been labelled a thief and a murderer to thousands of people, but she does. Spine stiff, she makes her way to the door and opens it, ushering him inside and shutting it quickly.

The two of them stand in silence in the hallway, and it dawns on Nadine that the last time he was here was the night they slept together. It seems like an eternity ago now. She can't bring herself to meet his eye, so she crosses her arms and stares at his shoes.

'What do you want?' she says.

'Did you really do what they're saying you did?'

Nadine's shoulders curl. 'Which part? Committing fraud or committing murder?'

'Both.'

She draws a long, slow breath in through her teeth, then moves towards the kitchen.

'Drink?' she says, pulling out two glasses from the cupboard and uncorking a bottle of Chateau La Conseillante; the most expensive bottle of red she owns. She had planned to save it for a special occasion, but she supposes near imprisonment is as good an excuse as any. Andrew doesn't respond to her offer but she pours him a glass anyway, sliding it along the kitchen island towards him as she perches on one of the stools. Sighing, he comes to join her.

'I didn't kill Geneva.' She swirls the wine around her glass a few times.

'What about the money?' he says.

Nodding slowly, she takes a sip, allowing the liquid to sit on her tongue for a few seconds.

'I did do that.' She's still not able to meet Andrew's eye, but she can see him shaking his head in her peripheral vision.

'Why?'

Though she went through everything that happened with the police earlier, this is different. They didn't ask her why she did it, just the how, the when, the where. She slides her finger along the rim of her glass and finally brings her gaze up to meet his.

'I bought this house not long after I joined the company. Did I ever tell you that?'

Andrew's eyes roam the room. 'I don't think so.'

'Fresh out of law school, crippling student debts. I was going to rent a place in Westbourne, even got so far as paying the deposit. But, of course, it wasn't good enough for my mother. No, her daughter had to live in Sandbanks. She had to be able to tell people her daughter lived on Millionaire's Row. So she and my father chose the house, paid for the house, moved me into the house. Then proceeded to make my life a living hell, because from that day on I owed them. I thought if I managed to pay them back quickly, they might finally think I'm good enough.'

She takes another sip of wine and places the glass back on the counter with too much force, so that the clang echoes around the room. Andrew's forehead creases, the line in between his eyebrows deepening.

'I have to go,' he murmurs.

Nadine's stomach lurches. She hadn't wanted him to come in, but now that he's here she's not sure she wants to be alone again. She places a hand on his.

'Please don't.'

'I'm sorry.' He grimaces, looking down at her hand as if it's pure poison, then slips his out from underneath. 'You're not who I thought you were.'

He stands and steps back out into the hallway. The sound of the front door slamming shut makes Nadine flinch. Then there is silence. Cold, dark, lonely silence, apart from her quivering breathing as she tries to fight back the tears.

Chapter Twenty-One

Tuesday, 28th June

Zara

'Oh, Miss Garcia.' The cheeks of the woman behind the reception desk at the club go as bright pink as her long, obviously fake nails. She leans forward, keeping her voice low. 'Um, I'm afraid you're not going to be able to come in today. Your membership has been suspended.'

Zara exchanges a glance with Frankie, before turning back to the receptionist and frowning, perplexed. 'I'm not sure what you mean? Did the payment not go through this month?'

She has the extortionate membership fee set up on a direct debit, so doesn't usually check to make sure it's been processed each month, but she's never had an issue before.

'No, nothing like that.' The receptionist's cheeks progress from pink to red. 'It's one of our policies that all members need to be in good standing with the community and, well . . .' She drops her gaze and starts fiddling with the pen on her desk. 'Owing to the risk of . . . negative publicity for the club . . . the manager has taken the decision to halt yours and Miss Howe's memberships, and your guest privileges,' she adds, looking at Frankie. 'I'm ever so sorry.'

'We haven't done anything wrong,' Zara says, biting back the curse words filling her mouth.

Becca Day

'I really am sorry. It's not my call. If you want to speak with the manager about it, you can send an email.' She slides a business card towards them, which Zara snatches up a little too roughly. She knows it's not the girl's fault, she's only following orders, but between this and her clients cancelling their appointments she feels as though her life is being torn away, ripped out from under her feet like a rug.

'Come on.' Zara marches towards the entrance doors, not even waiting to check that Frankie's following. 'Let's go to mine.'

The water is ice cold as it laps around Zara's ankles. She shuffles, runs her fingers along the ridges in the wood of the jetty. As much as sitting out here instead of in the luxury of the club hadn't been their first choice, it's probably worked out for the best. This stretch of ocean is private, only accessible by the owners of the mansions on Millionaire's Row. The staring and whispers at the club are becoming too much to bear.

'What were you going to tell me, Frankie?' She stretches out her legs, hoping against hope that she's not about to get into yet another argument. 'When we were outside Nadine's office?'

'Oh, nothing.'

She feels Frankie tense beside her, and she places a tentative hand over hers.

'You said you didn't cheat on Mike. So how could it be that Callie isn't his?'

The pinched expression, the tremble of her lip, the way she sucks in a shaky breath, is enough to confirm what she's suspected ever since their conversation got cut short.

'Did someone hurt you?' she ventures, her own voice growing unsteady too.

Frankie nods, almost imperceptibly, and Zara's eyes fill with tears.

'I'm not even completely sure who it was,' Frankie whispers. 'I went to a house party, this was back before we moved to Millionaire's Row, and my drink must have been spiked because I totally blacked out. All I know is I woke up lying on a bed and could tell something was wrong.'

'Oh, Frankie. Why didn't you go to the police?'

Frankie lets out a half-laugh. 'Come on, Zara, you really think that would have done any good? Why do you think women like me never speak up? These things always turn out the same way. There's never enough evidence, especially when I didn't even know who had done it, and there would have been the question of whether I'd asked for it or not. I couldn't put myself through that. So I decided to pretend it had never happened, try to erase it from my memory, and then I found out I was pregnant with Callie. I was in total denial. Just told myself she was Mike's. But every now and again it would gnaw at me. The uncertainty. I had this recurring nightmare that would make me wake up in a cold sweat. So when she was fourteen I ordered a paternity test and . . . that's when I finally knew.'

As she finishes speaking, she finally moves her gaze from the ocean to Zara, whose cheeks are now soaked.

'I'm . . . I'm so sorry.'

Frankie shrugs.

Hating herself, Zara thinks back to every moment she's resented Frankie for thinking she, too, had had an affair. Every time she's scoffed at her perfect marriage, at her desire to be wife and mother and nothing else. Every time she thought she was prudish for never wanting to go to parties, preferring the relative exclusivity of the club or, even better, their homes.

'I'm such a shit friend,' she says, sobbing.

'Don't be silly. How could you have known?'

Zara doesn't know what to say to that, so she just continues to attempt stifling her cries. The two sit in silent contemplation for some time, and then Frankie says, 'Anyway. I've not exactly been a stellar friend recently. I was wrong about Nadine.'

'We were wrong, you mean,' Zara mutters. She peers back to look at Nadine's house, where the curtains remain tightly pulled shut. They tried knocking earlier and sent her a message saying they were outside, but didn't get a response.

'We still don't know anything for sure, though. There's a chance she knew we were onto her. She could have shared her own secret to throw us off the scent.' But even as the words leave Frankie's mouth, Zara can tell she believes that just as much as she does. There's no way. Nadine is potentially facing prison time. She'd have been mad to let this get out on purpose.

'I can't believe we're back to square one.' Zara kicks at the water, sending droplets flying into the air and splashing back down. She watches the rings ripple across the surface, so calm and serene, the complete antithesis to the thoughts racing around her head. She thinks back to their scribbled timeline of events, to the feeble list of people who could have broken into Nadine's house. 'It's got to be Elliot, right? I mean, who else could it have been?'

'He certainly does seem the most likely. And the fact he's disappeared off the face of the earth since he came after you at the clinic doesn't bode well for him.' Frankie leans forward, her elbows on her knees, thinking. 'We need to talk to him. Why don't you try calling him?'

'What?' Zara's eyes widen with horror. The prospect of facing him again sends panic flaring through her gut. She never wants to see him again for as long as she lives.

'If anyone's going to be able to bring him out of hiding, it's you. If we make him think he's meeting up with you to discuss your relationship, he might buy it. Then if we face him together, corner him, it'll take him by surprise.'

Begrudgingly, Zara pulls out her phone and navigates to Elliot's number. She puts it on loudspeaker and rests the phone on her thigh instead of pressing it to her ear, as if she's afraid he'll reach through the receiver and grab her. It goes straight to voicemail.

'His phone must be switched off,' Zara says, quietly relieved. 'I didn't think he'd answer anyway. He thinks I hate him.'

'We need to try to get a message to him.' Frankie tilts her head back, face angled to the sun, as she thinks. After a few moments she sits up straight. 'I've just had a really stupid idea.'

The block of flats Zara arrives at is far rougher than anything they'd see in Sandbanks. The bricks are dirty grey, decorated with colourful graffiti, and the cracked glass front door has been haphazardly covered with brown packing tape.

Referencing the instructions she received via Messenger, she checks the flat number and presses the appropriate buzzer. A voice sounds almost instantly.

'Hello?'

'Hi, it's me. Zara.' She wishes she didn't sound so nervous.

'Great! I'll be down in one moment.'

Zara bounces on the balls of her feet as she waits, burying her hands in her pockets and praying no one will see her. Not that anyone she knows would hang around these parts anyway. She checks the time and sees a message from Frankie, asking to let her know as soon as she's done. Zara agreed to go straight back to the jetty to give her all the details as soon as this is over anyway, but clearly Frankie is as anxious about this as she is.

A flash of blonde hair appears in the hallway as Zara curses inwardly. It's too late to turn back now.

'Thanks for coming! I thought we could go film in the park. My place is a right mess.'

'Sure thing.' Zara forces a smile as she follows Juniper away from the block of flats. She's got what she has to say, disingenuous as it is, rehearsed in her mind, but as she walks she completely draws a blank. What the hell is she thinking? This is bound to be a mistake.

TRANSCRIPT

Video published 28/06/2022

Subscriber count: 82,175

Welcome back to *True Crime Over Wine*. Today marks a historic moment on this channel as finally I've managed to get one of Geneva's friends, lead suspect in your guys' books, Zara Garcia, to agree to an interview with me. I spoke to her just an hour ago and have rushed to get this filmed and edited for you. Now, I know you're going to be as desperate as I am to hear what she has to say, but before that let's have a quick word from today's sponsor.

– Sponsor Ad break –

Thank you so much to BodyBlast Supplements for sponsoring today's video. As always, let's quickly go over the current suspect list.

—Nadine Howe has shot into the lead after the revelation that she committed fraud, with most of you convinced that that's the dirt Geneva had on her. I have to admit, she seems to me like the kind of ruthless person who would do anything to keep that kind of secret safe, though, of course, I try to only deal with facts on this channel as opposed to gut feelings.

—The second most common theory is that the three of them worked together, with Nadine being the driving force behind it. Definitely a possibility.

—The rest of the list stands as it did yesterday. Zara Garcia is coming in third place.

—Frankie Crawford is in fourth.

—Mike Crawford is in fifth.

—Elliot O'Connor is coming in sixth place.

—Ana Castillo, Zara's maid, is coming in joint seventh place with Stephen Pollard, Lou's ex-boyfriend.

Right, I'm not going to hold you in suspense any longer. Let's see what Zara has to say for herself.

– Cut to interview footage with Zara Garcia –

INTERVIEW FILMED AT 12.38 ON 28/06/2022

Juniper: Ready?

Zara: Mm-hmm.

Juniper: Firstly, let's talk about the night of the murder. You, Nadine, Frankie and Geneva were doing wine club at Nadine's house, right?

Zara: That's right.

Juniper: Did anything happen? Anything out of the ordinary?

Zara: Nope. It was a nice, relaxed evening. Geneva left first and we all filtered home after her. That was the last we saw of her.

Juniper: And you definitely all went straight home?

Zara: Yes. It was late.

Juniper: Geneva didn't go straight home though, did she? Any idea why she'd have gone to the beach?

Zara: I have no idea. No one really ever knew why Geneva did anything.

Juniper: OK. Now, I hate to ask this, but can you explain what happened with Geneva and your sister? Forgive me, I know it's probably a very sensitive topic.

Zara: I mean . . . I think you know most of it from your interview with Stephen.

Juniper: Yes, but the viewers really want to hear your take on it.

Zara: Because it could be my motive for killing Geneva?

(Pause)

Zara: It's just like he said. Geneva shared their sex tape online. That's the reason she took her own life.

Juniper: And you're sure it was Geneva?

Zara: It could only have been her. She was convinced Lou was sleeping with Elliot.

Juniper: Was she?

Zara: *pause* No.

Juniper: How do you know?

Zara: You're really going to make me say it? Because it was me. Happy? I was the one sleeping with Elliot.

Juniper: Right. When did the affair start?

Zara: It was about two years before Geneva died.

Juniper: Were you ever worried that Geneva would find out? That she'd do to you what she ended up doing to Lou?

Zara: It crossed my mind. You had to be either really brave or really dumb to cross Geneva.

Juniper: Which one were you?

Zara: Well, I'm not brave.

(Pause)

Zara: I was in love with him. That made it seem like Geneva potentially finding out just . . . didn't matter. To be honest, I still am in love with him.

Juniper: On *The Todd Lane Show* you said you were convinced he was the one who tried to kill you.

Zara: I was angry. Scared. I honestly don't know what to think anymore. I wish I could talk to him and try to make sense of everything that's happened.

Juniper: So, if you loved him as much as you say you did, why didn't you stick by him when the world turned on him? I mean, when I spoke to him he told me he had absolutely no one in his corner.

Zara: Because I honestly thought he might have killed her. I've been back and forth on it so much over the past five years it's driving me insane. I'm still not a hundred per cent sure either way. I'd give anything to have a proper conversation with him.

Juniper: Yes, I've been having trouble reaching him these past few days. Have you heard from him at all?

Zara: I wish I had.

Juniper: OK, let's go back to your affair. A few episodes ago, I spoke to Geneva's co-worker from *Copperdale Street* and she revealed that the day before Geneva died, she was ranting and raving about you, calling you a bitch. Do you think that may have been because she found out about you and Elliot?

Zara: I'm not really sure. Maybe.

Juniper: She didn't say anything to you? Didn't confront you at all?

Zara: No.

Juniper: But you were at wine club together that night. Surely, if she was calling you every name under the sun the day before, you'd have at least sensed something was up that night.

Zara: Not if she didn't want me to. She didn't just reserve her acting skills for the screen.

Juniper: Did you know Elliot was considering asking Geneva for a divorce?

Zara: Yes. He was going to leave her for me. That was our plan before . . .

Juniper: Before Geneva was killed?

Zara: I've been so consumed with guilt for so many years. Not just about what happened with Lou, but with Geneva too. Believe it or not we really were all friends. We might have been a bit . . . dysfunctional . . . but she made us a kind of family. I never wanted to hurt her. I still . . . I still go to her grave on Tuesdays at 8 p.m. on the dot every single week. Just to sit there and be with her.

Juniper: In the name of clearing your conscience, is there anything else you want to share with the people watching at home? About you or your friends?

Zara: I don't think so. I wish I could be more help. Now, though, none of us have anything to hide. We'll help with your investigation in whatever way we can.

Juniper: I appreciate that. OK, Zara, I just have one last question for you.

Zara: Shoot.

Juniper: Do you completely trust Frankie and Nadine?

Zara: Of course I do.

Juniper: There's not a tiny part of you that's thought maybe one of them did it?

Zara: *pause* Let's just say, if there ever were any doubts, they've been put to rest now.

– Cut back to studio –

So, I've watched that interview back three times now, and I can't quite figure out what she meant by that last remark. 'If there were any doubts, they've been put to rest now.' Does that mean she did think one or both of her friends killed Geneva at one point? And if she did, what is it that's changed her mind?

I feel like we're so close to cracking this case. There must be something someone hasn't come forward with yet, some tiny, seemingly insignificant piece of evidence that will blow this whole thing wide open. And now that the police are starting to take an interest again, I can only hope that they'll have the resources I've been lacking that will allow the truth to finally come out. I'm more convinced than ever that the killer is one of Geneva's three friends. We just need to figure out which one, or whether they worked together.

Let's quickly revisit what we know about the three women so far.

Zara Garcia

- Zara was having an affair with Elliot O'Connor.
- Elliot was planning on divorcing Geneva to be with Zara, which would have left Geneva destitute. Could she have

blackmailed Elliot with what happened to Ana Castillo's sister as a way to stop him from leaving her, and then Zara killed her to get her out of the way?
- Geneva ranting to her co-worker and calling Zara a bitch suggests she may have found out about the affair. Could her death have been an argument gone wrong?
- Zara also held a grudge against Geneva for sharing the sex tape that ultimately ended in her sister taking her own life.
- Finally, she was locked in the sauna by 'someone'. Could it have been the killer? One of the other two girls who knew she was in there, perhaps?

Nadine Howe

- Nadine committed fraud by swindling a large sum of money from an elderly client, which we can assume is the secret that Geneva had on her.
- Which, in turn, makes her the only known criminal in this case.
- She has also been eerily in control during this case, as if she has some kind of hold over the other two.

Frankie Crawford

- Frankie took a paternity test to determine whether Mike Crawford is her eldest child's biological father or not, and we know that Geneva knew about the test.
- Three days before Geneva was murdered, she sent a text to her that read 'I swear to God, Geneva, if you tell Mike, you're dead to me.'

I mean, they all had pretty good reasons for wanting Geneva dead. Zara seems to have the most motive, but the only thing that's bothering me is how she let Elliot take the fall. If she killed Geneva to get rid of her so that they could be together, why would she distance herself from him like that?

Chapter Twenty-Two

Tuesday, 28th June

Nadine

'You're a free woman,' Nadine's lawyer's gruff voice says through the phone, and she can't help but grimace. He had called with good news. Since her crime was so long ago, and the victim of her crime is no longer alive, she's been let off, though she's agreed to pay the money she stole back to the family. Technically, her lawyer is right – she's free. She's no longer facing the prospect of going to prison for fraud, and she's trying to hold on to the relief that comes from that. It's being superseded, though, by other worries. She's facing a different sort of prison. She's lost the only thing that ever really mattered to her – her career – and will probably end up losing the very house she went through all of this to get as a result. Not to mention she's going to be afraid to even walk outside, or to answer the phone.

Oh God. Her parents will know what she did.

On top of that, she has to consider the possibility that being let off in the eyes of the law could only be temporary. The police have their eye on her now. She's not going to go down for fraud, but there's still a very real chance that she could go down for murder.

She's crawled back inside her hard, protective shell since Andrew left, regretting her display of weakness. Frankie and Zara tried to knock but she wasn't in the mood to face anybody else. By the time she hangs up with her lawyer and finally moves from her spot on the sofa, her limbs are stiff and her joints click. She looks around her house, which no longer really feels like hers now she knows she's not going to be able to pay for it. It feels odd knowing the police were here just yesterday. Everything seems dirty, tainted. Even her bedroom, when she drags herself upstairs in the hopes of sleeping away the day, feels alien. The ghost of her night of passion with Andrew lingers, now soured with the memory of how everything turned out with him.

She shuffles across to the window and squints as she peers out through the crack in the curtain. The sea glistens under the too bright sun like a bed of shattered glass. She wonders, as she watches the gentle movement of the water, if this was the last thing Geneva saw that night. Had she watched the waves lap against the beach as she faded away? Or had her eyes been fixed on her killer, the person holding her by the throat and choking the life out of her? Who was it? There are too many unanswered questions, and now that she doesn't have the charade, the lies, to keep her occupied, she can't stop turning them over in her mind, going through all the possibilities with a fine-tooth comb.

Movement over to the right distracts her and she twists to look down at the jetty a couple of houses over. Frankie and Zara are sitting out there, no doubt talking about her. Dropping the curtain and plunging the bedroom back into blackness, she makes a start towards the bed, then hesitates. Those two women out there are possibly the only people she has left in this world. At least they'd knocked. At least they had wanted to see her, penniless as she was about to become, which is more than she could say of her own parents or anyone at the club. And at least they understood. Maybe Geneva was right after all. Maybe their secrets would be the thing to keep them close, even after they've been exposed.

'Oh my god, Nadine!' Zara jumps to her feet as Nadine approaches, sliding her sunglasses up to perch on top of her head. 'What happened? We tried knocking as soon as we realised you were back.'

'I know. Sorry, I wasn't really in the right head space to talk to anyone.'

She doesn't miss the awkward expression on Frankie's face.

'Please don't judge me,' Nadine says. 'I'm going to have enough of that from everyone else.'

'No, we're not!' Zara cuts in, not allowing Frankie to speak. 'We just . . .'

Nadine watches the two women make eye contact. What the hell is going on?

After a pause, Frankie heaves herself up from her spot on the jetty and comes to join them. 'OK, you have to understand the pressure we've been under since all this speculation started up again. And both of our secrets had been leaked and yours hadn't and it just seemed a little . . . suspicious.'

Nadine shakes her head, confused. 'Suspicious? You mean you thought I was the one dishing the dirt to Juniper?' There's that look between them again, and this time the penny drops. 'Wait. You thought I killed Geneva?'

'We didn't so much think it. More like briefly considered it.'

Nadine stares at them, stunned.

'But now we know it definitely wasn't you,' Zara is quick to add. 'I even went on Juniper's YouTube channel saying as much.'

'Hold on, you went on her channel?'

'Well, yes.' She shuffles her bare feet on the wood, staring down at her French manicured toenails. 'Actually, it wasn't just to say we thought you were innocent. It was Frankie's idea.'

Nadine's stomach lurches. This is what happens when she's not around to keep an eye on things, to keep the both of them in check. They go off and make rash decisions without thinking things through.

She takes a breath, centring herself. 'Tell me what you've done. Slowly.'

This time, Frankie is the one to speak. 'We figured we need to confront Elliot. For real this time. Maybe if the three of us come face to face with him, he'll get nervous and slip up. Except we don't know where he is. We figured that if Zara said she was still in love with him, he might make himself known to her, that he might turn up at Geneva's grave tonight?'

'What?' Nadine frowns.

'I told Juniper I visited her grave every Tuesday at eight,' said Zara, sheepishly.

While Frankie details more of their plan, Nadine forces herself to keep her mouth shut. Only once Frankie finishes and looks nervously her way for approval does she speak.

'So, you're banking on him having watched Juniper's video, understanding Zara's hint that she'll be at the grave tonight, and going to meet her there. Of course, that's if he even wants to see her at all.'

'It's better than sitting around doing nothing.'

The flaws in Frankie's plan are glaring, but she does have a point. Besides, Nadine hasn't been able to come up with anything better while she's been holed up in her misery with the curtains drawn. She rolls her eyes and glances at her diamond Chanel watch; no doubt another soon-to-be casualty of her secret coming out. It's coming up to 5 p.m., so they have three hours until they need to be at Geneva's grave. Not that she thinks he'll actually be there, but there isn't a whole lot to lose at this point.

'You couldn't have said you went to visit the grave at lunchtime?' Nadine says, as they make their way through the iron gates of the cemetery. She's not a particularly superstitious person, certainly doesn't believe in ghosts, but being here in the dead of night with what she's sure is a storm rolling in above their heads certainly isn't her idea of a good time. They make their way along the main path, framed either side by tended lawns dotted with headstones. At least they don't have to venture as far as the northern end of the cemetery, the old part where the scattered graves are abandoned and forgotten, left to succumb to the weeds and be weathered unreadable by years of rainfall. This end, the area where Geneva is buried, is newer and still looked after, though it doesn't do much to quell the creepiness.

'Can you remember where it is?' Frankie asks.

'Over on the right. Near those trees.' Nadine nods her head in the direction, where the graves are shadowed by the woody surroundings and cut off from the light of the lamps on the main path. Her stomach flips as she feels someone grab her arm, but it's only Zara, bundling up close to her as they shuffle into the darkness. The sky flashes bright white and they all jump in unison.

'That's about right,' Frankie mutters, as the lightning is followed by a distant grumble of thunder.

'Oh hell, let's just go.' Zara is bouncing nervously now, gripping onto Nadine's arm so hard it's starting to hurt. 'He's not going to come out here in a thunderstorm.'

Nadine shakes her head. 'It was your stupid plan in the first place. We're here now. Let's at least have a quick look around.'

'It was Frankie's stupid plan,' Zara mumbles under her breath, but Nadine ignores her, turning on the torch on her phone to guide their way. They press on, shivering as a few light raindrops land on their faces.

Nadine can't bring herself to look at Geneva's grave as they approach. There's a reason none of them have visited since the funeral. In all of their minds, Geneva still lives. Her dominating, sometimes even captivating personality, her flaws, all still vivid, taking residence in their memories. Looking at the grave and picturing her decomposed body lying there under the dirt is too much.

'Let's get out of here,' Zara says, but as she does another flash of lightning illuminates the sky and Nadine is sure she sees a figure standing by one of the nearby trees. Watching them. She lets out a shriek, dropping her phone and grabbing both Frankie and Zara's hands, which makes them scream too. The lightning finishes and they're once again plunged into darkness. When the next flash of lightning comes, there's no one to be seen. Breathless, Nadine picks up her phone and pivots, spinning on her heel, whipping her torch from one tree trunk to the next.

'What is it?' Zara whimpers beside her. It sounds like she's crying, but Nadine can't bring herself to answer. Her heart is racing, panic thundering in her chest. The light of her torch lands on another tree, closer to the chapel, and catches a flutter of movement.

'Hey!' Nadine stumbles forward, the rain now beating heavy on her head, making her hair stick to her face. She tries not to pay attention to the fact she's venturing deeper into the trees in the middle of a thunderstorm. Her own safety isn't a priority anymore. The priority is getting to Elliot and putting an end to this madness. She breaks into a sprint, weaving around gravestones, the light of her phone thrashing around wildly as she runs.

'Elliot!' she shouts into the darkness. Behind her, she can hear Frankie calling her name, but she doesn't stop. Her feet beat the sodden ground as she wildly scans the surrounding trees, searching for any sign of more movement. The breath is snatched from her as her toe catches on a protruding tree root and she flies forward, face hurtling towards the mud, and she stretches out her hands to save herself. Her phone skids forward as she lands. Pain shoots through her knees, her shins, her palms. She makes a desperate grab for her phone and shines it around her, but all is still, save for the falling rain and the swaying of the trees. Maybe she hadn't seen anyone at all. But even as she thinks it, the sense of being watched is still strong, making every inch of her skin tingle.

Wincing and gasping for breath, she clambers back to her feet, and Frankie's calls drift into her ears again.

'Nadine! Come back! You have to see this!'

Her stomach is breaking into a cramp but she fights past it, hobbling back to Geneva's grave.

Zara storms towards her as she approaches. 'What the hell do you think you're doing? You could have broken your ankle! Or been electrocuted!'

'I thought I saw someone,' Nadine says, feebly wiping at her coat which is now caked in mud.

'Yeah, well, wait until you see what we've seen.'

Nadine's gaze follows Zara's arm as she points towards Geneva's grave. Steeling herself, she angles her torch towards it.

At first, she doesn't notice what they're talking about. Her eyes skip across the engraving on the stone.

Geneva O'Connor.
Born 29th February 1992. Died 17th June 2017.
Loving wife and daughter. Heaven has gained an angel.

It's only as Nadine's eyes travel down that she sees it. Propped up against the stone, half dug into the soil of Geneva's grave, is a shovel.

Nadine recoils. 'What the hell?'

'I don't know,' Frankie says. 'It was just there. We only spotted it after you ran off.'

'Maybe someone's just been tending to the grave and left it there by mistake,' Zara suggests, but as the words leave her mouth Nadine's phone buzzes in her hand. The sense of dread hits Nadine before she even looks at the screen. She just has a gut feeling that this is something bad, something she's going to wish she hadn't read. Still, she has no choice but to open up her notifications.

It's a withheld number. There's a picture attachment.

Nadine lets out a half-cough, half-choke as her eyes focus on what she's seeing. It's Elliot. It's unmistakably Elliot, but he's sat on what looks like a dining chair in a dark room, with his wrists and his ankles strapped to the wood, a thick roll of fabric wedged into his mouth.

Breathless, she whispers the message that's written underneath the photo.

Do as you're told or I'll kill him.

Zara falters beside her, falling to her knees, hands clasped around her mouth. Before Nadine can bend down to comfort her, her phone buzzes again. Another message pops up beneath the previous one.

Pick up the shovel and start to dig.

Chapter Twenty-Three

Tuesday, 28th June

Frankie

'It doesn't mean . . . surely it can't mean . . .'

Frankie's words are lost to the thunder, now raging relentlessly away from them, and Zara's cries. Her eyes keep flicking between the message on Nadine's phone and the shovel. This has to be some kind of sick joke. Surely they're not being expected to dig up Geneva's grave.

'Give me that.' Frankie plucks the phone from Nadine's trembling hand and opens up the photo again, zooming in to get a proper look. Millions of tiny ants crawl down her spine. That look in his eyes. It's pure terror. There's no clue as to where he is. The room he's in looks sort of like a living room – there's the edge of what looks like it could be a sofa in the corner of the picture – but whoever took it did a good job of not capturing any distinguishing features. This must be why he disappeared straight after his run-in with Zara at the clinic. They had assumed it was because he had gone into hiding in case she reported him.

Frankie swallows the lump in her throat. Whoever sent this has to be the killer. They're talking to Geneva's murderer.

'We have to show this to the police,' she says suddenly. 'This proves it wasn't us. They'll probably be able to figure out where it came from.'

'No!' Zara's shriek is so loud it echoes around the cemetery. She lunges forward, snatching the phone from Frankie's hand. 'Didn't you read what it said? They're going to kill Elliot if we don't do as we're told!'

'You actually think if we dig up Geneva's grave, they'll let him go? He's probably seen who they are! They're never going to let him go. His best chance is for us to go to the police.'

Zara backs away, her grip tightening on the phone. She turns to look pleadingly at Nadine.

'We should take a vote,' Nadine says, and suddenly Frankie is right back there. On that beach. Staring down at Geneva's lifeless eyes.

'Fuck you and your votes.' Zara's words come out with so much hostility they seem to surprise even herself. Before Frankie knows what's happening, Zara makes a grab at the shovel, lifts it up and slams it into the earth below.

'Zara, you can't!' Frankie moves to stop her but Zara shoves her back. She trips as she tries to steady herself. Clumps of mud fly as Zara works at the grave.

'Stop, Zara,' Nadine says, and Frankie expels a short breath of relief. Finally someone is seeing sense.

Zara's refusals stutter out between angry sobs. 'No. I won't let him die. This is all my fault. I should have trusted him.'

'No, stop digging. I see something!'

There's a moment of stillness as Nadine's words sink in, before they lean in to inspect what Nadine has seen. A smooth corner of something is poking out from the disturbed dirt. For one ridiculous second Frankie panics that it might be a human bone, but she's quick to reason with herself that Geneva's body would be much, much deeper than the little Zara has dug.

Nadine steps forward and curls her fingers around the object. She tugs, loose earth falling away, and wriggles it free. It's a metal case. Frankie chews on her lip as Nadine pops the latch and lifts the lid. Realisation hits all three of them seemingly simultaneously, because they all gasp in unison.

'Geneva's laptop,' Frankie says. 'Does that mean the anonymous source is working with Geneva's killer?'

Nadine nods. 'That or it's the same person.'

'Shit!' Zara drops the shovel and holds up Nadine's phone, blinding Frankie with the sudden light. 'There's another message. It's telling us to open the laptop and then wait for instructions.'

'They're watching us!' It's Frankie's turn to spin around now, staring aimlessly into the thick of the trees. Whoever is doing this to them, whoever has Elliot, whoever killed Geneva is here, now. 'What do you want?' she screams into the blackness, but all she gets in response is her own echo.

The Windows start-up sound is too loud in the relative quiet of the cemetery, bouncing off the gravestones, and the light that floods out of the screen as Zara opens it bathes everything in a ghostly white glow. Whoever planted the laptop obviously charged it in anticipation for this moment.

'Oh my god.' Zara's voice is little more than a whisper. Frankie stops searching the trees and focuses on the laptop, tries to make sense of what she's seeing.

'No,' Nadine says.

'Is . . . is that . . .' Frankie stutters.

It is. There, planted on the screen so that it would be the first thing to show when they opened up the laptop, is a slightly blurry photo of her, Nadine and Zara standing on the beach, staring down at Geneva's lifeless body.

'You know what really gets me,' Nadine says as they sit around the laptop, staring at it as if it might explode at any second, their backsides damp from the wet grass and soil, though thankfully the rain has stopped. 'They could have just messaged us that photo. But instead, they decided to put it on the laptop, bury the thing and then make us dig it up.'

'They're clearly messing with us.' Frankie presses her head against her knees. She wishes the ringing in her ears would stop. 'They want to see how far they can push us. That's why they're making us wait for instructions. It's a power trip. What can they make us do?'

'Anything now we know they have this,' says Zara. 'We're completely screwed. Even if we did go to the police all they'd have to do is send them that photo and we're done for.'

'Maybe we could say it's been photoshopped?'

Nadine shakes her head. 'But it hasn't been. It's a real photo. The police would be able to prove that eventually.'

Frankie barely hears what Nadine says, because another sound has caught her attention. A poppy tinkling noise that sounds strangely familiar.

'Can you hear that?' she says, trying to lean in to where the sound is coming from. Zara and Nadine stop to listen too.

'It's coming from the grave.' Zara lurches forward and, not even bothering with the shovel this time, starts digging her freshly manicured nails into the soil. It only takes a couple of seconds for her to retrieve the source of the music. They could have guessed. Geneva's phone had been buried along with the laptop, protected from the damp inside a plastic Ziploc bag, and it's ringing.

'I'm not answering it,' Zara says, thrusting the phone towards Frankie. Nadine tries to snatch it but Frankie is faster. She's not going to make the mistake they made before. Nadine called the shots, told them what to do, and look where it's got them. Frankie needs to look out for herself this time.

'Hello?' Her voice catches in her throat as she answers the phone. It seems ludicrous, as if she's about to have a good old natter with a friend, but she's not sure what else to say.

To begin with, she doesn't think anyone is going to reply, but then there's a crackle on the other end of the line. A deep, mechanical voice sounds like something out of a horror movie, turning Frankie's blood to ice. It would be laughable if it weren't so terrifying.

'One of you will confess to Geneva's murder,' the voice says. 'If you don't, I'll kill Elliot and frame you all.'

'Wait, what do you . . .' But before Frankie can ask the mystery voice to explain what the hell they mean, the line goes dead.

Chapter Twenty-Four

Tuesday, 28th June

Zara

Drained and quiet, the three of them sit at Nadine's kitchen island, staring at the laptop and phone lying before them. The distinct sense of being watched had followed them all the way back to Millionaire's Row, although none of them saw any people or cars they recognised. Nadine had made them all cups of tea to warm them after their ordeal in the cemetery, but none of them are in the mood. The cups sit cold and abandoned, adding to the dismal mood. Between the lack of sleep, the rain and the mud from the grave they could easily be mistaken for the three witches from *Macbeth*. They feel just as tragic. All signs of glamour, of the women they have made themselves become, are gone.

No one has mentioned the elephant sitting in the room, but they're clearly all thinking the same thing. They're done for. There's no way out. Apparently money can't save you after all. Various barely thought-out plans have flitted through Zara's mind since the call. Maybe they could find Elliot before anything happens to him, rescue him, get the police on it, put up missing posters, rally the club members to look for him. But she knows it's pointless. He's not missing. He's been abducted by Geneva's killer. If they try anything, anything at all other than what they've been instructed to do, Elliot will die. And it's all her fault for not trusting him, for letting other people's suspicions get into her head. She replays the day in the clinic in her head. He was confrontational, definitely, totally out of bounds and should have listened to her begging him to leave her alone, but he didn't actually hurt her in any way. In fact, the only time he actually touched her was when he had tried to help her up after she fell over. Where she thought his actions were those of a dangerous murderer, now it seems they were just the last attempts of a desperate man pleading with the woman he loves to give him a chance.

Geneva's phone flashing up and ringing makes all of them jump out of their skins. Zara's hands thrash out, knocking the cold cup of tea in front of her and sending it sloshing over the counter. She grabs the phone and fumbles to answer it.

'Yes? Hello?' she practically screams.

There's a slight crackle, and then, 'Time is running out. Elliot is waiting for you.'

'How do we know you haven't killed him already?' Nadine calls, leaning in close.

At first, there's silence and Zara thinks they've hung up again, but after a few seconds a familiar voice sounds through the speaker.

'What are you doing? No!'

Zara drops the phone as Elliot's howls of agony echo through the room. She clasps her hands to her ears and shakes her head. 'Stop! Please don't hurt him!'

'You have two hours,' the voice says, before Elliot's earth-shattering screams get cut short and the line goes dead.

'We have to help him.' Zara's voice cracks from the strain of all the sobbing. 'He's suffered enough.'

'Zara's right. We have no choice,' says Frankie, glancing at a message from Mike asking when she'd be going back to the hotel and promptly ignoring it. 'I suppose we deserve it. We're terrible people after all. Terrible things happen to terrible people.' Her eyes gloss with tears. 'Do you think the kids will be able to visit me in prison?'

Nadine throws her head back, exasperated. 'Oh, for God's sake, stop it. Neither of you are going to prison.'

'Why? Do you have a plan?' Zara eyes Nadine, allowing herself to feel the tiniest flicker of hope. As much as Frankie seems to have had enough of Nadine's plans, she can't deny they've got them out of a sticky situation or two in the past. If anyone is going to figure out a way out of this, it's Nadine.

As if reading Zara's mind, the corners of Nadine's mouth quirk up. 'Of course I do. I'm going to say I killed Geneva.'

Frankie screws her face up. 'Don't be ridiculous.'

'I'm not. I'm deadly serious. This is all my fault. I'm the one who made us take the phone and laptop that night. If anyone deserves to go to prison, it's me.'

Zara stands, her stool screeching against the kitchen tiles. 'No. I should be the one. This is penance for what happened to Lou because of me.' She scoops up the phone and laptop and powers, almost stumbling, towards the hall. There's no time to stop and think or second guess herself. If she falters, she'll lose Elliot forever.

'Zara, just stop for one second.' Frankie's forceful hand grabs her shoulder and yanks her back, making her nearly drop the phone and laptop. 'Nadine, I expected more of you. Since when do you just give up? Both of you need to use your brains. Even if we do exactly as this person says, they could still kill Elliot. We have to be smarter than them.'

Both Zara and Nadine stare at Frankie expectantly, waiting to hear what better alternative she could come up with. Frankie purses her lips, thinking, then raises her eyebrows at Nadine.

'Do you still have that address book you found?'

For a moment, Nadine looks as if she has no idea what Frankie is talking about, but seconds later she digs her hand into her pocket and retrieves a small leather book.

'If Geneva knew her killer, maybe there's a clue in there somewhere,' Frankie says.

Nadine's eyes narrow and she starts flicking through the pages. Zara ignores the twisting sensation in her stomach. Even with Geneva long gone, she can't help but think how much she'd fume knowing they were snooping through her possessions.

'Anything?' Frankie says, though her voice sounds about as hopeful as Zara feels.

'Nothing obvious.' She continues making her way through the book, every turn of a page chipping away at the remnants of possibility.

Zara is about to spin back to the door and continue with her resolution to turn herself in, when Frankie sucks in a sharp breath.

'Wait,' she says, placing a hand on the book and stopping Zara in her tracks. 'Does that say what I think it says?'

Zara cranes to see what she can see. Her eyes flick to Nadine, and the expression on her face confirms that it is exactly who they think it is.

Andrew.

Chapter Twenty-Five

Tuesday, 28th June

Nadine

Outside, the sky is still a threatening grey, as if the heavens are ready to release another storm at any moment. Nadine presses her foot harder down on the accelerator, ignoring Frankie's pleas from the back seat to slow down a little. There's no slowing down, not now that the paralysing fear Nadine felt in the cemetery has been replaced with hot, burning rage. Her first instinct had been right. It had to be Andrew who'd been feeding information to Juniper. She had just known it. And he had the nerve to make her feel guilty for thinking such a thing. Who was Andrew to Geneva? Had they been sleeping together? The fact that she could ever have let him put his hands on her makes her feel sick.

The car screeches to a halt outside of Andrew's house, a fairly small semi-detached, modest considering his income at the firm. She bursts out, leaving the car door wide open, and storms up the steps before pounding at the door. It isn't long before the rattling of the chain lock sounds and the door swings open, revealing a rather stunned Andrew.

Nadine doesn't even say anything. She forces her way past him, pushing him into the wall.

'Elliot! Elliot, where are you?' she calls, and Frankie and Zara behind her do the same.

'What the hell do you think you're doing?' Andrew yells, but they ignore him and go from room to room, kicking open doors and calling Elliot's name. Resisting Andrew's protests, they check every room. Elliot is nowhere to be seen.

'Where is he?' Returning to the entrance hall, Nadine turns on Andrew, spittle flying from her mouth.

'Where is who? Have you lost your mind?'

'Don't give me that shit! It's over, Andrew!' She lifts up Geneva's address book in a dramatic gesture, his name plastered on the open page.

Andrew frowns, peering at the book for a second, before realisation dawns.

'All this time,' Nadine says, her voice trembling, 'and it was you all along, wasn't it?'

Taking her completely by surprise, Andrew bursts into laughter. 'You think I killed Geneva?'

He continues to chuckle, which only angers Nadine further. 'You never told me you knew her. There's only one reason you'd have kept that a secret.'

'Because it's none of your goddamned business!' His laugh morphs, now filled with disgust. 'She was my cousin. Actually, no, she was more than that. She was the person who stuck up for me when I was bullied in school. Who got me out of my abusive marriage. She meant a lot to me. I moved this way to be closer to her. How the hell was I supposed to know that one of her friends would be working at the same legal firm I got a job at?'

'But you could have told me afterwards. When we got to know each other.'

'I didn't want it affecting our friendship. I liked you. Before I realised you were fucking crazy!'

An ice-cold breeze flows in from the still open front door, and Nadine shivers. 'So you have no idea who killed her?' She lowers the address book, exasperated.

'You don't think I'd have said something to the police if I did? You really are something else, Nadine. First you accuse me of talking to some YouTuber I'd never met at the office, then you come to my home and accuse me of murdering my cousin? You know, I was actually going to call you today. I had some information I thought you might want to know. But no, screw you. Get the hell out!'

Nadine barely hears his ranting. She's distracted by movement behind Andrew, someone else entering the house. She can't tell who it is because their face is covered. They're dressed head to toe in black fabric. Nadine blinks, fear stabbing the base of her stomach, and for a second she's paralysed. It's only when she glimpses a flash of metal in the person's hand that adrenaline kicks in.

'Andrew! Behind you!'

But it's too late. The intruder is faster. Their hands move with such speed, it's happened before Nadine even finishes shouting out. Andrew's head is yanked back by his hair, exposing his throat. The knife whips across from left to right. Terror and realisation spark in Andrew's eyes as the blood, his life, starts to pump out of him. Nadine lunges forward, hands reaching out, and Andrew's heavy frame falls into her, crumpling in her arms. Her knees buckle and she drops to the floor. She cradles him, crimson coating her fingers as she desperately tries to hold the wound closed, her screams mingling with those of Frankie and Zara's behind her

She madly scans him over, trying to tell herself that she's not seeing what she's seeing.

'Call an ambulance!' she shrieks at Frankie and Zara, who are standing huddled together behind her, unable to look at the bloody scene before them. She directs her attention back to Andrew. 'Hold on. Please hold on.' But of course he doesn't respond. He's already gone. He's staring at her, through her, empty.

Fire of guilt and anger burn under Nadine's skin as the tears flow. Her eyes flick up to the doorway, to where the killer had been standing. They're long gone. Fled from the scene. Sirens sound in the distance, rapidly growing closer. Nadine didn't hear the others call an ambulance, but then again she can't think straight. It's too late for an ambulance anyway. Andrew hadn't stood a chance. He was dead within seconds.

But it isn't an ambulance. Before Nadine knows what's happening, a swarm of police officers burst into the cramped hallway. Chaos ensues. They're shouting, Nadine can see that, but what they're saying she has no idea. Everything has distorted, shifted into another reality.

She shakes her head, her ears popping.

'Hands above your head! Right now!'

She can't speak. Her mind is a void. It doesn't even feel like she is the one controlling her movements as she releases Andrew's body and lifts her hands in the air. It's like she was a puppet on a string. Men lunge for her, grabbing at her and yanking her up. At some point the cold metal of handcuffs are clamped around her wrists, but she's barely aware of it. All she can do is stare helplessly at Andrew as she's dragged away from him, leaving him alone in a pool of his own blood.

Chapter Twenty-Six

Wednesday, 29th June

Frankie

'The trouble is . . .' DS Paulsen shakes his head as he sits on the opposite side of the interview table, 'every one of you could be guilty. I don't think I've ever seen so many possible motives in a case.'

Frankie clamps her jaw together, refusing to take the bait and wishing she could punch the mildly amused look off his face. The fact that he thinks this is even the slightest bit entertaining just goes to show he shouldn't be a police officer.

She takes a sip of her coffee, and the other man, DS Hogan, shuffles beside his colleague. The coffee is vile, as it always is when served from a dispenser into a plastic cup, but the warmth is helping to settle her stomach.

'Look, I'm going to level with you.' DS Paulsen leans forward, his elbows on the table. 'We already know one of you killed him. And we know one of you killed Geneva O'Connor too. We just have to figure out how much each of you is involved.'

Her lawyer – the very best she and Mike could afford – leans in and whispers in her ear. 'They don't know anything for sure. Don't say anything to confirm or deny.'

As if he knows exactly what was just said, DS Paulsen rolls

his eyes and slides a plastic bag across the table. Even without the items inside being removed, Frankie can see it contains the laptop and phone.

'Can you explain why these were in Nadine's house?'

Frankie exchanges a glance with her lawyer, who shakes his head.

'No comment,' she says.

'OK, let's try a different question. Why did you send a message to Geneva the night she died, asking her to meet you at the beach?'

Frankie freezes, her breath hitching. 'I'm sorry?'

DS Paulsen nods at DS Hogan, who slides a printed screenshot towards Frankie.

'This was recovered from Geneva's phone.'

Frankie's eyes flick across the message.

Hey, meet me at the beach in ten mins. It's urgent.

She reads it once, twice, three times, the words blurring and contorting before her very eyes. She takes in the date, the timestamp. It doesn't make any sense.

'I didn't send that,' she says, looking pleadingly up at DS Paulsen. There's been some kind of mistake. They have to believe her. She can sense her solicitor tensing beside her.

'It came from your phone.' DS Paulsen quirks an eyebrow at her. 'Who else could have sent it?'

'I don't know. But I sure as hell didn't!' Her voice is getting shrill. She's losing her composure, which is exactly what she hadn't wanted to do.

'OK, let's forget the message for a moment and focus on a different question. Why is there a photo of you and your friends standing around Geneva's dead body on this laptop?'

She blanches, her back straightening. Between the bloodbath at Andrew's house and spending the night in a cell, she'd almost forgotten about the photo.

'I . . . I . .'

'Was Andrew the one sharing all your secrets, all your motives, with the YouTuber Juniper Rose? Is that why you killed him?'

'I'd like a moment with my client,' the lawyer interjects, but Frankie barely hears him. She slumps forward, runs her fingers through the roots of her hair and tugs until it hurts. She can't do this anymore. She can't lie anymore.

'We didn't kill Andrew! We went there because we thought he had killed Geneva and someone attacked him. They obviously wanted to frame us for his murder. They've got Elliot and they threatened him in the same way. Someone is messing with us.'

'That's awfully convenient, Mrs Crawford. Is someone trying to frame you with that picture too? Reckon they hired lookalikes to stand around your friend's cold dead body?'

'No, that was us.' Her voice is barely a whisper, choked with tears. 'We found her. She was already dead. We should have called the police straightaway. Trust me, I've regretted the decision not to every day since.'

DS Paulsen leans back in his chair. 'Why wouldn't you?'

'She . . . she had so much on us. All of our secrets. We knew they would make us look guilty. None of us could afford to be murder suspects. We all had too much to lose. So we took the phone and the laptop so there wouldn't be any evidence of it. But now we've all lost everything anyway.'

She hunches over and sobs, great big snotty sobs that make her face blotchy and her breathing laboured. DS Paulsen just watches her, waiting for her to finish. Once she eventually regains a semblance of composure and wipes her nose with the tissue DS Hogan has slid towards her, she feels surprisingly lighter. She's kept all this locked to her chest for so long, to finally share the terrible secret they've all been harbouring is both freeing and damning all at the same time.

Frankie's skin is still itchy from the rough cell bedcovers, and she desperately wants a shower. She wishes she could know what her kids are doing right now. When she spoke to Mike on the phone, he assured her he wasn't going to tell them she'd been arrested, though she's not sure what excuse he'll have come up with. She prays they'll be distracted enough with the water slides at the hotel to think much about her, though she's sure Callie will know something is up.

She ended up telling DS Paulsen everything. Once she'd started she couldn't stop. Though she's not sure how much he believed. Now that she's back in her cell and going over everything she said in the interview room, she's not sure she even believes what they did. How could they be so stupid as to think they'd get away with all of this? She wonders if Zara and Nadine are in their cells too, and how much they will have spilled in their interviews. Maybe if they all went the truthful route and their stories match up, the police will actually believe them.

Unable to sit still, she hauls herself up from the bed and begins to pace her cell, claustrophobia tearing at her insides as she faces each of the four walls. She's still pacing when DS Hogan comes and unlocks her cell, letting a welcome, albeit artificial, stream of light into the dimness.

'You're free to go.'

For a moment Frankie thinks she's misheard, or perhaps DS Hogan is playing some kind of cruel trick on her. She frowns. 'You're not charging me?'

'Not today. Come on, unless you want to spend another night here?'

Shaking her head, she scurries out of the cell and flinches as the door is slammed shut behind her. Questions flood her mouth as she struggles to keep up with him.

'Did you figure out who's been messing with us?' she asks, but DS Hogan ignores her, weaving through corridors until they emerge out into the main booking room. Her questions continue to be blanked as paperwork is filled and her belongings are returned to her and she's led to the entrance.

'Frankie!'

At the sound of her name being called, she spins around to see Zara hurrying over to her. When she reaches her, she throws her arms around her and they hug in silence for a good few minutes, relief flooding the both of them. When they separate, Frankie peers around the car park.

Nadine is nowhere to be seen.

TRANSCRIPT

Video published 29/06/2022

Subscriber count: 101,246

Welcome back to *True Crime Over Wine*. Well, what can I say? Just two weeks ago the name Elliot O'Connor was mud amongst those who knew it. Here was a man who couldn't leave his house without fear of being attacked. A man who has suffered emotional, financial and physical hardship, as well as not being able to properly grieve for his wife, all because the keyboard warriors decided he was guilty of murder. Today, I am able to say these words not just as a hunch, but with absolute certainty:

Elliot O'Connor did not kill his wife. He is innocent.

Yesterday, the Dorset police issued the following statement. Quote: 'Earlier this afternoon, Nadine Howe confessed to the murder of twenty-five-year-old Geneva O'Connor. She remains in custody and we ask that the family's privacy is respected at this incredibly difficult time.'

Since this news broke yesterday, I have been inundated with messages, mostly very well meaning, congratulating me on solving an unsolvable case. Calling this a momentous victory. But this is not a victory. Amongst the relief of finally seeing Geneva's killer brought to justice, let's not forget how this YouTube series started. Elliot O'Connor will never get these past five years of his life back.

He'll have scars from this ordeal that will last a lifetime. A real victory would have been the police arresting Nadine five years ago.

Unfortunately, I've still been unable to contact Elliot since the twenty-third, but it is my deepest hope that he can now finally begin to move on. To think I played even a small part in allowing that for an innocent man makes me proud. Proud of this channel. Proud of the people who were brave enough to come on and be interviewed. Proud of you in the comments, leaving your theories and your suggestions. I started this case with no idea whether we would actually be able to solve it, but this experience has been a shining example of how hard ordinary, everyday people will fight for justice.

Now, a lot of you have been asking if the case being solved means the end of this channel. Don't worry. I was making these videos long before Geneva O'Connor and I'll continue making them long after. I am, however, going to take a little break now. I've been releasing these videos every single day for the past two weeks and, not going to lie, I've basically had no life for the entire duration. But I will be back in a couple of weeks so make sure you subscribe and hit the notification bell so that you're the first to know when I start my next investigation. I'm going to be doing another deep-dive, this time investigating the bizarre case of Lacey and Norah Williams. You won't want to miss it.

Chapter Twenty-Seven

Wednesday, 29th June

Zara

Mike ended up coming to collect them from the police station, and Zara wishes he hadn't. As much as Frankie had been thrilled to see him and the kids, there were so many journalists waiting to snap a photo of them leaving the station, they had to drive at a crawl, with Frankie telling the kids to duck down so they wouldn't be in any of the pictures. It's like stepping back in time to when Geneva was first killed. Only now there's another murder victim. The body count of this sorry situation is growing.

The paparazzi were waiting outside Zara's house too, so Mike suggested she come and stay at the hotel with them. Now, she's sitting in the bar of the hotel nursing a glass of wine, and as much as she appreciates the gesture, she's starting to think she should have just braved the journalists and fought her way into her house. She feels awkward being here. Frankie is with her and she shouldn't be. She should be with her husband and her kids, not babysitting Zara out of a sense of obligation.

When Frankie's phone flashes with a notification that Juniper Rose has uploaded a video entitled 'The Geneva O'Connor Case: The Final Resolution', they both sigh in unison. Nadine has taken the ultimate fall for them. Not only did she confess to Geneva's murder, apparently she said she'd only tell DS Paulsen what happened if he could assure her that Zara and Frankie would walk free.

'Did you see?' Zara says, flicking mindlessly through news story after news story covering the 'notoriously unsolvable case'. 'There's rumours Juniper has been offered a Netflix deal. They're going to make a whole series with her investigating unsolved murders apparently.'

Frankie scoffs, draining the last of her wine and picking up the bottle to refill. 'Whoever would have thought Geneva would end up making some unknown YouTuber a celebrity.'

'Yeah. I bet she's set for life now. At least someone got something good out of all this.' As the words leave Zara's mouth, she pauses, allowing that last sentence to sit on her tongue, percolating. Something shifts in the deepest corners of her mind, pulling at her consciousness, a cog turning. She squeezes her eyes shut, tries to grasp at it.

Refocusing on her phone, she taps into one of the news reports that focuses on Juniper's sharp rise to fame. Her hands are growing sweaty, and damp fingerprints mark the screen as she scrolls, forcing herself to slow down and really take in the words she's reading. After a brief introduction to the case there's a paragraph about Juniper's life before her YouTube success. Zara's eyes flit across the text, picking out the key bits of information.

. . . from pauper to princess of the true crime world . . .
. . . came from humble beginnings . . .
. . . grew up in Surrey . . .

Surrey. Zara sits back in her chair. That's where Geneva grew up too.

She clicks off the news report and this time navigates to Facebook, where she types *Juniper Rose* into the search bar. They've already done this twice, but something is telling her to look again. Countless posts from people talking about the case pop up, including a group called 'Juniper Rose's Army' which appears to belong to a group of fans who spend all their free time theorising about Zara and Frankie and Nadine's guilt. And there's Juniper's profile, locked and private, just as it was the last time they looked.

She tries Instagram, Twitter, LinkedIn, every social media platform she can think of. No luck.

Frankie can clearly see the determination on Zara's face, because she frowns and says, 'You OK?'

Zara shakes her head, not wanting to lose the thread of suspicion she's clinging on to. She goes to one more website; that of Geneva's secondary school. She navigates to *Gallery*, and then *Yearbooks Archive*, scrolling carefully through the albums, watching as the date descends under her thumb. She finds the one Geneva would have been in and narrows her eyes as the old school photos buffer into focus. She spots Geneva instantly, but none of the grinning headshots confirm Zara's suspicions. Maybe she's clutching at straws. She clicks onto a few of the other photos – some snaps from a school production of *Oliver!*, a couple of group pictures of girls sporting pen-covered shirts that they've all signed, a few students proudly holding up mathematics awards.

And then she sees it.

It's an action shot from a sports day. Teenagers in baggy colour-coordinated tops and shorts are running a race, steely looks of determination on their faces. Geneva is, of course, near the front. A little in the background, the clearly less athletic students are huffing and puffing to catch up, and one of them catches Zara's eye. A rather frumpy girl with frizzy hair and glasses that are way too big for her and look as though they're about to fall off. Zara wouldn't recognise this girl for any other reason, wouldn't know to pick her out from a crowd, were it not for one detail. Something that no one watching Juniper's YouTube videos would be aware of. Something that only she saw that day Juniper had dropped to her knees beside a bleeding Elliot after Mike had punched him.

On this unrecognisable girl's thigh is an intricate, quite unique tattoo of a rose.

She's right. She's got it.

Zara feels light-headed as Frankie drives. They might be too late. Elliot could already be dead.

When they reach Juniper's street and approach the block of flats, she doesn't even wait for Frankie to fully stop the car before she opens the door and unbuckles her seat belt. Frankie's arm reaches out and grabs her.

'Hang on, let's be sensible about this.' Zara watches impatiently, her leg jiggling with anticipation, as Frankie dials 999 and tells the operator they think Juniper is behind all of this and is holding Elliot prisoner. When Frankie hangs up, she looks at Zara, eyes glassy. 'We should just wait for the police,' she says.

But the words are like a shot of adrenaline flooding Zara's body. 'No. Every second we wait, Elliot could be that much closer to dying.'

There's no time to try to convince Frankie. She will not lose him this way. Flinging the door wide, she lurches out of the car and runs to the entrance of the block of flats. Her finger hovers over 4C – Juniper's flat – but then she decides better of it and presses the button below just as Frankie catches up with her. A shrill buzzing sounds, followed by ''Ello?'

'Amazon delivery,' Zara says down the speaker, trying to keep her voice steady and assured. Another buzz sounds and the door clicks, the lock disengaging.

Holding her breath, the two of them edge into the entrance hall. Unlike the apartment complex at Sandbanks, there's no doorman to advise which floor to take in the lift. In fact, there's no lift at all, just a dimly lit staircase with fraying stained carpet. They climb the four floors, wondering how long it will take for the police to arrive. When they reach Juniper's door, Zara eyes it up and down, then turns to Frankie.

'Looks pretty flimsy,' she whispers, noting the way the door bows at the bottom as if it's not properly fixed to the hinges.

'You're not suggesting we break it down?'

'If we knock, she won't let us in.'

'What if we're wrong?'

'We're not.' She says the words with more conviction than she's felt in the last five years. She's never been so sure of anything in her life. Juniper is the key. It all makes sense, all finally slotting into place.

She turns back to the door and bends her knees, readying herself. Begrudgingly, Frankie does the same.

'Three,' Zara murmurs, praying that her theory is correct and that the door will easily buckle. 'Two, one.'

They bring their legs up in a sharp kick, slamming the soles of their trainers against the wood of the door. Luckily, since their night in the police station, neither of them have bothered with heels. The door creaks, the sound of wood splintering, and it swings back, crashing into the interior wall. They sprint into the tiny entrance hall, making a sharp left into a slightly larger open space. In a flash, Zara surveys the room; a cracked leather sofa that looks as if the central support has gone, a couple of cheap-looking pieces of art hung on the dated stripe wallpaper, a small TV.

It's what's taped to the walls next to the TV that makes her stomach constrict. Instead of wallpaper, the entire side wall is covered with photos of Juniper at various ages, ranging from small child to young adult. Some of the photos look as if they've been slashed at with a knife, removing the eyes. Others have scribbles across them, black marker pen circling areas of Juniper's body. Post-it notes have been dotted across the pictures, and Zara squints to read the chaotic writing.

'Idiot'.

'Boring'.

'Unwanted'.

'Disgusting'.

'Fat'.

'Ugly'.

'Worthless'.

'Gross skin'.

'Flabby'.

'Greasy hair'.

'I hate myself'.

'What the fuck . . .' Frankie whispers behind her, and they unwittingly grip on to each other's arms. They move along the wall, taking in the bizarre display of self-hatred, until they reach more photos. This time they're of Geneva.

'Perfect' – the photo closest to them has been labelled.

'Beautiful'.

'Rich'.

'Talented'.

'Good-looking husband'.

'Thin'.

'Blonde glossy hair'.

'Big boobs'.

'Flawless'.

The dots connect horrifyingly in their heads as they take it all in. This is the work of total obsession.

After they've had a few moments to come to terms with the wall, they remember why they're here and continue to search for Elliot. The house is empty though, completely abandoned.

'Hang on.' Zara grabs Frankie's arm, a moment of realisation hitting her. 'Wasn't she supposed to be moving in with Elliot? Maybe she's there with him!'

'Wouldn't we have seen if someone had been moving around in that house though?'

Zara squeezes her eyes shut, trying to remember the photo of Elliot tied up. It had kind of looked like a living room he was being held in, but it certainly wasn't his living room. She'd recognise the bright flamingo-print wallpaper that Geneva had picked out if it was. No, the room Elliot was being held in was dark.

Her eyes snap open.

'The cinema room!'

Geneva had the cinema room installed in their basement just a few months before she died. She had wanted an at-home spa, Elliot had wanted a games room, so the cinema was their compromise. The girls had only been down there once, when Geneva first unveiled it to them, which would explain why they didn't immediately recognise it. But now she's thought of it, Zara couldn't be more sure of herself.

The drive back to Millionaire's Row feels agonisingly slow, and Zara finds herself growing more and more frustrated with herself. All this time that she's been panicking about Elliot and he's been right next door.

Frankie lets herself into Nadine's house, now eerily quiet from her absence, and retrieves the spare key to Elliot's mansion. Frankie takes the lead as they enter.

'As long as Juniper hasn't changed the code to the alarm, it's Elliot and Geneva's wedding anniversary,' she whispers.

As it turns out, they don't need the alarm code. It hasn't been set. They're met with deafening silence as they step into the hallway. Either Juniper has forgotten to set the alarm, or she's somewhere in the house.

Holding their breath, they tiptoe to the basement door. It creaks mercilessly as Frankie opens it, and it's all Zara can do not to grab hold of Frankie's arm and squeeze. Together, they make their way down the steps, descending into the darkness. The only light source at the bottom of the stairs is a fluorescent strip over where the projector is, but it's just enough for them to be able to see his outline.

'Elliot!'

Forgetting the need to be as quiet as possible, Zara runs to him. Her stomach lurches as she gets close enough to be able to take in his appearance. He's tied to a dining chair, his wrists and ankles bound with cable ties just like in the photo they received. His head is slumped forward. Heart pounding, Zara reaches for the side of his neck, presses her fingers against his cold skin and feels for a pulse. At first she thinks her worst fear has been realised, but after a couple of seconds she feels it; faint but rhythmic beneath her fingertips.

'He's still alive!' she shouts. 'Quick, see if there's some kitchen scissors upstairs or something. We need to untie him.'

She starts working at the knots, long nails snapping as she struggles to loosen them, but then notices Frankie is standing quite still, staring at Elliot.

'What are you doing?' she hisses.

'What if this is a trap?'

'What?'

'This could all be part of a plan that he and Juniper have concocted together. He could just be pretending to be held hostage.'

Frankie's words are like a bucket of ice water being thrown over Zara. She can't. She can't go through this again, flip-flopping between trusting him wholeheartedly and considering that he could be pure evil.

'That's ridiculous,' she says, eyes flicking back to Elliot, but even as she says it she's trying to look for any twitches of the facial muscles, any indication that he could be listening to what they say right now. Heart and mind at odds with each other, she buries her face in her hands, nails digging into the skin on her forehead.

She's so preoccupied with the emotional battle going on inside her, she doesn't even hear the footsteps. Doesn't realise there's someone else in the cinema room with them. But she feels the blow to the back of her head.

Chapter Twenty-Eight

Wednesday, 29th June

Frankie

It's so dark when Frankie's eyes flicker open that she wonders if she's still passed out. But then the pain settles in, and she knows she's conscious. A dull throbbing at the back of her skull makes her grimace. Memories filter back: breaking into Juniper's flat, finding Elliot in the cinema room, seeing Zara go down, and spinning around just in time to see the figure in black. Dread churns in the pit of her stomach and she wriggles, but her hands won't move. They're tied tightly to the chair she's sitting on, her ankles too. She breathes noisily through her nostrils, increasing in pace as the panic mounts.

A low murmur from behind her makes her crane her head to see who it is, but it's too dark to see a thing.

'Zara?' she says, praying that it is indeed Zara she heard and that she wasn't killed by the impact to her head.

'Hmm?' Zara grunts.

'Thank God. Are you OK?'

'I'm . . . oh shit . . . I'm tied up.'

Even though Zara's voice still sounds drowsy, Frankie can hear the fear in it.

'I know. I am too. We're going to be OK. I'm going to figure this out.'

The words, of course, are completely empty. She doesn't even know who they're up against, let alone how to free themselves. But she can't allow the terror she feels to take over. If she does, she may as well give up. She's starting to sweat, her damp fringe clinging to her forehead.

'What do you think . . .' Zara's words are snatched away by a blinding light streaming into the room. It's as if the entire wall of the room they're being held in has fallen away.

Frankie jolts, snapping her eyes shut and trying to twist away from the light. Music fills her ears and she wonders if this is all some bizarre psychedelic dream. Maybe she's been drugged. Or maybe she's dead.

Wincing, she prises her eyes open ever so slightly and peeks at the source of the light and music. As her eyes adjust, and the spots dancing across her vision subside, she realises what it is she's seeing. The cinema screen has been lit up. There's a movie playing.

She blinks, confused. The video on the giant screen is of a stage. Teenagers dressed in red and white costumes flock from the wings, moving to the music and singing along. Frankie sucks in a breath, her hands gripping the arms of her chair, as she spots someone she recognises, someone whose movements are far more exaggerated and over the top than the other girls. It's Geneva. Young, slightly less glamorous Geneva. As the song comes to an end everyone on the stage freezes in unison, pointing to a screen at the back of the stage. The words 'Merry Christmas from St Pauls' appear in a swirly font on the screen. But just as quickly as they appear, they flicker and vanish, replaced instead with a hand-held video of a girl alone in what looks like a school changing room. She has mousy, frizzy hair and her face is covered in the telltale signs of teenage hormonal acne. Clearly unaware that she's being filmed, the girl begins to undress, changing out of her PE kit. As items of clothing are removed the murmurs of laughter begin to emerge from the girls on the stage. A flustered teacher hurries up onto the stage and fumbles with the bottom of the screen, trying to turn it off, which only makes the students laugh harder. And that's when Frankie sees it. The girl who had been filmed undressing is amongst the dancers on stage. Tears stream down her face as she flees to the wings. Once she's gone, the rest of the girls fall about laughing, some pointing, Geneva in particular looking utterly overjoyed, while the teacher frantically tries to shoo them off the stage.

'That was just one of the terrible things Geneva O'Connor did to me as I was growing up,' says a voice, as the video pauses.

Frankie struggles to angle her head towards it. Juniper is standing at the back of the cinema room, near the door, eyes fixed on the screen. The light of the video catches on the knife she's clutching in her hand, making it glint.

'Pretty, talented, perfect Geneva,' Juniper says softly. 'Except she wasn't perfect at all, was she? You girls know that better than anyone. She was a bully who made a habit of ruining people's lives. Who got enjoyment from it.'

'You're . . . you're Janet Rowland, aren't you?' Frankie stammers, remembering the yearbook photos Zara had pulled up on her phone. The hair and complexion and weight were vastly different, making her look unrecognisable. Had it not been for the thigh tattoo giving her away, which she was always careful not to show on her videos, they'd never have known it was her.

'Very good.' Janet smiles. 'And Janet Rowland was the laughing stock of the school, thanks to Geneva. My grades began to suffer, I started cutting myself, I even ended up in hospital for bulimia thanks to her constantly criticising my weight.'

Inwardly, Frankie cringes. She knows exactly what Geneva was like, but somehow it seems even worse thinking about her doing it to a fellow teenage girl, when those years of desperately trying to find your place in the world are hard enough as it is. It's one of the things she's always been terrified of as a mother, that her kids would end up having the light that makes them unique snuffed out by the pressure of attempting to fit in.

'After school I made a promise to myself,' Janet continues, 'that I'd never be made to feel bad about myself ever again. Geneva was always popular. I had to mould myself to make myself like her. So I watched her. And I studied her. And I replicated her. Dyed my hair to match hers, figured out which beauty products she used and bought the same, starved myself so that I'd fit into all the clothes that she wore. I even changed my name to be more like hers. Did you know the meaning of the name Geneva is actually Juniper tree?'

As Janet rants, Frankie allows her fingers to feel around her bindings, trying to figure out if there's any room for her to slide her wrists out.

'It wasn't enough though!' Janet shrieks, making Frankie start. 'I tried getting into acting like her, but apparently I wasn't good enough. I started a YouTube channel that never got anywhere . . . not for years, anyway. That's all I've ever been told my whole life. I'm never good enough. And the more I watched Geneva with her sickeningly perfect life, the more I grew to hate her. And all of you, her rich entitled friends who always think they can get away with anything. Adultery . . . theft . . .' She pauses, angling the knife towards Zara, chest rising and falling. 'Even causing your own sister's death didn't stop you from living your disgusting glamorous life! How is that fair? I resented your lives and coveted them at the same time.'

Frankie's eyes widen with horror as she realises this isn't all about Geneva after all. Janet wants to see all of them suffer.

'So I came up with my final plan to replace Geneva for good, steal her identity, everything she had that was rightfully mine. Once and for all. I knew that if I did this kind of series on my YouTube channel, it would gain me an audience, so I created the perfect crime for me to investigate. It was a win-win. After killing her, I just had to bide my time, wait for my eventual rise to fame. It was just a bonus that you stupid bitches had so many reasons for wanting her dead too. It was so easy to pin it on any of you. And then you went and made it even easier for me by stealing her phone and laptop. Incriminating you would be the perfect punishment for all the awful things you've done in your lives.'

'But you'd got away with it!' Frankie can't help but want to understand. 'Everyone thought it was Elliot. Why wouldn't you just let people believe that?'

'You're not listening. It wasn't enough just to get rid of Geneva. I wanted to *be* Geneva. That meant getting famous, through investigating this case, and clearing Elliot's name so I could take him for myself. Once I looked like Geneva I was suddenly his type, and he was so broken when I approached him at New Year's, it was easy to seduce him. He even invited to me to move into Geneva's house and sleep in Geneva's bed! Of course, that was all working perfectly until *you* decided to start fucking him again!'

She jabs the knife towards Zara again, who lets out a small whimper.

'I thought locking you in the sauna and getting rid of you might have been enough to make Elliot forget about you and choose me instead. I should have stayed and made sure the job was done.' She sneers in Elliot's direction. 'It only made him want you more, anyway. It didn't matter what I said, he still couldn't see that everything I've done has been for the both of us. He could be so much happier with me.'

'It's ironic,' Frankie says, trying to draw Janet's attention away from Zara, 'that you were able to forgive all Elliot's mistakes since it was convenient to you. He's an adulterer too, remember. And he covered up that girl's death at his club.'

'He suffered for his sins too!' Her expression hardens. 'For five years his life was hell on earth. I thought the five-year anniversary of her death would be the perfect amount of time to wait. Maximum impact, you know? And it was enough time to allow you all to let your guards down. To make you think you'd all got away with it. But of course, I wasn't expecting you to move away. That did put a wrench in my plan, I have to admit. I'd have preferred for Eleanor to have lived. She seemed like a nice lady. But I needed a way to bring you all back together and I knew that would do it.'

'You . . . you killed my mum?' Zara's haunted whisper sends a shiver down Frankie's spine.

'She'd have died eventually anyway. I didn't give the woman cancer. But it's much easier to speed things along when all you have to do is slightly over-administer the drugs someone's on.'

Frankie hears the screech of Zara's chair on the floor as Zara thrashes against her restraints. 'I'm going to kill you! I'm going to fucking kill you!' she screams.

Janet just laughs at Zara's attempts, and Frankie closes her eyes against the chaos, trying to make sense of all this.

'What about Andrew? Why did he have to die?'

But as she asks the question she already knows the answer. Andrew's words replay in her mind. 'I was going to call you today,' he had said. 'I had some information I thought you might like to know.'

'He'd started to suspect me,' Janet says, confirming Frankie's suspicions. 'I didn't realise he was her cousin. Apparently I'm not the only one who had a glow-up. I didn't recognise him at all. But he recognised me . . . eventually. He confronted me to tell me to stop making the videos – I don't think he liked that I'd ruined Nadine's life – and I could see it in his eyes. The flicker of recognition. So he had to go. I have to say, I didn't expect you lot to actually go to his place. I'd been watching you ever since the graveyard and was most pleased when I saw you heading in that direction. It made framing you much, much easier. You do that a lot, don't you?'

Frankie thinks about the picture of them crowded around Geneva's body. Janet must have thought that all her Christmases had come at once when she saw them. Another thought occurs to her, then. Something that DS Paulsen had said, and her eyes snap open.

'How did you manage to send a text from my phone to Geneva asking her to meet us at the beach?'

At this, Janet's face contorts into a knowing, malicious grin. 'You didn't think I could do all this on my own did you?'

Frankie swallows, her heart skipping. There's someone else behind all of this? Who?

Possibilities flit through her mind as Janet turns to the door and knocks three times. The clicking of a lock opening sounds, and the handle lowers. Frankie squints and leans forward as she tries to make out who is entering the cinema room. When the realisation hits, it's as if the floor has been removed from under her feet and she's free-falling.

It can't be.

Chapter Twenty-Nine

Five Years Ago

Callie

Callie wakes up to the sound of them arguing. It takes her a moment to figure out what's going on, but she quickly recognises the voices as those of her mum and of Geneva. She doesn't really like Geneva. She gets a bad feeling from her. But her mum seems to get on with her most of the time, so she doesn't say anything. She's not getting on with her now, though. Callie's never heard her mum so angry, not even when she's argued with her dad.

Knowing she shouldn't really be eavesdropping on her mum's private conversation, she creeps out of bed and pads to her door, listening intently.

'I mean it, Geneva,' her mum's voice says. 'This isn't one of your games. This is my family we're talking about.'

'Did I say I was going to do anything to your family? No. All I'm saying is that it's all very well blowing off your friends for a man, but we're the ones who know all your dirty little secrets.'

'And by that you mean the paternity test, yes?'

'Hey, I'm the one who convinced you not to say anything to Mike, remember?'

'Yes, so that you could use it against me later down the line! I'm not stupid, Geneva. I know how your mind works.'

'I resent that. I suggested it would be best not to tell Mike because I didn't want it to affect his relationship with Callie. She's at a sensitive age. The last thing she needs is to find out her dad isn't really her dad.'

'Don't pretend like you care about my kids, Geneva.'

There are more words after that, more snipes from Geneva, more curses from her mum, but Callie barely hears any of them. She presses her hands to her ears, unable to bear listening to any more. Someone may as well have come along and ripped her heart straight out of her chest.

Her dad, the man who brought her up, who taught her to ride a bike, who hoisted her up onto his shoulders as they walked to school. He's not her dad at all.

Tears start spilling from her eyes and she runs back to her room, burying herself under her duvet and willing this to all be a dream. A nightmare.

He doesn't know. Does that mean her mum cheated on him? It must do. They were together for three years before she was born. Her chest twists and her fingers tremble from the rage building within.

Pressing her face into her pillow to muffle the sound, a scream rips from her throat. She cries into the pillow, pressing it against her mouth, her nails digging into her skin. It stings, but it's almost a relief, taking her mind off the hurt inside.

She hates her. She hates her mum for doing this to her, to her dad, and for lying all these years. And she hates Geneva for daring to threaten her family.

The internet is a weird place. Buried among the usual sites that everyone visits on a daily basis, there are dark corners and hidden crevices. The forum Callie has found herself on is one such place. It describes itself as a commentary website on public figures, but actually it seems it's just a place for angry, bitter keyboard warriors with nothing better to do than to slam those in the public eye, hiding behind their anonymity. She's ventured onto this icky page for one reason only; to see if she can dig up some dirt on Geneva.

All last night, as she lay sobbing in her bed, she thought about the situation and decided that she will do whatever is necessary to stop her dad from finding out. If it's only she that knows, maybe their relationship can continue on as it always has. But if he knows, he could decide to turn his back on her. Maybe he wouldn't even be able to face her anymore knowing she's not truly his flesh and blood. Maybe the very sight of her would be too much to handle, too much of a reminder. She can't risk it. She won't.

So she has to shut Geneva up, hence why she's sitting, bleary eyed with dark circles, scrolling through vile messages commenting on Geneva's weight and marriage and lack of acting ability, hoping she'll stumble across something she can use.

She's been reading this particular thread for so long she's starting to lose faith in humanity, when a post catches her eye.

> I've despised the woman for over a decade. Bitch made my life a misery at school. God, what I'd give to see her knocked from her pedestal and left to rot in the dirt where she belongs.

Callie's hand moves of its own accord, not allowing herself to properly think through what she's doing. She taps into the person's profile; *WobblyThighs19278*. A faceless avatar stares back at her. She holds her breath as her fingers tap away at the keyboard, typing a message into the DM box.

> *Saw your message about Geneva O'Connor. Thinking maybe we could help each other out.*

Over the next couple of weeks, as Callie and WobblyThighs19278's relationship grows, her mum's warnings about strangers on the internet ring at the back of her mind, but she shuts them down as quickly as they appear. The more she talks to this mystery person, the more her hatred of Geneva swells, and the less what she's doing feels wrong. To begin with, it's all very harmless anyway. Geneva's old school victim shares many a tortured memory, but none of them are quite what she needs. She needs something she can actually use against her, that will be enough to get her to keep quiet about the paternity test. Give her a taste of her own medicine, and all that.

The suggestion that they meet up to discuss a plan comes after a few days of silence. Callie had actually started to assume WobblyThighs19278 was done talking to her, so a flutter of excitement hit as she opened the message. Now the words on that DM circle her mind as she grips the straps of her backpack, eyes pinned to the pavement as she walks to school.

Let's meet up face to face.

The request is a non-stop jab at her brain as she sits through her classes attempting, in vain, to concentrate. It clings to her thoughts like bubble gum as she hangs around with her mates at lunch, putting her quietness down to it being her time of the month. At home, she rushes straight past her mum in the kitchen – who keeps on asking her why she's being so out of sorts and is doing her absolute nut in – and makes a beeline straight for her room, where she falls onto her bed and stares up at the ceiling, thinking.

It's dangerous meeting up with people you talk to online. All the internet safety flyers say so. It would be so easy, so much wiser, to say no. To apologise for wasting this person's time and to go back to quietly hating Geneva in the background, hoping and praying she won't do anything to destroy her life. But Callie already knows she's not about to rest the fate of her family with someone as manipulative as Geneva. She knew she'd say yes to the meet-up as soon as she read the message.

She's careful about it, takes all the appropriate steps, suggesting they meet in a public space so that if this person does actually turn out to be an old man with a hunger for teenage girls, she'd be able to cause a scene. She is told that the person she's speaking to is called Juniper, and that she'll be able to recognise her by her bright red turtleneck jumper.

When she reaches the café, heart jittering as she steps off the bus and peers through the window, she's pleased to see that her choice of venue is a good one. It's fairly busy, lots of people to ask for help if she feels in any way threatened by this encounter. Three elderly women bunch around one table. Another is occupied by a gaggle of mums with pushchairs. And then there's one table, tucked into the corner, where a woman sits alone. She's found her.

Juniper's head is bowed. She's writing furiously on a collection of Post-it notes, bringing her eyes up every now and again to survey her surroundings. As Callie's hand rests on the door, she hesitates. Maybe this isn't such a good idea after all. She doesn't even know what this plan is that Juniper has. She refused to tell her any more over DM. What if it's something illegal?

But as she falters outside, Juniper looks up and moves her gaze to the door, her eyes staring straight into Callie's, and Callie knows she's reached the point of no return.

Callie stands frozen to the spot as she and Juniper wait on the beach, cold sea breeze whipping around them. Juniper has gone over the plan with her endless times, assured her that very little can go wrong, but still she's breathing so rapidly she's sure Juniper must sense how nervous she is.

The first part of the plan was nerve-wracking enough. She'd forced herself to stay awake while her mum was at wine club at Nadine's house, waiting for her to return. When she did eventually stumble in, dumping her belongings on the console table as she always does, Callie had to stealthily retrieve her phone and send a message to Geneva, pretending to be her mum, asking her to meet her at the beach. It worked. The blunt response from Geneva – 'fine' – came within a few seconds, and Callie had just enough time to delete both messages and replace her mum's phone on the console table before her deception was discovered. She then pretended to go back to bed, arranging her pillows under the duvet to look like a sleeping person, and sneaked out of the house.

That had been the easy part though.

Now, they're waiting for Geneva to turn up at the beach so that they can give her their ultimatum. Juniper has expertly compiled every evil thing that Geneva has done, right from school all the way up until now. They're going to present her with the file and tell her that if she doesn't leave Callie and her family alone, they'll spill it to the press. Her career will be over, her husband will probably leave her, her picture-perfect life will crumble. An eye for an eye.

'Just let me do the talking,' Juniper whispers, giving Callie's arm a reassuring squeeze. Callie forces a smile. She's grateful to Juniper really. This total stranger has gone out of her way, done so much, all to help her. She can't let her down and chicken out now.

Movement catches her eye on the other end of the beach, and her body tenses as she recognises Geneva's slender outline. *Breathe*, she tells herself, as she and Juniper start to move towards Geneva, the gap between them shrinking. Recognition flashes on Geneva's face as she spots Callie.

'Is your mum here?' she asks. 'I'm supposed to be meeting her.'

'Your friends aren't coming,' Juniper says before Callie can answer. 'No one is.'

Geneva frowns, looking Juniper up and down. 'Do I know you?'

'I'm just one of the many people you've hurt.' Juniper smirks, then circles Geneva, stopping to stand directly behind her. She points at Callie over Geneva's shoulder. 'Just like you're planning on hurting this poor young girl. What did she ever do to you, eh?'

Geneva flinches away from her. 'What the fuck do you think you're . . .'

It all happens so quickly. Juniper grabs something out of her pocket and lunges for Geneva. Callie stumbles back, confusion ripping through her. The sound Geneva makes – a choking, spluttering that gurgles in her throat – is like nothing Callie's ever heard.

'Stop!' Callie screeches, as the reality of what Juniper is doing descends on her. She wants to run forward and prise Juniper's hands off of her, to pull the cord away from Geneva's throat, but she's paralysed. Her limbs are locked with fear, and all she can do is cover her face and scream.

When it's done, when Geneva lies dead on the sand in front of her, Callie's body shakes so much she can barely stand. Sweating and panting, Juniper releases the cord and comes to stand beside her.

'That was harder than I thought it would be,' she says. Her voice is so carefree, as if she's just run a relay as opposed to murdering someone with her bare hands, that Callie immediately recoils.

'You . . . you killed her . . .' she stammers.

'You wanted to shut her up, right? Mission accomplished.'

Callie shakes her head, causing fresh tears to spill down her cheeks. 'That wasn't . . . I didn't mean . . .'

But before she can stutter out any more words, Juniper turns to her and wraps her arms around her. She pulls Callie close to her chest, shushing her like a baby, and as much as Callie wants to tear herself away, she's still too terrified to move.

'It's a lot to take in, I know,' Juniper is saying, gently brushing Callie's hair with her fingers. 'But it's for the best. We did this for all the right reasons.'

Callie stiffens, looks up at Juniper. 'We? I didn't kill her.'

'We were both here. You didn't stop me. If I go down, you will too. And your dad will find out about the paternity test and all this will have been for nothing.' The smile that creeps onto Juniper's lips is haunting, making every hair on Callie's arms stand up on end. That was a threat. She's warning her to keep quiet. 'But it's all going to be OK. No one will track this to us. Not when we've got so many people we can pin it on.'

'W-what do you mean?'

'I'm not finished with you yet, Callie. This is just the first play of a long game. You're going to get the ultimate revenge on your mum for cheating on your dad,' Juniper says, simply.

Chapter Thirty

Wednesday, 29th June

Zara

'It took her a while to get on board if it makes you feel any better.'
Janet smirks. Zara can't see Frankie's face from her position, but
she can imagine what it must look like. 'She really hadn't expected
things to go down that way, bless her, but after a lot of talking she
came around. It's remarkable how impressionable teenage girls
can be. I needed that phone and laptop, though I could never
have guessed just how many brilliant, juicy secrets they held. But
I'd never have been able to get them. Callie here had all the right
access. Access to your phone, Frankie. Access to the spare key
to Nadine's house. She was the perfect option. My "anonymous
source". She even had the brilliant idea to bug Nadine's handbag
when she couldn't find the phone and laptop the first time she
broke in. That was just sheer genius. I could never have succeeded
without her.'

'Callie, darling.' Frankie sobs. 'How could you do this?'

'How could I?' Suddenly, Callie's face twists, eyes flashing. 'How
could you? How could you do that to Dad? To me? Yes, that's right.
I found out about the paternity test five years ago. We shut Geneva
up. But you still have to pay for what you did . . . Mum.' She spits that
last word, the venom in her voice making Zara wince.

'Is this why you've not been eating? Because you've been living with this awful secret? Oh, Callie . . .'

'Don't!' Callie screams. 'Don't pretend to care now. Don't pretend to be a good mother. I've had five years of this bullshit, quietly hating you, biding my time. I don't have to listen to your lies anymore.'

'Callie, you don't understand,' Zara says, attempting to turn in her seat. 'Your mum didn't cheat on your dad.'

'Enough!' Janet's shrill voice bounces off the walls of the cinema room, making Zara's heart stutter. 'We don't care about your excuses. All we care about is seeing justice done. Geneva had her punishment. So did Elliot. Nadine is going down for the murder.' Janet steps towards them, bouncing the knife in her hand. This is all a game to her. She's probably had this planned out for years. And Zara knows that if Janet had any intention of letting either of them go, she wouldn't have made her grand confession. If Zara and Frankie are going to get out of this alive, one of them needs to come up with a strategy and fast. Where is Nadine when they need her?

'Now,' Janet continues, 'what will your punishments be? What do you reckon, Callie?'

Janet lunges towards them with the knife. Frankie lets out a scream.

'Wait! Stop! Frankie shouldn't be punished!' Zara shrieks above the noise, completely acting on impulse. 'She didn't do anything wrong! Punish me instead!'

There's a brief silence as her words linger. Janet cocks her head to one side. 'How noble. Protecting an adulterer.'

'No. Callie, listen to me.' Zara cranes her neck, ignoring Janet and her glinting knife and instead focusing her attention on Callie. She looks completely different from the last time she saw her five years ago. No longer a teenager but a hardened, scorned young woman. 'Your mum was raped. That's why she hid it. She's just an innocent victim, like you. She doesn't deserve any of this.'

Callie's eyes widen, a flicker of something – hesitation? – flashing across her face. Janet steps between them, breaking their eye contact. She purses her lips, looking between Zara and Frankie, and Zara shrinks back against her seat as her entire body begins to tremble. The seconds tick by. Zara's mouth is so dry she can't swallow.

Janet tucks a stray hair behind her ear.

'Fine,' she says, the vein in her forehead throbbing. She takes a step towards Frankie, knife aimed at her, and Zara struggles against her restraints. But Frankie's cry of pain doesn't come. Instead, out of the corner of her eye Zara sees Janet cut Frankie's cable ties. 'It's your lucky day, Francine.'

Confused, Zara watches as Janet places a hand on Frankie's shoulder, the other hand with the knife hanging menacingly beside her, and leads her around to face Zara.

'Callie, come here, sweet,' Janet calls. Callie, clearly as unsure of what Janet is up to as Zara, shuffles forward. As she approaches, Janet grabs Callie by the throat.

'No!' Frankie jolts, her immediate reaction causing her to reach for her daughter, but Janet holds up the knife.

'Ah, ah, ah. Not so fast. We're playing by my rules now.' The corner of Janet's mouth curls, insanity dripping off her. 'Zara says that she's the one who should be punished, and I've always thought she's a little too vain for her own good, so, Frankie, you're going to take this knife' – she holds out the knife to Frankie – 'and scar that pretty little face of hers.'

Zara's chest constricts as Frankie recoils, distancing herself from the knife.

'You're insane. I'm not going to do that.'

A wave of relief laps over Zara's fear, but she knows Janet will have anticipated this. This entire time, since the day Geneva was killed, they've been pawns playing her little game, and every step of the way they've done exactly as she wanted without even realising it.

'That's fine. You don't have to punish Zara if you don't want,' Janet says, pulling the knife back. 'But that means I'll have to punish you instead by killing your daughter.'

Zara sucks in a breath, clawing into her armrests.

'Juniper, what the hell are you doing?' Callie squirms under Janet's grasp, eyes darting between Frankie and the weapon. Clearly this was not part of their joint plan. Janet is changing the rules.

'Do whatever you want to me,' Frankie says gravely. 'But let Callie go.'

Janet throws her head back and laughs, an empty, hollow sound. 'Nah, this is far more fun.'

Reality hits Zara: Frankie's kids are her kryptonite and Janet knows it. It's obvious Frankie will do whatever Janet wants as long as she's threatening her daughter.

'Come on then, we haven't got all day,' Janet says. 'Punish Zara or punish yourself. Your choice.'

'Mum...' Callie's voice is wobbling, returning her to the teenager Zara remembers, and the tears that have started spilling down her cheeks betray how scared she is. Zara tries to meet her eye, to tell her that it's OK, that her mum will never let anything happen to her.

Frankie's eyes flit to Zara and she can already see she's made her decision. Zara's muscles tense, already imagining the blade digging into her cheek, dragging across her skin, carving a thick bloody line through her flesh. Her jaw tightens as Frankie's shaky hand lifts and takes the knife. She wonders fleetingly if Frankie would be able to turn the knife on Janet, but there's no way. Janet's grip is tight around Callie's throat. She could snap her neck in a second if they tried anything.

As Frankie turns to her, Zara's heart starts pounding as if it's battling to break free from her chest. Frankie takes a step forward. And another. Saliva pools in Zara's mouth as her breathing turns desperate.

'I'm so sorry,' Frankie whispers.

Zara tries to shake her head to tell her it's OK, that she doesn't blame her, but her body is so stiff her head barely moves. Slowly, Frankie raises the blade, and Zara squeezes her eyes shut, readying herself for the pain.

Except it doesn't come.

Chapter Thirty-One

Wednesday, 29th June

Frankie

The commotion is so sudden that Frankie can do nothing but watch. Elliot, clearly having woken up while Janet was talking and managing to loosen his ties, throws himself towards Janet and Callie, completely knocking Janet off balance. He kicks hard, his shoe impacting with Janet's knee. Grimacing, she topples sideways, legs buckling underneath her as her arms flail, releasing Callie from her grasp.

A flicker of hope: now that Callie's free, Frankie can lunge at her, attack her with the knife . . .

But Janet is faster. She grabs Callie's arm as she falls and pulls her down with her. As Elliot continues to attack, all that can be seen is a mess of flailing limbs, striking each other with jabbing elbows and knees. There's no way Frankie can get to Janet with the knife without the risk of accidentally hurting Callie in the process. Or Elliot for that matter.

Elliot sucks in a ragged gasp as Janet punches him, catching him in the throat. Frankie drops the knife and dives, throwing herself on top of the scrum and pushing against Janet. Between them, she and Elliot wrestle Janet away. Anger mixing with adrenaline, Frankie grabs her by the shoulders and throws her with all her might, slamming her head against the floor.

There's a sudden, deafening silence as Janet goes limp.

Behind her, Zara bursts into tears. 'Elliot, I'm so sorry . . . so sorry . . .'

Frankie scrambles up, grabbing the knife from the floor, and hurries over to Zara. She can't bring herself to face her daughter right now.

'I didn't want to do it,' Frankie sobs, sliding the blade underneath the cable ties and freeing Zara's wrists.

'I know. I don't blame you.'

Once free, Zara jumps up and flings her arms around Frankie. They grip on to each other tight for a few seconds.

'Elliot.' Zara peels herself away and moves to him. 'Are you OK?'

'I am now.'

They take a moment to embrace too, and Frankie peers down at the floor, an apology to Elliot dancing on her tongue. It's not the right moment though.

'We need to get out of here,' Frankie says eventually, making sure the knife is still firmly in her hand.

Zara glances at Janet, still lying motionless on the floor. 'Is she dead?'

'I'm not sure, but let's not wait around to find out.'

Finally, she faces her daughter. 'Are you coming?'

Callie's eyes flick between Frankie and Janet. She squeezes her jaw together and nods. Grabbing her daughter's hand, Frankie leads them to the door. She hasn't got the brain capacity to process everything that's happened with Callie right now. That's going to have to be dealt with later.

They reach the door and Frankie releases Callie's hand to grab the handle. It's stiff. Locked.

'I locked it when I came in,' Callie says, suddenly jumping into action and fumbling about in her pockets. She retrieves the key and tries to insert it into the keyhole, but she's shaking so much it won't go in.

None of them hear the movement behind them, but Frankie feels the hands on her shoulders. She's yanked back with such force the air is ripped from her lungs. As she hits the floor, she looks up just in time to see Janet looming over her, a crazed look on her face. Still clutching the knife in her hand, Frankie jerks it up, thrusts it towards Janet. She feels the pressure of metal against clothing, against flesh, as it gouges Janet's shoulder.

There's a howl of pain. It's enough for Janet to fall sharply back. Frankie takes her opportunity and flings herself around, lumbering on top of Janet and pinning her to the floor. The movement is so vigorous her hand loosens on the knife and it skitters across the tiles, but she's quick to snatch it back up again. Eyes narrowing to slits, she presses the blade against Janet's throat, so that the skin whitens and puckers.

'Enough!' Her voice is shrill. 'This is over now.'

Frankie holds her breath, waiting. She doesn't want to kill Janet but she will if she has to. Time seems to drag as she watches Janet's face. Her eyes don't seem to be looking at her anymore. They've travelled past her, around her, to the cinema screen where the paused vision of Geneva standing on the stage still stares back at them.

Epilogue

Two Years Later

Callie

'If it helps, I never intended for it to turn out like this.' Callie smiles across the visiting room table. On the other side, Janet looks less than impressed with her unexpected visitor.

Callie had been in two minds about whether or not to go to see Janet. In the immediate aftermath of their ordeal in the cinema room, there was no way she'd have been able to so much as mention her name without everyone around her acting like she was uttering some forbidden curse.

The trial had been long and ugly. Janet had pleaded guilty to it all – in fact, she almost seemed proud of herself as she stood up and declared that she had enjoyed taking Geneva's life. That portion of it had been relatively quick. The difficulty came with Callie's trial. The jury were tasked with deciding whether she should be held responsible for her actions. On the face of it, it seemed like she should most certainly face prison time. After all, her crimes were numerous. Helping Janet to lure Geneva to the beach that night. Not reporting the murder to the police. Not reporting the fact that Nadine had stolen the phone and laptop to the police, and subsequently breaking into her house and searching high and low for them so that they could use the information on them. Standing by as Janet locked Zara in the sauna so she could have her precious Elliot. Not to mention assisting Janet with the kidnap of not only Elliot, but of Zara and her own mother too. But, the deliberation came due to Callie's age when she met Janet. Her defence, drummed into her by the hotshot lawyer Nadine had organised for her, was that she was just a vulnerable kid influenced by a manipulative psychopath. She had been lured into a situation that she didn't know how to get out of, and tricked and pressured into doing things she'd never normally have done. It worked wonders, resulting in her leaving the courtroom not only a free woman, but one with a shiny new identity to protect her from the kind of people who hounded Elliot for all those years. Sure, she had to sit through months of excruciating therapy, saying all the right things to all the right people, playing the role of victim, grovelling for forgiveness from her parents, but it was worth it in the end.

Judging by the look on Janet's face, this is a bone of contention.

Callie smiles at her. 'You played your part awfully well though.'

'What are you talking about?' Janet says though gritted teeth.

Callie leans back and cracks her knuckles. Janet, bless her, really isn't that bright. The fact that she didn't put all this together years ago, still amazes Callie.

'Getting rid of Geneva for me,' Callie says simply. 'I mean, when we met up and you suggested blackmailing her, I had been planning on killing her all along. But then you went and saved me the trouble.'

Janet's eyes widen. 'But you . . . you were so scared. You told me to stop.'

'Mmm. Good, wasn't it? The thing is, I knew you were crazy enough to actually do it. You really can find some dangerous people on the internet.'

'I'm not the only crazy one in this room,' Janet sneers.

'Perhaps not.'

'You fucking turned on me.'

Callie raises an eyebrow. 'I believe it was you who turned on me. Hurt Zara or I'll kill your daughter? I don't recall that being part of the plan.'

'I knew she'd never let me hurt you. Obviously, I was never going to. It was a spur of the moment thing.'

'Ah, see, that's where you made your mistake.' Callie crosses her arms, enjoying the bitterness seeping off of Janet. 'Always stick to the plan. If you had just killed Geneva and quietly taken her place like you had wanted to, it probably would have worked. I'm sure Elliot would have fucked you eventually.' At this, Janet looks as if she's about ready to tear Callie's throat out, but she continues none the less. 'But no, you wanted more. You couldn't just be satisfied with making Geneva suffer. You wanted all her rich, overindulged, immoral friends to suffer too. That's where you made your mistake. You got greedy, and it was your eventual downfall.'

As her words, and the understanding that comes from them, sink in, Callie watches Janet, appraising her. She then leans forward, one corner of her mouth quirked up.

'Tell me, Janet. Has that changed these past two years?'

Janet's eyes narrow. 'What do you mean?'

'Do you still want Geneva's friends to suffer? I mean, you can't do a lot from in here, can you? That would drive me mad, personally. Wanting to take action, to finish what I started, but being locked in here unable to do anything. That would definitely keep me up at night.' She smiles. 'The thing is, the courts insisted on me going to all these therapists. Lots of getting me to open my mind to my true feelings, pinpointing the source of my pent-up anger, trying to deal with it rather than trying to bury it. And it has been pretty enlightening, though not, I imagine, in the way they had hoped. All that thinking about it made me realise that I don't think our plan is finished yet. I still hate my mum for keeping that secret all of those years. And I still want her to suffer.' She pauses, resting her elbows on the table. 'Do you still want them to suffer, Janet? Because if you do, I say we put our heads together and make it happen.'

The corners of Janet's mouth lift, and as her eyes burn into her, Callie recognises the insanity that had first drawn them together.

'What did you have in mind?' she says.

Acknowledgements

Writing books has proven to be more challenging than I ever anticipated, yet the rewards have surpassed my wildest imagination. As I embark on this journey for the third time, I must acknowledge the unwavering support of my incredible husband, Sam. Without his constant encouragement, none of this would have been possible. I would also thank my daughters Elise and Evie, but I can't lie and say they made writing this book any easier. They most certainly did not! I love them anyway though.

I am eternally grateful to my agent, friend, and emotional pillar, Emily Glenister. Two years ago, she took a chance on me. Since then, she has been the epitome of being by my side through thick and thin. Emily, never leave me . . . I'll cry.

To Cara Chimirri, the most extraordinary editor I could have asked for. Your enthusiasm for my books and career is boundless, and I am truly fortunate to have you on my team. I also want to express my gratitude to my previous editor, Hannah Smith, who believed in me from the start and acquired my debut in 2021, giving me the launching pad I needed.

The Embla team is an absolute powerhouse, and I am deeply honoured to be a part of it. While it's impossible to mention every individual who dedicated their valuable time to work on this novel, I want to give a special shout-out to Emily Thomas, Anna Perkins, Hannah Deuce and Ellie Pilcher.

A heartfelt thanks to my mum, grandad, dad, step-mum, brother, sister, and all my wonderful in-laws. Their unwavering support and encouragement have allowed me to pursue this crazy dream of mine. Thanks also to the lovely team surrounding me at Jericho Writers, for allowing me to amalgamate my day job with my writing career so flawlessly.

Lastly, I want to express my gratitude to Sarah Bonner, Mira Shah, Vikki Patis and Eve Ainsworth, William Shaw and Lauren North, who are always there when I need a friendly face or someone to moan to. It's true what they say. The friends you make are the best bit about being an author.

About the Author

Becca Day lives in the middle of the woods in Surrey with her husband, daughters and cocker spaniel. She studied acting at Guildford College and went on to start her own Murder Mystery theatre troupe. It was this move that inspired her love of crime fiction, and when she sold the company she threw herself head first into crime writing. Aside from penning novels, she is also Marketing Manager for leading literary consultancy and writing community Jericho Writers.

About Embla Books

Embla Books is a digital-first publisher of standout commercial adult fiction. Passionate about storytelling, the team at Embla publish books that will make you 'laugh, love, look over your shoulder and lose sleep'. Launched by Bonnier Books UK in 2021, the imprint is named after the first woman from the creation myth in Norse mythology, who was carved by the gods from a tree trunk found on the seashore – an image of the kind of creative work and crafting that writers do, and a symbol of how stories shape our lives.

Find out about some of our other books and stay in touch:

Twitter, Facebook, Instagram: @emblabooks
Newsletter: https://bit.ly/emblanewsletter